"Will Sanders is one of the better-kept secrets in science fiction. The problem is, with his talents he ought to be a household name. Hopefully this novel will set matters right."
—Mike Resnick

"Sanders' prose and dialogue is wry, and funny, and serious, and gripping. The book swallows you whole from the first page when Billy's grandfather talks to him through the body of a blue jay and doesn't let you go until the end, with not a wasted page in between. Rather, there's a wealth of intriguing incident and story, character and interaction, high flights of fancy and down to earth horrors."
—Charles de Lint in *Fantasy & Science Fiction*

"William Sanders is a throwback to the time of Sturgeon and Dick, a talent mad, generous, individualistic and brilliant."
—Rick Bowes

"There aren't many SF writers these days whose work I automatically pick up in a bookstore as soon as I see the author's name. Will Sanders is one of them."
—S.M. Stirling

Also by William Sanders

The Wild Blue and the Gray
Are We Having Fun Yet

Hugh B. Cave

The Witching Lands
Larks Will Sing
The Cross on the Drum
Drums of Revolt

Lafcadio Hearn

Some Chinese Ghosts
Fantastics and Other Fancies

Brian McNaughton

The Throne of Bones
Gemini Rising
Nasty Stories
Even More Nasty Stories
Downward to Darkness
Worse Things Waiting

Stephen Mark Rainey

Balak
The Last Trumpet

Lawrence Watt-Evans

The Misenchanted Sword
With a Single Spell
The Blood of a Dragon
The Unwilling Warlord
Taking Flight
The Spell of the Black Dagger
The Nightmare People

Also from Wildside Press

Masque of Dreams, by Bruce Boston
An Alien Darkness, by Adam-Troy Castro
Storm Over Atlantis, by Adrian Cole
Moonlight, by Susan Dexter
Wind Over Heaven, by Bruce Holland Rogers

THE BALLAD OF
BILLY BADASS
AND THE
ROSE OF TURKESTAN

William Sanders

WILDSIDE PRESS
PENNSYLVANIA • CALIFORNIA • OHIO • NEW YORK

THE BALLAD OF BILLY BADASS
AND THE ROSE OF TURKESTAN

Copyright 19xx by William Sanders.
All rights reserved.

Cover illustration by xx.

No portion of this book may be reproduced by any means, electronic or otherwise, without the prior written authorization of the copyright holder. For more information, please contact:

Wildside Press
P.O. Box 301
Holicong, PA 18928-0301
www.wildsidepress.com

TO BAYAN
AND TO ROGER
WHO BELIEVED IN THIS BOOK

AUTHOR'S NOTE:

This being a work of fiction, and fantastic fiction at that, certain considerable liberties have been taken with geography and cultural background. There is no Blacktail Springs Reservation in Nevada—or, as far as I know, anywhere else—and the Paiute band described as living there exists only in these pages.

Many of the details of Cherokee tradition, especially concerning ritual matters, have been deliberately altered; for the author to give an accurate and specific description of, for example, a tobacco-remaking procedure would be sacrilegious. The traditions described are valid in general outline but not necessarily so in all details.

The matter of illegal dumping of radioactive wastes and other toxic materials is, of course, a nationally notorious reality; however, nothing in this story is to be taken as referring to any actual case.

The information in Chapter 8, however, concerning Soviet nuclear-weapons testing in Central Asia and the effects on the population of Kazakhstan, is factually correct according to the author's personal sources.

1.

BILLY BADASS WAS SITTING on a big rock above Barren Fork Creek when his grandfather spoke to him for the first time. Or rather it was the first time in the five years since his grandfather had died.

It was early morning, the sun just starting to filter through the dense leaf cover and spot the floors of the hollows with yellow. April was almost over and the birds were everywhere; birds of every kind, from the little blue-gray gnatcatchers having microscopic hysterical rages over territorial borders to the solitary great blue heron flapping unhurriedly along above the spring-high creek. Which was probably why Billy Badass took no particular note of the large bluejay that flew down and sat on a bush facing him, six or seven feet away. Not, that is, until it looked at him and said, "'*Siyo, sgilisi, gado haduhne?*'"

Billy stared at the bluejay for a couple of seconds. "Holy shit," he said finally. He said it in English, there being no way to say "Holy shit" in Cherokee.

The bluejay clicked its beak in a somehow disapproving way. "Picking up bad language from the *yonegs*," it said. "Picking up bad habits from those Kiowas you've been hanging around with, too. Didn't I tell you enough times to stay away from that peyote crap? Just look at you," the bird went on, "sitting there trying to remember which end is your head and which is your ass. Not even enough sense to speak properly to your grandfather."

"*Eduda?*" Billy said dazedly. "Grandfather? It's you?"

"Of course, you jackass," the bluejay said impatiently, speaking English now. "Jaybirds can't talk, for God's sake."

Billy shook his head hard. The effort didn't seem to do any good; the motion merely aggravated an already vicious headache. "You mean," he said, "you've been—what do they call it? Reincarnated? As a bird?"

The bluejay snorted. At least it made a snorting sound, or seemed to.

"Worse messed up than I thought," it said, "if you've took to believing in that New Age horse shit. Next thing you know you'll be wearing a quartz crystal around your neck and hunkering over a pyramid. Reincarnation my Native American ass."

Well, Billy thought foggily, that settled one thing anyway. Hallucination or spirit vision or whatever the hell was going on, it was definitely Grandfather Ninekiller speaking to him. Nobody and nothing else, in any of the worlds, was that sarcastic.

HIS NAME WASN'T really Billy Badass; the nickname had been hung on him in high school, when he had looked like making state champion in wrestling, before getting kicked off the team in a best-forgotten scandal involving some bootleg whisky, a hot-wired Buick, and the coach's teenage daughter.

His enrollment card in the Cherokee Nation of Oklahoma gave his name as William E. Badwater. Even that represented a bit of sloppy work on the part of the official interpreter when his great-great-grandparents had been forcibly enrolled, back around the turn of the century; in Cherokee the name more precisely referred to dangerous waters, as for instance a hazardous rapid or a whirlpool.

He had another card, issued by the Bureau of Indian Affairs, that said he was a full-blood Cherokee. ("Four-fourths" was the Bureau's odd terminology; he often wondered why they had chosen to express it that way rather than, say, sixteen-sixteenths or sixty-four-sixty-fourths.) His Oklahoma driver's license said he was twenty-eight years old, five feet eight, a hundred and eighty-five pounds—off a trifle, but not enough to matter—with black hair and brown eyes, and that he was licensed to operate a motorcycle on the public highways.

His wallet also contained a folded and ragged photocopy of a page of military gibberish that, decoded, stated that Badwater William E. had been honorably discharged a bit less than two years ago from the United States Army, having attained the rank of Staff Sergeant. That was just about all the wallet contained at the moment. Eight years of military service, including participation in a violent if short-lived war, had generated a great deal of paper, but very little of it had been of the green sort.

He was a dark, wiry young man, with the classic mountain Cherokee build: long arms and legs, narrow high-boned straight-nosed face, big chest, and almost no ass. He wore tight-cut jeans, a black T-shirt printed with a Jerome Tiger design of an Indian on horseback, cheap running shoes from the Wal-Mart in Tahlequah, and a sweaty red bandanna for a headband. His coarse black hair was starting to reach the point where he would soon have to make a decision either to get a haircut or let it grow long. He was inclined to the latter choice—maybe he'd even braid it, Plains style, though that would piss the Cherokee traditionalists off—less from a desire to look Indian than as a delayed reaction against years of military hair-length regulations.

He had been back in Oklahoma since January, having walked off a construction job in Florida in a fit of homesickness. He still didn't have a clue what he was going to do with himself, though a white man at a security-guard company in Tulsa, where he had applied for a job, had made a somewhat impracticable suggestion.

The grandfather/bird/whatever was right about his present condition, though. He had been hanging out lately with a bunch of Southern Plains types, Kiowas and Comanches mostly, who had been trying to get him into the Native American Church. The previous night he had finally gone to one of their services, over near Tulsa, out of curiosity and a vague idea that it might help him get his shit together. Even before he had risen to his feet and lurched hastily out of the peyote lodge and off into the night, puking every few staggering steps, he had known this was not for him. He had no clear recollection of how he had gotten back to Cherokee County; he only knew that he had been out here in the woods since just before daybreak, trying to clear the weird alkaloids from his brain cells.

Now here he was seeing talking birds—or, more exactly, a talking bluejay that claimed persuasively to be his dead grandfather. It's finally happened, he thought dully. I've lost my God-damned mind.

THE BLUEJAY SAID, "What's got into you, *chooch*? You used to be a pretty bright kid, even if you do look too much like your daddy's side of the family. I know I didn't have you long, but I thought I taught you better than this."

Billy said, "If you're Grandfather, then why are you speaking English?"

"Because," the bird said, "if I spoke Cherokee you wouldn't understand half of it. And you might talk Cherokee back to me, and you speak it so bad it makes my teeth hurt. Well, my beak, just now."

Unfortunately that was true enough. Orphaned at age nine, Billy had been raised by mixed-blood foster parents who hadn't spoken the language, and a series of summers spent with Grandfather Ninekiller hadn't entirely taken up the slack. He could get by in Cherokee, but just barely. In fact, to his private embarrassment, he was—thanks to a year at the Army Language School in Monterey, California—considerably more fluent in Russian than in his own native tongue.

"Probably doing good to talk at all right now," the bluejay went on. "Didn't I warn you about those Mexican cactus buds? If a bunch of Kiowas and Apaches and whatever want to chew that stuff, fine, they're all crazy anyway, can't hurt their brains any worse. But it's not part of *our* medicine, God damn it."

"There were some Osages there too," Billy muttered defensively, and immediately wished he hadn't.

"Osages," the bluejay said scornfully, somehow packing several centuries of blood-enmity into the one word. "Gets worse and worse, *chooch*. I can see I got my work cut out for me, getting you straightened out."

Billy leaned back against the big limestone boulder behind him and studied the bluejay. It didn't look any different from any other jay; maybe a little on the fat side, but nothing freakish.

"How does this work?" he asked after a moment. "I mean, you said you hadn't been reincarnated—I know, I know, that's not part of our tradition either—but what's the story? Is the bird part just a hallucination I'm having, or what?"

"Oh, it would take weeks to explain," the grandfather-bird said. "And even then you wouldn't understand it. Some things you just can't grasp until you're in the spirit world yourself. Which, by the way, you're going to be very soon if you don't quit trying to ride that damn motor-sickle with a head full of half-cured peyote. I just about shit, watching you take those curves over by Hulbert last night."

"You've been watching me?"

"Well, of *course* I've been watching you. You're the only surviving direct descendant I've got, you know," Grandfather said. "Since your mama died in that car wreck and your Uncle Jimmy got killed in Vietnam. What the hell do you think ancestors *do*—sit around in the spirit world playing dominoes?"

The jay hopped up onto a higher branch and looked at Billy from eye level. "Of course we do some of that too," it added in Grandfather Ninekiller's voice. "It's not all work and no play. Meet some damn interesting people here, too. You get here, don't ever play dominoes with this old *yoneg* named Ambrose Bierce. He'll skin you alive."

"About this business with the bird," Billy said faintly.

"Oh, that. Like I say, it's kind of hard to explain. Look," Grandfather said, "if I just came at you out of nowhere—like a disembodied voice, you know?—you'd get crazy. That's one of the things they warn you about when you get to the spirit world: don't go speaking in disembodied voices to the living, it just screws up their minds. Every now and then some damn fool—well, anyway. Point is, I have to show myself to you in some way, give you something to focus on. The jaybird was handy and didn't seem to be doing anything important at the moment."

"You—what? Took over the bird's body?"

"In a manner of speaking. Of course he's not actually *talking*—you're really hearing my voice inside your own head—but it's a kind of a what-do-you-call-it act. Like the guy who sets the dummy on his lap and makes him talk."

"Ventriloquist."

"Whatever. Anyway, I just sort of borrowed the jaybird. Hm," Grandfather mused. "I wonder if he'll have any recollection of a blank spot in his morning. I guess not. Jaybirds aren't too smart."

"So," Billy said, "you could have appeared to me in some other form? No particular significance to the bluejay?"

"Well, I always did wonder what it would feel like to be a jaybird. They seem to have so much fun. Next time," Grandfather said thoughtfully, "I might try showing up as a tomcat. Been a hell of a lot of years, live and dead, since I had any of *that* kind of fun."

"Next time." Billy considered the implications of the words. "Does that mean you're going to be—"

"Why, sure. Like I say, high time somebody took ahold of you and cleaned up your act. Been thinking about doing this ever since you got back from the war, but I was waiting for the right time. I ain't happy about you eating that peyote, but I admit it did give me a good opening. Loosened your head up a little, so you weren't quite so surprised to meet a talking jaybird. Even so, I ever catch you chewing that crap again, I'll appear as a mule and kick your ass."

The bluejay flared its wings and flew suddenly toward Billy, dropping at the last instant to land on his left knee. Its claws dug painfully through the worn-thin denim of his jeans.

"Better get used to the idea, *chooch*," Grandfather said. "I'm gonna be with you for a long spell."

Billy groaned involuntarily. The jay opened its beak and seemed to laugh, a scratchy old man's cackle. "Don't take it so hard, *chooch*. Go on, now, get up. You remember what I told you to do when your head gets mixed up?"

Billy thought about it for a few seconds. "The river," he said finally. "Sit and watch the river."

"Right. Watch the river flow until you feel it flow through you. I wondered if you'd remember."

"I tried it a few times," Billy said. "All it did was make me need to pee."

"Well, try it again. The creek will do all right. See that gravel bar down there, by that old willow? Go sit there in the sun and let the creek run through your spirit, the way I taught you. Really need to make a smoke, but I don't guess you've got any of the makings."

"Not even a light."

"Never mind. Time for that later. Get up, now."

The jay fluttered up into the nearest tree and watched while Billy got slowly and painfully to his feet. "Careful, now, *chooch*, don't go falling into the creek. . . ."

As Billy started toward the trail that led down to the creek, he said, "Are you going to stay with me?"

"No, no. For this, you've gotta be alone. I'd just distract you. Don't worry, though. I'll be seeing you again real soon."

"I can hardly wait," Billy muttered.

"Think I'm just in time," Grandfather Ninekiller added. "I

never was strong on telling the future, but I've picked up a few tricks in the years since I died. I can read sign some now—and I think there's some really interesting shit about to go down. In your life, and a lot of other people's."

2.

Billy Badass met the Rose of Turkestan the following Saturday night, at a powwow at the community building in Tahlequah. The week had gone by with no further manifestations or visitations by Grandfather Ninekiller, and Billy had decided the whole thing had been merely a peyote hallucination. He had told no one about the experience.

The community building was a big concrete-floored structure on the south side of Tahlequah, down near the Department of Human Services where you applied for food stamps. When Billy arrived the parking area was already full of old cars, pickup trucks, and vans, though there was still light in the western sky. Indians of various tribes stood around parked vehicles, getting into dance outfits or just talking and smoking. A couple of men recognized Billy and waved as he pulled into the lot. He found a parking spot, leaned his motorcycle on its sidestand, took the key from the ignition and his hat from the fiberglass box bolted to the Honda's luggage rack, and went inside.

The sound hit him as he came through the doorway, a deafening *BOOM BOOM BOOM BOOM* from the big drum in the center of the floor, and over it the high-pitched singing of the eight Indian men who sat around it in a folding-chair circle. Their long whippy drumsticks rose and fell in unison. Their voices tried to do the same, with a bit less success in the unison department. Billy didn't recognize any of the singers, but if this was a typical eastern-Oklahoma pickup drum group, most or all of them would be from eastern tribes—Cherokees, Shawnees, Quapaws, this side of the Grand River you got all kinds. The Kiowa gourd-dance song they were singing would have been learned phonetically, by rote, with no vested cultural interest at all in its content. Still, they had a good beat going and the sound brought back pleasant memories; it was the first powwow Billy had been to since coming home. He stood in the doorway a moment, his head moving slightly as he let the rhythm flow through him.

Around the drum, in a big loose approximate circle, a dozen or so gourd dancers moved in the curious small mincing steps of their dance, shaking long-handled rattles made from metal canisters or bell gourds, holding feather fans in their left hands. The swishing *shick-shick-shick-shick* of their rattles cut softly but insistently through the booming of the drum and the wailing of the singers. Most were older men, veterans of Vietnam or Korea or even the Second World War; their dark faces were relaxed and expressionless as they danced, and there was great dignity to the set of their backs and shoulders.

Billy nodded appreciatively and walked on into the building, easing through the crowd, speaking to a few acquaintances and relatives, heading toward the concession stand to get himself a soda pop. He lived several miles from town and the windy ride had given him a serious thirst.

He didn't really notice the young woman standing beside the concession-stand window, not at first. But when he had paid for his Coke and turned away—wondering as always why, with diabetes so common in so many tribes, the powwow concessions never seemed to sell diet drinks—he glanced over and saw that she was looking at him.

"*'Siyo,*" he said politely, and she nodded and smiled, and so then he stopped and looked her over more carefully.

What he saw at first was nothing all that remarkable, at least not around an Oklahoma powwow. She was small, almost tiny, even by Indian standards; she couldn't, he guessed, stand over five feet tall, and she was slight of build, though with just enough fullness of hip to miss the skinny-little-boy look that white women always seemed to try for. She wore a simple, inexpensive-looking dress of some thin blue-and-yellow material, the hemline cut good and high, revealing nice legs that were maybe just a trifle too thin for his taste.

She had long thick hair, glossy black like his own, and prominent cheekbones. Her eyes were dark and oblong in shape. It was the eyes that got him; they were genuinely beautiful eyes, and at the moment they were fixed on him with more than casual interest.

She was, in fact, looking at Billy as if he were all of the basic food groups.

He was glad, now, that he'd taken the trouble to dress up a little for the occasion. He had on his good ribbon shirt—the black one with the red and white ribbons—and his best jeans, and the fancy Tony Lama cowboy boots that had taken a painful but worth-it bite out of his G.I. separation pay. Around his neck he wore a bone-hairpipe choker, Southern Cheyenne style. On his head sat another piece of discharge-money extravagance: a genuine Resistol Western hat, dead black, with a beaded headband made by a cousin of his who was learning

Indian crafts from books written by white people. The hat also bore a long eagle feather, left to him by Grandfather Ninekiller.

He figured he looked pretty good. And evidently this girl—or woman; he couldn't guess her age, late teens to middle twenties maybe—agreed.

Say something, asshole. . . .

He said, "Would you like something to drink?" and held up his Coke.

Still smiling, she shook her head. "Thank you, no." She held up a paper cup of her own and tilted it to show him the bottom was full of crushed ice. "I have just had," she said.

Her voice was high and musical, with an odd accent Billy couldn't place. He stepped away from the concession-stand window, toward her, trying to identify the accent and the features. She was no Cherokee, that was for sure. Apache, maybe? No, the bridge of the nose was wrong. For all he knew she could be Eskimo or even Aleut.

He said, "Excuse me, what tribe are you?"

She looked momentarily baffled. Billy thought the drum had drowned out his question, and started to repeat himself, but then her face cleared and she said, "Oh, yes, tribe, you mean nation, yes? I am Kazakh."

Billy's mind flipped rapidly through its files and came up blank. What the hell, maybe a Canadian tribe. He said, "Uh, I don't guess I know—"

"Kazakh," she repeated. "From Kazakhstan. Formerly part of Soviet Union, you know?"

"Oh. Oh, yeah, sure, Kazakhstan, I know where that is." Actually he didn't, except vaguely—somewhere in Central Asia, wasn't it?—but he wasn't about to admit that, not just now anyway. Then a delayed circuit closed in his head and he grinned at her.

"*Nu, tak,*" he said, "*v'i govoritye po-Russki?*"

"*Da, konyechno,*" she answered automatically. Then her eyes went round and she whispered, "*Bozhe moi!*"

"*Ya govoryu nyimnoshko,*" Billy went on modestly. "*K sozhalyeniu, mnye nuzhno praktika.*"

"My God, it is impossible," she said, also in Russian. "The first time in this country I meet a man who speaks Russian, and he is an Indian. How can it be?"

"I studied in the army," Billy said in English. "I'm afraid it was several years ago and, like I said, I'm out of practice."

She raised an eyebrow. "You have a school in your army which teaches Russian?"

"And just about any other language you can name. I had a buddy who was studying Swahili."

"Fantastic," she said.

The recruiter had been right after all, Billy thought; you learned all sorts of things in the military that you could use in civilian life. . . .

"Come," she said, "let us sit down. I want to watch this dancing."

The hell of it was, he reflected as he followed her through the crowd, they hadn't taught him the kind of Russian you needed in a situation like this. His memory served up a number of phrases: *provolochnoye zagrazhdyeniye*, barbed-wire entanglement. *Gvardeiski minomyot*, heavy mortar. *Nabliudatel'niy punkt*, observation post. Not exactly the sort of thing you could work into a romantic conversation.

The gourd dancers were moving in to surround the drum now, coming up on the balls of their feet and bouncing on their heels, shaking their rattles furiously as the singers belted out the final song. Some of the dancers were letting off shrill yipping cries.

"This dance, what does it mean?" she asked as they found a couple of unoccupied folding chairs. One thing about Tahlequah, they always provided plenty of chairs. At most powwows you brought your own or you stood up.

"Warriors' dance," Billy explained. "Originally Kiowa, if you ask a Kiowa. Cheyennes and Crows claim they started it. I don't think anybody really knows. Kind of a ceremony for a returning war party, in the old days. Now it's just a dance for Indian veterans."

She nodded. "You are veteran too, I think," she said. "Were you in the war with Iraq?"

"Such as it was. It didn't really amount to enough to qualify me as a veteran, at least the part I was in," Billy said. "I sure don't feel like any kind of a returning hero."

"It is only important that you returned," she said in Russian. "My brother was killed in Afghanistan."

Billy could think of nothing to say to that. He sat back and watched the dance. Or pretended to; mostly he watched her watching the dance.

The song came to an end, the drummers following with a flurry of out-of-rhythm bangs to signify the end of the set. The gourd dancers broke ranks and began leaving the arena, shaking hands and talking among themselves. The drummers were lighting cigarettes, casually ignoring the NO SMOKING signs posted about the building. Up on the stage the emcee, an overweight Kiowa with a tendency to mumble, began announcing upcoming powwows in various towns, while costumed dancers began lining up for the grand entry. Billy looked at his new acquaintance and said, "Well, what's your story?"

"Pardon me?"

"How did you wind up here in Oklahoma? Long way from home, aren't you?"

She laughed softly. "What is the American idiom? It is a long story."

"Tell me," he said. Somehow it had become important to know about her.

Her name was Janna Turanova and she was twenty-seven years old, though Billy did not learn this last until much later. Her home was in the city of Almaty, formerly Alma-Ata, at the foot of the Tien Shan Mountains, but she had been born in a village on the steppes to the northwest.

"A tiny place," she said, "you have never heard of it." Billy, having never heard of Almaty or Alma-Ata before either, didn't argue the point.

She was a medical technologist, a researcher in pediatric cancer and genetic defects. Back home, she was part of the staff of a new medical center that worked with children suffering from the effects of radiation exposure, the legacy of generations of Soviet nuclear-weapons testing on the plains of eastern Kazakhstan. She was in the United States on a kind of exchange program, funded by an international nuclear-disarmament coalition, studying similar cases among the Indians of Nevada and Utah. A professor at Northeastern State University, in Tahlequah, had brought her here as a guest speaker.

"It was in the newspapers," she said. "Perhaps you saw."

Billy shook his head. He never read the local papers, or any others except occasionally the *Cherokee Advocate*. Even that was strictly for laughs, checking out the funny letters from outraged Cherokee Baptists pissed off about the tribe getting into bingo, or funnier ones from white people trying to find out if they had Indian blood. ("Dear Editor: My mother told me before she died that my grandmother was a Cherokee princess. Can any of your readers help me? All I know is that she was from Missouri and her name was Smith—")

"I spoke last night at the university," Janna said. "Tuesday I go back to Nevada."

Damn, Billy said to himself, you finally meet somebody you really like and she's practically on her way out of town already.

"Some teachers from the university brought me here," she added. "I have never been to one of these dances before."

The announcer was calling for the grand entry. The drummers began banging and bellowing and the first dancers came stepping into the arena, eagle feathers jerking with the rhythm, brass bells jingling at knees and ankles. The leading male dancer, a middle-aged Comanche built along the lines of an armored personnel carrier, bore a large American flag on a pole. Everybody stood up.

"We're supposed to stand," Billy explained, getting to his feet and taking off his hat. "Well, of course, you don't have to, it's not your country's flag."

She stood up beside him. "That is all right. I will observe the courtesy," she said in Russian. "But I do not understand this with the flag. I would not think your people would have much love for this nation, the way it has treated you."

"Most Indians," Billy said, also in Russian, trying to remember the correct case endings, "are very patriotic."

"I don't understand this." She shook her head. "I am sorry."

"Well—" It didn't, Billy reflected, make a hell of a lot of sense when you thought about it that way. Why *did* Indians always fall all over themselves to follow that flag? It was, after all, the emblem of a nation that had been founded on the basic principle that the North American continent was much too good for a lot of God-damned Indians, who had no rights and were probably not human anyway. And had operated on that principle, pretty consistently, right up to the present day. . . . "I don't know," Billy admitted, speaking English now. "I don't really understand it myself."

The grand entry went on until all the costumed dancers were in the arena. Then everybody remained standing for the flag song—Billy was relieved that Janna didn't ask what that was all about—and a seemingly interminable prayer, over a squealing and fading PA system, by an aging Osage preacher. At last the opening ceremonies ended and the drummers fired up again. The dancers began a round dance.

"Fantastic," Janna said. "Excuse me, please, I must—you know?"

He watched as she moved off through the crowd, heading toward the women's restroom. The building was starting to fill up with Indians and quite a few whites, even one or two black faces in the crowd; there wasn't much to do around Tahlequah on a Saturday night, and powwows were free. He noticed several of the young men checking Janna out as she passed.

Billy sat and watched the dancing, waiting for her to return. The round dance ended and the emcee started another announcement: "At this time we'd like to honor our head dancer, Marvin Blackhorse—" He had, Billy estimated sourly, used the phrase "at this time" at least a dozen times in less than an hour. So much for the proud traditions of Indian oratory, that used to impress the whites so highly. "From where the sun now stands" to "At this time" in one lousy century. Well, they probably had boring windbags in the old days too, only nobody wrote their speeches down—

"Billy." A large shape materialized in front of him, blocking off most of the view of the arena. Billy's eyes traveled upward over a vast expanse of Sequoyah High School T-shirt and came to rest on a big round moon face that just now was split open in a wide grin. Minnie Badwater, a cousin from Delaware County; damn near two hundred pounds of pure jiggling blubber, but sweet as pie. They'd been close friends as children; she'd been the only relative to write to him while he was in the army.

"Billy," she said again, flashing her overbite, "what are you doing to that Russian girl?"

"She's not Russian, she's Kazakh," Billy said. "Probably likes being called Russian about as much as you'd like being taken for an Osage. What do you mean, doing to her?"

"She's in the ladies' room, talking to some *yoneg* woman from Northeastern, telling her all about this fantastic man she's just met." Minnie did a pretty good imitation of Janna's accent, "fahn-*tahs*-teek," rolling her eyes comically. "I don't know what you're up to," she added, "but you're sure going at it right."

"Thanks for the information," Billy grunted, and Minnie laughed. Then she looked more closely at his face.

"Hey," she said, "you're not just fooling around this time, are you? Something more than just trying to get into her pants, huh? Looks to me like you're getting a case of the real thing."

"For God's sake, I just met her."

"Hah! Sometimes it doesn't take long," Minnie said seriously. "Boy, I ought to know."

He knew what she meant. She was two years younger than Billy but she had already been married three times, the first time at sixteen. The last he had heard, she had five children, one by an anonymous fourth party. If anybody knew about impulse love it was Minnie Badwater.

"Go for it," she said, tapping his knee with the tips of her fingers. "Good luck."

He watched her waddle off through the crowd, leaving a wake like a *Wisconsin*-class battleship. After a minute he laughed softly to himself and turned back to watch the dancers, who were now circling the drum in an intertribal war dance.

Janna reappeared and sat down beside him. "Please," she said, "you must tell me all about this. The costumes, the dancers, tell me what they mean."

He gave her a quick rundown, while the dancers milled and wheeled about the floor in a swirl of feathers and beads and bright-colored shawls. "The men in the cloth outfits are what we call straight dancers. Southern Plains style, maybe a hundred years old, pretty hard to master."

His pointing finger picked out a burly young man in breechcloth and fringed leggings, upper body bare except for a hairpipe breastplate, face painted black and yellow. Long dark-brown feathers sprouted from the bustle at his rear, making him look like a huge bird. "Northern traditional dancer," Billy said. "See how he dances all crouched over, looking around and down at the floor? He's imitating a warrior on the track of an enemy. Then the guys in the wild outfits with all the bright-colored feathers, they're fancy dancers—free style, you might say, modern costumes and moves based on traditional patterns. They get really outrageous."

He showed her the various women's outfits: buckskin, cloth, jingle dress, fancy shawl. "Each of these clothing styles goes with a particular style of dancing," he said, "and each style has its own songs. Right now they're all dancing together, but later tonight they'll have the contest dances for each group. Then you'll see something."

"Contest?" She looked puzzled. "I thought these dances were . . . *religioznii*," she said, shifting to Russian again. "Ceremonial. Sacred."

Billy snorted. "Maybe they used to be. Maybe some of the older people still remember when they were, maybe some people like to pretend they still are, but they're kidding themselves. Nowadays the average powwow's just a social event, and some of the big ones are as commercial and phony as Buffalo Bill's Wild West Show."

He wondered if he'd thrown her with that last bit. She wasn't likely to know what it meant. But she only said, "That's sad. Do you dance?"

"I used to, a little, when I was a teenager. Never had the money to put together a first-class outfit, though." He lifted his shoulders. "Now I think of it, I don't guess I've danced at a powwow in nine or ten years."

"But you should," she said, looking at him. "You should help keep alive the traditions of your people."

"My people?" His mouth twisted at the corners. "Not *my* people's traditions. This is mostly Plains stuff. Cherokees only got involved in the powwow scene in recent times, mostly because the young people saw other Indians doing it and it looked like fun. It's not part of the Cherokee way."

He looked at her a moment longer, an idea crystallizing in his mind. "Wait just a second," he said.

He got up and worked his way through the crowd, looking about him. At last he went up to an old man who sat near the arena, arms folded, watching the dance with unreadable eyes. "'*Siyo, eduji,*" Billy said, "*dohiju?*"

The old man looked at Billy for several seconds. "You're Billy Badwater," he said finally. "Annie Ninekiller's boy. The one they used to call Billy Badass," he added, saying the nickname in English, chuckling softly in his throat. His eyes glittered like those of a mischievous ancient turtle.

They talked for a few minutes, making polite inconsequential conversation, inquiring after family; it would have been gratingly rude for Billy to approach an elder with a direct and immediate question, though plenty of young Cherokees wouldn't have known any better. Finally Billy said, "Where are they dancing tonight, Uncle?"

The old man looked thoughtful. "Which Saturday is this?"

"Third," Billy said after thinking.

"Then they'll be down at Redbird. Ought to be a pretty good one, too." The old man looked wistful. "Wish I could go, but I got nobody to drive me."

Billy excused himself and went back to where Janna was sitting. "Listen," he said, "you want to see how we do it? Real Cherokee dancing?"

"I'd love it," she said, standing up. "You can take me?"

"If you don't mind riding a motorcycle."

"Oh, that will be even better." She looked almost childishly excited. "Wait one minute," she said. "I must tell some people I am leaving."

He watched as she went over and began talking to a middle-aged white couple who stood near the side doors. Almost immediately their heads turned and they stared straight at him—Christ, *yonegs* could be so damn rude—and he saw that they were talking to her now, both of them at the same time. They looked pretty unhappy. It didn't take a lip reader to figure out that they were trying to talk her out of going with him. For an instant an old anger flared in his blood and tightened his throat, but then he told himself it wasn't a racial thing, not this time. White, black, red, it didn't matter; if you weren't connected with some university, these people figured you walked on your knuckles.

Finally Janna turned and began working her way back toward Billy and he moved to meet her, conscious of the white couple's eyes still tracking him like a Patriot battery locked onto an incoming SCUD. Ignoring them, he said, "Ready to go?"

"Please," she said.

Out in the parking lot he took his hat off and carefully stowed it in the bike's topbox, taking Janna's small purse and putting that in too. Ought to have a helmet for her, but he hadn't even worn his own tonight. Come to think of it, she wasn't really dressed for the occasion in any respect. He said dubiously, "You sure you don't mind riding, well, like that? I mean it's dark and all, but still—"

He gestured at her short thin dress. "You know," he said self-consciously.

She laughed. "It's all right. In my country it is very common to see women riding on bicycles or motorcycles or horses wearing skirts." Her lips turned up at the corners. "Of course in my country we don't have the strip dancers like in America. Maybe this is because the men have already seen everything."

He straddled the old Honda 750 and held out a hand to help her as she climbed on behind him. She wore cheap-looking wooden sandals and it was hard for her to get aboard, but she made it. "Oh, I love this," she said, wrapping her arms around his waist.

He kicked the sidestand up and turned on the ignition. The engine fired as soon as he hit the button.

"Hang on," he said, and toed the Honda into gear and let in the clutch. A moment later they were turning down Muskogee Avenue, headed south. Big white moths fluttered across the headlight beam like demented ghosts.

3.

For the rest of his life Billy would remember that ride in every detail, with a sharp and sometimes aching clarity: the rush of the night air against his face, the blare of the old 750cc. engine and the whine of the tires on the blacktop, the smell of cedar from the woods along the road, the nighthawk that fluttered suddenly into the bright cone of the headlight and almost hit the windshield, and most of all the feel of Janna's arms around his waist and her small body pressed against his back, molding herself to him.

She was a good passenger. A lot of women, Billy thought, got silly on the back of a bike, squealing and panicking if you went faster than a walk, or leaning the wrong way on curves, but this one took to riding pilion as if she'd been born there. Well, she was—if he had his geography and history right—the descendant of Central Asian nomads who had lived and fought and for a time conquered a lot of the world on horseback, so maybe riding was in her genes.

They couldn't talk over the blast of the wind in their ears and the roar of the Honda's non-stock exhaust. Still, during that hour-long ride south from Tahlequah, they achieved a kind of communication, maybe better than anything they could have managed with words. There was nothing much of an overtly physical nature; once she reached up and touched the side of his face with her fingertips, and in response he took his left hand from the handgrip and briefly stroked her knee where it rested against his hip, but that was all.

Down the crumbly old two-lane snaketrack of Highway 82, then, across the scary narrow iron bridge above the upper end of Lake Tenkiller, up into the Cookson Hills, laying the bike over and jamming hard through the squirming uphill turns, down across Terrapin Creek and Chicken Creek with the exhaust popping and booming under deceleration, then up over the shoulder of Buckhorn Mountain and down again to cross the Sequoyah County line at Snake Creek, past the lights of the groceries-gas-and-bait one-stop store at Blackgum and on down a roller-coaster straight, the Honda squatting briefly on its shocks at the bottoms of the dips, and at last a long fast sweeping curve and then Billy grunted softly and started braking and shifting down, flicking on the right turn signal. The turn signal indicator threw a soft off-and-on glow against the rear surface of the windshield as he swung off the highway and aimed the Honda down the narrow asphalt ribbon of Moonshine Road.

Janna stirred slightly against him, raising her head from its resting place against his right shoulder. "Nearly there," he yelled, and felt her nod an acknowledgment.

A few minutes later he began slowing again. A rough gravel road led off to the right, disappearing into a patch of dense woods. A large sign, unevenly lettered on a four-by-eight sheet of plywood, appeared in his headlight beam:

REDBIRD SMITH
NIGHTHAWK KEETOOWAH SOCIETY
RELIGIOUS CEREMONIAL GROUNDS
ABSOLUTELY NO ALCOHOL OR DRUGS ALLOWED

The legend was repeated in the curling letters of the Cherokee alphabet. "Cousin of mine painted that sign," Billy said, and gunned the Honda gently up the rutted track, staying in bottom gear on the loose gravel.

The dirt road wound through a grove of big post-oak trees and then forked to make a big loop around the perimeter of a broad grassy clearing. In the middle of the field seven open post-oak arbors formed a circle, facing inward; and in the center of the circle burned a large fire, around which shadowy figures moved in a counterclockwise orbit, silhouetted against the leaping flames. The Honda's headlight picked up parked cars and pickup trucks, scattered about the field or bunched behind the arbors. A trio of young men in T-shirts appeared ahead, strolling across the road; they looked toward the oncoming bike, waved, and moved off into the dark.

Billy pulled up next to a big tree and shut off the engine and kicked the sidestand down. "Here we are," he said.

He sat still while she climbed awkwardly off the bike, using his shoulders as handholds. When she was down he leaned the Honda onto its stand and swung his leg over the tank and stood for a minute letting his eyes adjust to the dim light.

"What is this place?" Janna asked, looking around.

"Stomp dance ground," he told her. "This is how we do it. Where we do it. What Cherokees do, I mean."

He took his hat from the topbox and started to put it on. Then, remembering, he took the eagle feather from the beaded hatband and stowed it in the topbox, laying it carefully atop the loose tools and spark plugs and road maps. By stomp dance protocol, only a dance leader—a man qualified to lead the call-and-response songs—was supposed to wear a feather in his hat at a stomp ground. If he couldn't lead, or for some reason was not prepared to do so on a particular night, he should remove the feather before going into the circle. The rule was seldom enforced nowadays, but Billy tended to be conservative in such matters. And, despite Grandfather Ninekiller's efforts to train him, he had never felt up to leading a dance; it was all he could do, he often said, to follow.

"Come on," he said.

She took his hand as they started toward the dance circle. As they came out from beneath the trees the sky opened up above them, huge and deep, lit with the silver explosions of countless stars. Off to the north, right down on the horizon, faint flickers of far-off lightning against a bank of clouds said that Kansas was getting another spring storm. The rest of the sky was blue-black and clear. Billy heard Janna catch her breath beside him. "So beautiful," she said.

At the edge of the circle, between two arbors where Indian families sat on wooden benches, they stopped and watched the stomp dancers circling the fire. Next to the fire, the leader crouched and gesticulated, waving his hands in a complex pattern, calling out the syllables of a song so ancient the language had long ago been lost. Behind him men in wide-brimmed hats or mesh-backed gimme caps followed in a flat-footed trotting step, singing the response chorus in unison, at certain times turning and extending their hands to the fire.

There was no drum. Instead women and girls of varying

ages, interspersed among the men, carried the rhythm with turtle-shell rattles lashed to their legs, moving their feet in a double-shuffle step to produce a steady pulsing beat. Farther from the fire, in a second line, danced younger boys, girls without shell rattles, and adults lacking sufficient skill or confidence to join the leaders next to the fire.

Janna said something, very softly, in a language that was neither English nor Russian. Her hand tightened on his.

The leader's voice rose in a high loud whoop, ending the song. The circle of dancers broke up, the men calling *"Wado!"* in appreciation. Billy heard a few cries of *"Mato!"*—some Creek visitors here tonight, or maybe Seminoles. Janna tugged at his arm. "Excuse me," she said with some urgency, "where can I go to. . . ?"

"This way." He led her back across the field, past the parked cars, exchanging greetings with men and women who sat in the darkness on fenders or in lawn chairs. At the edge of the woods stood an incongruously modern, painfully ugly concrete-block structure, lit by electric bulbs around which swarmed squadrons of insects. The doors were lettered "Men" and "Women" in both English and Cherokee. "Up-to-date facilities here," Billy said dryly.

She disappeared inside and he realized his own bladder was starting to signal for relief. When he tried the men's-room door, though, it refused to open, and a voice inside called out something unintelligible. Billy said, "Shit," under his breath and stepped back, looking around. It was, after all, ridiculous to wait outside a restroom door with a forest of perfectly good trees right at hand. Fine Indian he'd be if he couldn't even pee in the woods.

He stepped into the shadows under the trees, selected a good-sized post oak, made sure he was hidden from view, and unzipped his jeans. With considerable enjoyment he watered the post oak until he ran dry. Zipping up again, he moved back from the tree, but then he stopped, enjoying the smell of the spring woods, listening to the singing from the dance ground and the *shaka-shaka-shaka* of the turtle-shell rattles on the women's legs. There weren't, he thought, too damn many times nowadays when it was good to be an Indian, but this was definitely one of them.

A voice overhead said, "*'Siyo, chooch.*"

Billy jumped so violently his hat nearly came off. "Jesus!" he said, looking up.

The biggest raccoon he had ever seen lay stretched out along a low-hanging limb. "No," it said in Cherokee, "just your grandfather."

Not again, Billy thought wildly. He started to lean against the tree for support, but at the last second he remembered he'd just pissed on it.

"Actually," Grandfather's voice went on in English, "Jesus doesn't care much for stomp dances, told me once he doesn't like the music. Said he prefers that mournful-sounding Jewish singing. Although lately he's very taken with some Englishman name of Elvis Costello."

"So it's you again." Billy glanced nervously around. Hell of a thing to get seen talking to a raccoon. "Being a coon this time, huh?"

"I ain't playing Lone Ranger, *chooch*. Glad you finally came down here. I was getting tired of that damn Kiowa screeching."

"You were at the powwow?"

"*Chooch*, I'm like Candid Camera—any time, when you least expect it, I might be watching you." The raccoon grinned, exposing sharp teeth. "Got yourself a girl, have you?"

"I don't know. I just met her."

The raccoon snorted. "Well, if you let her get away, you're crazier than even a Badwater has any right to be. That's a lot of woman there, *chooch*."

"You like her?" The thought pleased Billy.

"Son, if I was alive and fifty years younger—" The ringed tail switched from side to side a couple of times. "Never cared much for *yoneg* women, but this one's something special."

"She's not a *yoneg*," Billy said. "Not exactly, anyway."

"That's right, she's not, is she?" Grandfather mused. "She's from back where we all came from. Real home girl there. Explains a lot, don't it?"

Billy looked curiously at the raccoon. "You never believed in that before," he said. "About us Indians coming from Asia. You said it was just *yoneg* bullshit."

"Hey," Grandfather said, "you learn things here in the spirit world, like I said before. Why, I got to meet some of the people that made the original journey, back in the time of the big ice. Hell of a walk, to hear them tell it. Guy said those mammoths were a son of a bitch to kill, too."

"Bullshit," Billy said fondly.

"Maybe. Maybe not. You'll never know, will you?" The raccoon grinned again. "At least not in this life."

Through the trees Billy saw Janna come out of the restroom and stop, looking around. "Go on," Grandfather said, "she's looking for you. We can talk later."

Billy hesitated. *"Eduda—"*

"Go on," Grandfather repeated. "Take care of her, *sgilisi*. I told you, I can see some things from here. Some way, her life and yours are all tied up together, in more ways than I can make out just yet. *Donadagohuh*."

"*Howa*," Billy replied automatically. And saw, now, only a fat old raccoon asleep in a tree.

He walked out of the woods and across the clearing, to where Janna stood. "Like it here?" he said.

"This is an amazing place," she said, looking toward the dance circle, where another song had started. "I see what you meant, that it's not like the powwow. It's very . . . spiritual here. Even I can see that."

"Come on," he said, "let's get something to eat."

Nearby, lit by several undersized electric bulbs, stood a large open arbor where people sat talking in comfortable old chairs and Cherokee women tended a long rough-plank table loaded with pots and bowls and dishes of food. Billy got a couple of paper plates and filled them from a big covered pot. "Grape dumplings," he said, handing one of the plates to Janna. "Cherokee specialty. Want some coffee with it?"

"Please," she said.

A little while later, as they sat eating, Janna paused and looked about her. "This place," she said, gesturing with her plastic fork, "I suppose it must be hundreds of years old?"

"No," Billy said, and frowned. Didn't she know? But of course, most white Americans didn't know about the Trail of Tears, how would she have heard? "Cherokees aren't originally from this part of the country," he explained. "We lived back east, until about a century and a half ago, when the government forced us to move to Oklahoma."

"I know about deportations," she said. "Kazakhstan is full

of people who were deported from other parts of the Soviet Union. It is a big problem now."

"It was pretty rough," Billy said. "We lost a third of the tribe on the march, or so they say."

She nodded, something dark coming into her eyes. "Stalin killed a third of our people in the nineteen-thirties," she said. "At least a third, maybe more, nobody really knows. Many were deported to Siberia and never heard from again. As many as two million starved."

"Christ!"

"Of course," she added bleakly, "later on, they did even worse—no." She shook her head and stabbed viciously at her grape dumplings with the plastic fork. "I will not talk of these things now. Tonight I want to forget."

Billy didn't know what to say. After a minute he drained his coffee and stood up. "Finish up," he said, "and I'll teach you to stomp dance."

THE DANCE WENT on through the rest of the night, the songs getting farther apart and the dancers getting fewer as people got tired and dropped out, until there were only a handful circling the fire. Children slept in back seats or the beds of pickup trucks. Up under the big arbor, girls and women took off turtle-shell rattles and wearily rubbed their legs.

As the sky began to grow lighter and the stars faded from sight, Billy and Janna rode back up the two-lane, the old Honda's exhaust sounding very loud in the morning quiet. The sun was coming up as they crossed the Cherokee County line. On the hillsides the dogwood and the redbud were in bloom. Little pockets of early-morning mist lay white and wooly in the hollows.

He turned off the highway, just below the Tenkiller bridge, and headed down a series of unnumbered county roads. If she realized they were not going back the way they had come, she gave no sign. When he finally turned up a one-lane dirt track through a stand of pines, she raised her head to look around, but still she did not speak; and when he pulled into a weed-grown yard and stopped beside a battered old trailer sitting on concrete blocks, all she said was, "Yours?"

"Belongs to my uncle," he said. "He lets me live here."

She nodded sleepily and climbed off the motorcycle, while he put the stand down and took the key from the ignition lock. She followed him across the yard and up the flimsy metal steps and into the trailer without another word. Inside, they tumbled into the unmade bed and fell asleep in an embrace that was less that of lovers than of very tired children. Neither of them noticed the big gray owl that came and perched on a branch outside the window and sat for a little while looking in, watching them, before flapping away.

BILLY AWOKE A LITTLE after midday with Janna's hands and then her mouth on him. Struggling to break the surface tension of sleep, he lay passive and blinking while she undressed him. She was already naked and her skin was the color of a ripe apricot in the sunlight that streamed through the trailer's windows. The dark points of her small breasts were hard against his body as she slid up along him and kissed him. When he rolled over onto and into her she made a small soft sound deep in her throat.

Considerably later, they took turns showering—after establishing by experiment that the trailer's tiny shower stall wouldn't hold them both at once—and she washed her dress and underwear in the sink and hung them up by the window to dry. "Give me a shirt," she said.

"Hell, sit around like you are," he protested. "Nobody's going to come calling. Or are you cold?"

"No, I just want to wear your shirt. I want to wear something of yours," she said in Russian. "To feel it next to my skin."

"That doesn't make sense. What if I wanted to wear *your* clothes?"

"I don't have to make sense, I'm a woman and a Kazakh." She wiggled her nose at him. "And in love besides. A Kazakh woman in love, you better not argue with me. Go get me a shirt."

So he got her one of his army dress-uniform shirts, and she looked better in it than he ever had. "I love it," she said happily, pirouetting, making the long tails fly up around her thighs, exposing momentarily her round naked bottom. "What kind of soldier were you? Infantry, artillery, tanks?"

"Special Forces. What they call Green Berets."

Her eyes went round. "Oh, I have heard of them. You were a parachute jumper?"

"Among other things."

"Fantastic. How long did you serve?"

"Eight years." The subject still made him uncomfortable but if she wanted to know he'd tell her. "I enlisted for four, but then there was that business in Iraq. My team wound up working with these Kurdish rebels. When the United States just backed off, once their usefulness was finished, and left them to starve or be massacred, it just turned something off in me."

He looked out the window. "They sent us back later to help the refugees. I'd see them struggling through the snow, half of them barefoot, mothers carrying babies and little kids carrying littler kids, and I'd think, this is what the Trail of Tears must have looked like. Another bunch of people, like us, who made the mistake of counting on the honor of the American government . . . because we made the same mistake, you know. The Cherokees helped Andrew Jackson fight the Creeks, figured that would get us better treatment, and the son of a bitch double-crossed us the same way."

He turned back to face her. "So finally I couldn't take it any longer, and I got the hell out. Had a few connections by then, had a good service record, I managed to get a transfer. Only I had to extend my enlistment," he said. "That's how I wound up at language school, in fact."

"And now here you are." She walked over to stand before him, putting her hands on his shoulders. "And I am glad you are. Now." She looked about the interior of the trailer. They were in the single room that served as living room, dining room, and kitchen. "We must eat," she said. "What do you have?"

She went to the refrigerator and glanced in, wrinkling her nose at the smell and shutting the door hastily, and then began looking through the shelves above the stove.

"Not much there," he said. "Pretty poor stuff, what there is of it. Mostly Indian commodities."

"Pfui. You forget you are speaking to former Soviet citizen. I am expert on dealing with food shortages." She picked up a couple of cans, studying the labels. "Do you have onion?"

"Wild onions growing right outside," he said. "I'll go pull some."

"*Harasho.*" She took the big pot from the stove and examined the inside. "*Bozhe moi*, I must wash this first. How do you live like this?"

He started for the door. Just as he opened it she said quietly behind him, "We are crazy, you know."

"Yes," he said, not turning around.

"I don't care," she said. "Do you?"

"No," he said, and went outside to look for wild onions.

SHE STAYED THROUGH the night, and the next day and the next night.

They made various kinds of love in various kinds of ways, and did other inconsequential things. They went for a walk through the woods (Billy keeping a slightly nervous eye on the wildlife, but nothing spoke to him) and splashed briefly in the creek, keeping to the shallows because neither of them swam well, and later they sat on the couch drinking beer and listening to country-and-western music on his radio. He showed her how to write her name in Cherokee, and taught her Cherokee words and phrases and didn't tell her when she messed up the tones. She taught him a little basic Kazakh and a couple of new positions.

She told him about her country: the enormous flat expanses of desert and steppe, the blast-furnace heat of the summers and the killing cold of the winters and always the keening, searching wind. And about her people, the battered inheritors of all that was left of an almost vanished world.

For centuries the land of Turkestan had stretched from western China to the Caspian Sea, from Siberia to the Hindu Kush, home to peoples—wandering tribes and citizens of fabulous ancient cities—with a rich and complex culture that was old long before Temujin became the Jengiz Khan. The Kazakhs and other Turkish tribes had ridden stirrup-to-stirrup with the Mongols in their glory days, had intermarried or at least interscrewed with them ("Look at my eyes," Janna said) and, under a homeboy named Timur-i-leng aka Tamerlane, had eventually gone into the conquest business for themselves for a brief and bloody time.

Sooner or later every team hits a slump. In the nineteenth century, around the time the United States began to get its Indian-shafting act really together, the Russians took over Turkestan in a long brutal campaign—except for some bits the Chinese managed to nibble off—and remained as overlords until the following century.

The Turkestanis didn't like Russian rule any better than anybody else ever has, and on hearing about the Revolution they declared independence. But the Bolsheviks, for all their anti-Imperialist rhetoric, weren't having any of that; the Turkestani nationalists got crushed in a vicious six-year war and their country was whacked up into five arbitrarily-defined "republics" of which Kazakhstan was the biggest but also the most brutally oppressed and exploited. Nomadic herders since time out of mind, the Kazakhs were forcibly resettled on collective farms—usually on land that was hopeless for farming—and the traditional chiefs and elders were replaced by Stalinist bureaucrats and secret-police bullies. Later, under Khrushchev, great numbers of Russian colonists were brought in to settle and farm the so-called Virgin Lands, evicting such few bands of traditional herders as still remained, and very soon turning the world's oldest and greatest grazing lands into a dustbowl.

"They took our land and our freedom," Janna said, "and they tried to take away our souls as well. They did their best to destroy our identity as a people. Russian was the only official language in the government and schools. Religious and social traditions were discouraged or forbidden. Children were taught in school that they must forget the old ways and join the progressive Soviet society, yet when they did they learned that the good jobs always went to Russians. But you are not interested in these things—"

"No, hell, I'm fascinated," Billy said sincerely. "Because it all sounds so familiar, you know?"

Actually he had not entirely followed her. His Russian was still coming back to him, better than he'd expected, but she still lost him sometimes. Still, he had understood more than enough.

"This is not just ancient history," she added. "Even a few years ago, right up to independence, you could not get a job unless you spoke Russian. When I was a child in school there were terrible riots in the city, people killed and injured. There will be great bitterness for a long time. . . . No more of this," she said, switching back to English. "Talk of something else. You promised to teach me to make the fried bread."

MONDAY AFTERNOON they took the old Honda for a long run through the hills south of Tahlequah. Once again Janna wore that bobtailed dress, giving everyone else on the road a fine display; Billy considered that if this were an Eastwood movie it would be titled *Every Which Thing You Got.* They would meet a car going the other way and then Billy would see it swerve in the Honda's rear-view mirror. He wondered if she was aware of the effect she was having and decided most likely she was but didn't give a damn.

As they came back up 82 a half-dozen-strong band of self-consciously scruffy-looking young men on big Harley-Davidson motorcycles rumbled out of a side road and fell in behind them, following them for several miles of winding two-lane with no place to pass. Finally they did it anyway, passing one by one on a blind S-curve, jamming hard with plenty of noisy revving and gear-changing and hostile looks as they passed, regrouping ahead and disappearing on up the road.

"Their motorcycles," Janna said in Billy's ear, "they are better than this?"

"Pieces of shit," Billy shouted back above the blare of the 750's exhaust. "This bike will outrun any Harley ever made."

"Then why did they pass us?" she wanted to know."

"Because," Billy yelled, "if they didn't that made my penis longer than theirs."

"Shto?"

Billy turned his head and grinned at her. "Because I've got the girl in the white panties and they don't."

"Ah," she said, and nodded in comprehension. "A man thing."

"You got it."

He turned off just beyond the bridge and drove the Honda slowly down to the lake. They got off and walked along the shore holding hands. It was a fine day and the broad waters of Tenkiller sparkled in the sun. Off near the far shore somebody was fishing from a small motorboat. There was nobody else in sight.

"So beautiful and green here," Janna said. "I love natural things like this lake."

He looked sharply at her, realized then that she didn't

know. "I hate to tell you," he said, "but this is a manmade lake."

Something very weird came into her eyes. "Manmade?" Her voice climbed almost an octave. "How was it made?"

Strange question. "They built a dam. Flooded a lot of good land, ruined a perfectly valid river. What the hell, don't they have manmade lakes where you come from?"

She snorted. "Oh, yes, we have manmade lakes in Kazakhstan. That is one thing the Soviet Union gave us. We should be grateful."

She stared out across the wind-choppy water. "Only they did not bother with dams. In my country a manmade lake is usually a rain-filled crater left by an underground atomic explosion."

"Huh," Billy said. "Wouldn't they be radioactive?"

"Of *course* they're radioactive," Janna said angrily. "But the people were never told. Most of the herders and villagers didn't even know what radiation was. They watered their flocks at the lakes and drank the water and even swam in it."

"Christ, you mean they just let people wander in where they'd set off an atom bomb? Didn't they post guards or something?"

"The soldiers didn't know either. The danger was kept secret even from them. I remember once a Russian colonel went swimming in a nuclear lake to show it was safe, and took his son along. After all, the Soviet government—like yours—always denied there could be any harmful effects from underground testing."

"I'm a son of a bitch." Billy sat down on a concrete bench.

"It's not just the test craters," she added. "In 1961 they set off a big bomb at the junction of the Chagan and Ashisy rivers to create a lake for the local water supply. The children in that area—" Her voice began to break up and she stopped. "The things that have been done in my country," she said with difficulty, "you have no concept. Nobody does, nobody in the whole world."

She turned away and took a couple of steps toward the lake, her back very straight. Billy sat silently, letting her do whatever she had to do within herself. At last she turned back and came to stand in front of him. "Billy, Billy," she said, taking his hands, "we have so little time left. Please let's not spend it talking about these terrible things."

"I'm sorry," Billy said helplessly.

"Don't be. Come," she said, pulling at his wrists, "I want to ride some more."

They walked back to where he had left the motorcycle. She ran a hand over the chipped and oxidized paint of the tank. "Such a fantastic machine," she murmured. "So fast, like flying."

"She's just an old seven-fifty," Billy said, getting on. "Old enough to vote, forty thousand miles on her, needs a top-end job and new shocks and a lot of other stuff. Probably have to really wind her up even to break a hundred, now."

"I don't care, I love it." She climbed aboard behind him, clasping him around the waist and laying her cheek against his shoulder. "I wish we could just ride on and on and never have to stop. Never have to stop," she repeated as he started the engine, "to deal with the world."

TUESDAY MORNING HE drove her back to Tahlequah, to the house where she had been staying. When he pulled into the driveway the white couple from the college came out on the porch and stood staring while Janna dismounted. They looked pissed off.

"I hate saying goodbye," Janna said, holding his right hand in both of hers. "You made me happy. Now I have to go."

"Get your stuff," he said. "I'll run you on over to Tulsa to the airport."

But she shook her head. "I have to talk with these people. It was very bad what I did, running away and staying so long without even calling. Besides," she said as he started to speak, "we would just have to go through it all again when I get on the airplane."

She raised his hand to her face, resting the palm against her cheek. "*Donadagohuh'i*, Billy," she said, almost saying it right. "See, I remember."

"*Howa,*" Billy said, "till we meet again," not believing it for a minute.

He watched as she moved up the walk toward the waiting couple, the wind blowing her thin dress against her body. Then he toed the Honda into gear and laid it over and gunned it hard out of the drive and back down Shawnee Street, going too fast and making too much noise and asking for a ticket but not giving a damn. At the corner he turned and glanced back toward the house, but she was no longer in sight.

ON THE WAY home he stopped at a liquor store and bought a fifth of Jim Beam. Back at the trailer, standing in the yard next to the bike, he opened the bottle and raised it in the general direction of Tahlequah. "To a classy lady, " he said aloud, and took a long drink.

He didn't want to go inside the trailer, where everything would remind him of her. Instead he sat down on the big old stump beside the trailer and had another drink. He had had nothing to eat all morning and the whisky burned his empty stomach like acid but that was okay, one pain to take his mind off another.

A voice overhead said, *"Gado haduhne, sgilisi?"*

He looked up and saw a large gray owl sitting in the tree that shaded him. "*'Siyo, eduda,*" he said without real surprise or even much interest. "I'm getting drunk, for God's sake. What the fuck's it look like I'm doing?"

The owl clacked its beak. "I was gonna apologize for showing up like this, figured I'd probably scare the shit out of you, but it looks like you got more on your mind than being boogered by owls. Hurts pretty bad, does it?"

Billy took another pull at the Jim Beam and considered the question. "About like somebody's cut a hole in my chest and pulled all my insides out. And replaced them with a bunch of big rocks."

"That bad, huh?" Grandfather's voice was almost sympathetic. "Yeah, I recall when I was young, Melissa Bearpaw and me—but hell, you don't want to hear about that."

"I don't give a damn one way or the other," Billy said. The bourbon was beginning to hit him. "About that or anything else."

"Well," Grandfather said, "what are you doing sitting here on your ass, getting soused and feeling sorry for yourself? What are you going to do about it, God damn it? Just let her go?"

Billy shook his head angrily, wishing Grandfather would go away and leave him alone. Right now he didn't need a lot of harassment from an old man. Especially a dead one.

"There's nothing I *can* do," he said. "She gets on the plane for Nevada this afternoon."

"That scooter of yours won't make it to Nevada?"

Billy shrugged. "I guess it would. But hell, she's only going to be there a few more weeks—some time around the end of May, she goes back to Kazakhstan." He waved the bottle at the owl. "Hey, we already talked about it, about me going out there. Just wouldn't be any future in it."

"Future? There's no future, period," Grandfather said. "The future's nothing but another *yoneg* superstition, *chooch*."

The owl watched with big yellow eyes as Billy took another drink. "Looks like you're about to get through this day real fast," Grandfather said. "I don't think I want to hang around and watch you do it. I'll come back when you're ready to get up on your hind legs again."

Billy stared drunkenly at the owl. "What am I going to do, *eduda*?"

"It'll come to you," Grandfather said, and flew away.

4.

Speaking of Nevada, something extremely strange was getting ready to happen there.

Of course, the proposition could be advanced that something strange is always happening in Nevada, strangeness being indeed inherent in the nature of the place. Even the geography tends to be strange: weird dry lakes, waterless "rivers" that wander off and peter out without going anywhere, disconnected little mountain ranges that hunch up out of the desert in the most arbitrary places.

What Nevada mostly is, in fact—barring a little bit of spectacular real estate along the California line—is miles and miles and *miles* of doodly-squat, covered with sand and rocks and scrubby, sullen-looking vegetation. There are deposits of valuable minerals here and there, but these have only led to the hideous scarring of an already less than lush landscape.

There are only two cities of any size. Las Vegas exists on gambling, whoring, divorce, and ill-considered marriages. Reno exists on the same activities but in a different order of priority and without Wayne Newton. The rest of the state is mostly given over to things nobody in the rest of the country would have around on a bet: bombing ranges, toxic waste disposal sites, Indian reservations, and of course the only atomic weapons testing ground in the United States. What other state would they use to set off atom bombs? True, the testing finally stopped - to the anguished protests of quite a few native Nevadans - but where else would it have been tolerated in the first place? Even New Mexico got smarter than that.

Possibly, then, strange things happen in Nevada because only very strange people ever go there—practically everybody there is from somewhere else—let alone hang around and get involved enough to make things happen. Even in the old days, the other Indians used to say that the Paiutes were nice people but maybe just a trifle weird . . . but that's getting ahead.

It could even be argued that the only truly strange thing that could happen in Nevada would be for nothing strange to happen.

Be that as it may, the thing that was about to happen was strange even by Nevada standards. Which implies an event of truly apocalyptic strangeness, yet so it was and so it went down.

ON THE MORNING of the day it happened, Magda Simone stood at the big windows of her office and looked out over her empire—the New Age Enlightenment Center and Guest Ranch—and saw that it was good.

She was a tall, strongly-built woman in her late forties, with dark Mediterranean features and a still-voluptuous body; she had not yet hit the point where people would start using the adjective "handsome," though she didn't have far to go. Her thick black hair was piled on top of her head in an elaborate arrangement that her hairdresser had copied, on her instructions, from a picture of a Minoan priestess.

This morning she wore a floor-length blue robe of light cotton material, pulled in at the waist with a silver concho belt she had picked up for nearly nothing from an old Navajo woman in Gallup who had needed to bail her son out of jail. Her feet were bare, the better to enjoy the feel of the expensive carpet that covered her office floor. Since it was still early and she had not yet made her official appearance to the guests, she wore around her neck only the basics: a large gold cross of more or less Celtic design, a silver-and-turquoise rendering of a Egyptian ankh, and a quartz crystal not quite as big as a Tomahawk missile, all on finely-worked metal chains.

It was a bother, she thought, clanking around like that when there was nobody to see her, but you couldn't be too careful. Despite posted regulations and the efforts of a first-class security staff, guests had a way of popping up at the damnedest times and places; it wouldn't do to have them see their chief spiritual guide with her image down.

From the windows she had a fine view of the whole place; the morning sun blanketed the grounds and buildings with a soft golden glow that was very pleasing, and she made a mental note to have some photographs taken at this time of day, for use in advertisements and promotional brochures. The light gave a suitably mystical aspect, too, to the fake-Pueblo lines of the main building; might be worth remembering, she thought, when they started shooting that series of home-study videos later this year. Open with a long shot with the hills in the background, come in to a full-length of herself standing in the entryway, wind blowing her robe and her hair, rig a fan off-camera if the wind wouldn't co-operate. . . .

Warmed by the thought, she raised the cup in her hand (let the silly bastards drink that herb-tea swill in the dining hall, Magda Simone's day needed jump-starting: hell-black coffee with a drop of Jack Daniel's to give it a handle) and drank. Going to be a long day, she reflected.

HER NAME HAD NOT always been Magda Simone. She had been christened Renee Lacolle by her French-Canadian parents, years ago in Boston. Stripping and occasionally hooking around the Combat Zone, she had gone by a variety of names before at last meeting a minor underworld character named Eddie Caravello. Eddie had brought her to Vegas, married her after some persuasion, and in time left her a bit of money and a bit of real estate. There had been nothing sinister about Eddie's demise; he had merely had the bad luck to meet, head-on, a speeding van driven by a drunk who hadn't survived the collision either.

The money had been nice but not enough to last long at the level Renee had gotten used to. The real estate had turned out to consist of an establishment called the Putty Tat Ranch. After a period of shock and anger—the son of a bitch hadn't said anything to her about owning a whorehouse—Renee had decided she didn't feel like becoming a madam at this stage in her life. Anyway, the place wasn't really doing all that well, Eddie having been too cheap to get really first-class whores or fix the rooms up to look nice.

The great inspiration had come to her one day while visiting a friend who had gotten into the New Age movement. Renee had just about quit going to see her, in fact, she was getting to be such a pain in the ass; and sure enough, once again she had insisted on loading Renee down with books and magazines and tapes that promised to teach you to channel alien entities, remember previous incarnations, attain freedom from all bodily illnesses, and get rid of ugly cellulite in 48 hours. Back home, bored without Eddie to fight with, Renee had thumbed irritably through the pile of silly crap, and found herself studying a number of advertisements in the back of one of the magazines. Evidently there were places where these people paid a hell of a lot of money to sit and listen to this horse shit. . . .

"Damn," Renee had said aloud, the whole concept coming into her mind all at once, "there's a buck in this."

The employees of the Putty Tat Ranch had been given their walking papers, the builders had been called in—Eddie's old business contacts had been invaluable—and the work of transformation begun. She had gone way into hock to pay for everything, but she hadn't worried; she'd known she'd make it back in no time, and she'd been right.

Renee had shelled out the money to attend a few New Age workshops in northern California, while the work was in progress, and had learned that it wasn't all that complicated. All you had to do was serve up a goulash of Indian mumbo-jumbo—both kinds of Indian, of course—and fake Egyptology and Confucius-say Oriental philosophy, spiked with old-fashioned gypsy fortune telling and topped with a thick layer of Little Men From Outer Space like in the Spielberg movies. A shot of subliminal sex kept the mixture hot, but you had to be careful; some of these nutballs got hard to control when their hormones started to cook.

She had read everything she could get her hands on, from Shirley Maclaine to T. Lobsang Rampa and even Helen Blavatsky. ("New Age my ass," she had muttered, "this old babe was working the same game back a hundred years ago.")

She had concluded that this wasn't all that different from stripping or whoring: you just had to make the damn fools believe they were getting what they thought they wanted. If anything these customers were less critical than her old clientele; faking orgasms under drunk sailors around Scollay Square had been much harder work.

Magda Simone, she had named herself, after the ancient magician Simon Magus—the guy Jack Palance had played in *The Silver Chalice*, the one who was going to fly and didn't quite make it. Renee, or Magda, had always had the hots for Jack Palance anyway; her videotape library contained every movie the big hunk had ever made. She thought of herself mostly as Magda, these days. She never had cared much for her given name, but then she'd learned early in life that the only things people gave you were things you didn't want.

Finishing her coffee, she set the cup on the window sill for the Mexican-illegal maid to pick up, walked briskly over to her desk, and pushed a button. Almost immediately the door opened and a thin, pale, blond-haired young woman came in. "Yes?" she said expectantly.

"Call a meeting," Magda told her. "Nine o'clock in the conference room. I'll want Chuck and Lenore and, let's see, who's running the Ninth Circle meditation class?"

"Guido," the secretary said after thinking a moment.

"Red Hawk, dear, Red Hawk," Magda corrected her. "How many times do I have to tell you, we use only the professional names even when the guests aren't around. Then everybody's less likely to slip up."

"Sorry." The secretary bit her lip. "Will I be punished?"

"Forget it," Magda said, and then, seeing the disappointment in the blue eyes, "Oh, Christie, there's no *time* for that this morning, we've got work to do. Maybe tonight, if everything goes right."

"Okay," the secretary said happily. "Anyone else?"

"No, just those three. Special ceremony," Magda explained, "strictly for our advanced students. Have to make sure we've got it worked out properly, you know. They're paying Ninth Circle rates, they deserve the best we can give them."

Christie nodded and departed. Watching the door close, Magda sighed. She'd had other plans for the evening, involving one of the security guards—the new one, the one who looked a little like Jack Palance—but that would have to wait for another night. You had to keep the help happy. It was one of the rules of sound business management.

THE NEW AGE Enlightenment Center and Guest Ranch occupied several acres of prime desert land, an easy couple of hours' drive (less if you didn't mind pushing it on a narrow two-lane) from Las Vegas. Rugged hills surrounded the place on three sides, giving a picturesque look to the bleak landscape. That was one minor problem: during the rare but sometimes violent rainstorms, water runoff from the hills tended to gully the grounds and occasionally washed out the road from the main highway.

The land had once been part of the neighboring Indian reservation, the property of a small and impoverished splinter band of Paiutes, until the sixties, when some of Eddie Caravello's associates had decided the area had development possibilities. They had, then as always, owned the necessary people in government offices; it had been dead easy to get the land transferred. The Indians had put up no serious resistance.

The Bureau of Indian Affairs had been running wild at the time, terminating tribes left and right, and the Blacktail Springs Paiutes had had all they could do just to hang onto any of their reservation at all.

(Later, this bit of local history had caused occasional embarrassment for Magda Simone. Most of the guests, despite or maybe because of their financial wealth, were ignorant as fence posts; but now and then an unusually well-informed arrival would raise nasty questions. This was particularly awkward since New Age canon held American Indians up as persons of great wisdom and enlightenment. Magda, however, simply explained that modern-day Indians who suffered poverty and injustice were actually the reincarnated spirits of white soldiers from the previous century, paying off the bad karma they had accumulated by killing all those Indians. So far everyone had been satisfied with the explanation.)

The development scheme had never come to anything, which was why Eddie had been able to get the place cheap for his whorehouse. Lately, however, it was starting to look as if the sixties mobsters had merely been ahead of their time. The Vegas area was booming; desert property, once worthless, was starting to attract attention. Now that Vegas itself had gone respectable, transcending its sleazy origins, the area had become more attractive for retirement and vacation operations, and surveying teams could be found laying out golf courses where men had once wandered and died in trackless wastes. The closing of the Putty Tat Ranch had gone far to clean up the valley's image; a couple of resort developers had already sounded Magda out about the chances of acquiring the unused land to the west of the ranch. She figured there'd be more.

Unfortunately for Magda and everybody else, there was something almost nobody knew. The romantic desert valley wasn't quite as natural and untouched as it looked. It had, of course—like the rest of Nevada and the Great Basin, like the rest of the United States and the rest of the planet for that matter—received a steady and thorough dusting of radioactive fallout from the atomic tests of the last forty-odd years, but that wasn't it. This was a special sort of dirty secret, going back to a different sort of crime and more traditional criminals.

Even before it had attracted the interest of the mobster bosses, the secluded valley had caught the eye of a lower echelon of the criminal world. The Mob was heavily involved in the trucking industry, so it was natural for them to get into the burgeoning business of toxic-waste disposal; in some parts of the country, such as New Jersey, you could hardly turn around for a while there without tripping over a pile of leaking drums of God-knows-what, stacked in an abandoned building or simply dumped alongside a country road.

Nevada had little heavy industry, but there were mining operations that generated a significant amount of lethal garbage, and the government was starting to demand that they at least go through the motions of disposing of it properly. And then there was the whole nuclear business in its various manifestations; supposedly only the most carefully cleared and regulated carriers got the contracts to haul radioactive wastes, but since when has anything in this country operated the way it was supposed to?

The area was still Paiute land—that was one reason it was chosen; nobody was going to give a shit what you did on some damn Indians' turf—when the boys began dumping various odds and ends in the canyons and the ravines of the hills surrounding the future site of the Putty Tat Ranch. Most of the stuff was ordinary chemical toxins, evil enough but nothing unprecedented. There were also a few human cadavers, the mortal remains of minor gangland types who had made disastrously ill-considered career moves.

But then there was the truckload of heavy steel drums painted with the trifoliate warning symbol that meant, anywhere in the world, *radiation*. The men who trucked the drums in and unloaded them into the ravine were unhappy about the job, though they had been assured that there was no risk if they were careful. Behind the clandestine dumping stretched a long and complex trail of official corruption and negligence, and the owner of the trucking company was doing something outrageous even by Mob standards, but they knew nothing of this. They covered the drums with dirt and rocks as ordered and got the hell out of there. All of them died within a few years, one in a prison-yard stabbing, all the others of leukemia. Their boss had a heart attack and slept with his fathers, and godfathers. The matter was forgotten.

And the drums lay there a long time in their secret grave, doing an admirable job of holding in their dreadful contents; but they had been designed for transportation, not long-term storage, and in time they began to corrode, the metal made brittle by radiation. Shock waves from underground nuclear tests, less than a hundred miles away, caused them to shift in place and to crack, as did a couple of earthquakes clear off in southern California.

The rains came, when they came, and the water soaked into the dry rocky earth and over and then through the crumbling drums and their contents, and if the rain was heavy enough the water ran across the valley floor and cut long gullies that made more work for Magda Simone's underpaid staff of Paiute groundskeepers.

The whole place, in other words, was hotter than a two-dollar pistol.

LATE AFTERNOON, NOW, almost dusk.

Magda Simone walked out the front door of the administration building and paused a moment, enjoying once again the view of her domain. Over to her right rose the big main building with its classrooms and its Japanese-style meditation hall that was also a multimedia auditorium. Next to that, connected by an enclosed walkway, stood the health-and-fitness building with its aerobics and martial-arts gyms, its sacred-dance studio, its saunas and Jacuzzis and holistic-massage rooms—a couple of the girls from the old Putty Tat Ranch had returned to develop new careers in there. Beyond lay the long dining hall with its attached kitchen; one bonus of this game, Magda had discovered, was that you saved a pile on kitchen help and utilities, since most of the meals consisted of raw fruit and vegetables.

To her left, as she started down the walk, were the guests' living quarters, built around the rooms of the original whorehouse. Some distance away were the staff accommodations, less palatial but still a damn sight better than most of these losers had had before they went to work for her. Her own private house, the only two-story building on the premises, stood beyond, reared dramatically atop a rise of ground.

All the buildings were designed along similar blocky, more or less Puebloid lines, complete with coatings of fake adobe and bogus roofbeam-ends protruding along the upper walls. Down near the gate, however, was an unfinished all-metal structure that was going to be a big steel pyramid. That would be a hell of an attraction when it was done, well worth the modest expense. You had to spend money to make money; Eddie never had understood that.

Quite a little spread, she thought with satisfaction, striding unhurriedly down the swept-gravel walk toward the assembly field. There was just no getting around it: anybody who wasn't making it in this country wasn't trying.

Walking along, she turned her face this way and that, testing the air, and decided she had been right to schedule the ceremony outdoors. Usually these things were held in the air-conditioned auditorium or the gym; for all the clients' talk about attaining union with Nature, very few of them cared to spend any time roasting in the desert sun, and the chilly high-altitude nights were not much better. But the air today was cooler than usual, perhaps because of last night's storm, so it should be all right. Unless, of course, there was another storm on the way, but that was unlikely.

"HELL OF A STORM," Chuck had remarked at the morning's meeting. "Never saw anything like it. Weird lightning, damnedest colors, and the loudest thunder I ever heard—and yet it never did actually rain, did it?"

"It made the guests nervous," Lenore said. "They were talking about it this morning after sunrise meditation. Some of them came up and asked me if we might have done something wrong, here, to bring it on."

"Can't have that, can we?" Magda thought for a moment. "Okay, fly this one—that was no ordinary storm. The government is testing secret weapons in the area." Over the chorus of admiring murmurs she added, "You know the routine. Leak it confidentially to six or seven of the biggest blabbermouths—by now you ought to have them spotted—and let them do the rest of the job."

"Woo hoo. Heavy." Chuck gave her a big white grin. He was a husky curly-haired beefcake who had worked briefly as a male stripper and the female guests were crazy about him, but he had a tendency to irreverence. "Better watch out about anything political. Most of our honored guests are so far to the right they think Rush Limbaugh's a dangerous liberal."

"Right or left, they'll buy it," Lenore said. She was a pale-faced woman in her early thirties. She had a long face and long straight black hair that made her look a little like Joan Baez. "People in this country are always ready to believe the worst about their government. And it's not as if the government didn't keep giving them cause."

Magda clapped her hands impatiently. "Enough. No time for these little discussions. We've got to plan tonight's ceremony. The one for our special guests."

"The high-rollers," Chuck said. "The ones who cough up the extra nut to go the whole nine yards. Or circles."

"The Initiates of the Ninth Circle of Enlightenment," Magda said, glaring at Chuck, "are scheduled for a major ceremony this evening, and they'll have it. Outdoors, this time. It ought to be cool enough at sunset, and I want to get some use out of that medicine-circle setup. God knows I paid enough for it."

Guido, aka Red Hawk, raised his hand. He was dressed in fringed and beaded buckskins and high-topped Apache moccasins. "Which drum do I bring? The big one's louder but with the smaller one I can dance and beat it at the same time."

"Yes, the smaller one," Magda said approvingly. Eddie's nephew sometimes showed real aptitude for this business. "That song you did last time, okay? Now I want to make the following changes—"

NOW, AS SHE WALKED toward the ceremonial circle in the fading light, she saw that everyone was waiting for her: Chuck, Lenore, Red Hawk, and the twelve "initiates" who had sprung for the top-level enlightenment course, the one she privately thought of as "Around the World."

The ceremonial ground was enclosed by a stone-and-fake-adobe wall, eight feet high and almost perfectly circular. The inner surface was covered with big impressive-looking designs, mostly copied from Navajo sand paintings with some Tibetan mandalas and Egyptian hieroglyphics thrown in. In the center of the circle a fire burned in a ring of large black stones. A dozen feet due north of the fire stood the altar, a chest-high free-form concrete lump covered with imitation adobe and studded with huge genuine quartz crystals, some the size of loaves of bread.

The three staffers stood by the fire in their ordained places: Chuck on the east, Lenore on the south, and Red Hawk on the west. Chuck and Lenore had on white robes. Red Hawk wore his fringed buckskins and held his drum under one arm. Behind them in a semicircle, facing the altar, were the dozen Ninth Circle guests, all of them wearing saffron-yellow robes and carrying unlighted candles. Magda nodded to herself in satisfaction and stepped up to the altar. There was a faint but audible intake of breath from the waiting initiates.

She paused a moment for effect, knowing she looked good this evening. She was wearing her special-occasions robe, the dark blue one with the signs of the Zodiac worked in silver thread. Around her neck, besides the usual items, she wore a heavy Navajo squash-blossom necklace, a large buckskin bag decorated with Indian beadwork (it contained nothing but some wadded-up paper to give it bulk, but nobody knew that), a big gold Maltese cross with a quartz crystal set at the center, and various other trinkets that had no identifiable significance but added to the general look. In her ears she wore huge gold rings.

That was literally all, since she was wearing nothing beneath the robe. She never did. It was her private joke.

She spread her arms, not dramatically, merely in a motherly gesture of welcome. "Brothers and sisters. Are we One?"

The initiates more or less snapped to attention. They knew the drill. "We are One," they chorused.

Magda smiled approvingly, looking them over in the reddish light of the sunset. Some magazines, she thought, would have paid good money for a photo of this little gathering. Talk about lifestyles of the rich and famous. . . .

There was a popular rock singer from England, his career perhaps slightly past its peak but still good for a sellout crowd at any concert. Next to him was a Hollywood actress, once something of a goddess of steamy love scenes and now trying to get recognized as a serious dramatic performer, having pretty much exhausted the possibilities of cosmetic surgery. There was a gray-haired but handsome man who had become incredibly rich in the junk-bond game, and been one of the few to get away with it. And so on around the semicircle; every one of them had made at least one *People* magazine cover, and several had already published their ghosted memoirs.

"The Earth is our Mother," Magda asserted in a strong voice. "But last night . . . you have all heard."

Their faces said they had. Lenore had done her job well.

"Once again," Magda went on, "Mother Earth is in danger from the foolish actions of a few misguided men. I shudder to think how many incarnations they will have to go through, the suffering they will endure, to atone for this karma."

She leaned forward over the altar, being careful not to brush against the protruding quartz crystals. They looked fantastic but the damn things could gouge the shit out of you.

"You all remember our channeling sessions, and what Vaadu told you, through me." Vaadu was the twenty-thousand-year-old space alien who frequently spoke through her. Doing his voice gave her a sore throat but the effect was well worth it. "How the destruction of his own planet was caused by just such weapons, and how he witnessed the end of Atlantis from the same cause."

She had their attention now, and then some. The middle-aged actress in particular looked ready to wet her panties.

"This afternoon," Magda cried, "Vaadu spoke to me again. As you know, this place where we stand is at the convergence of two major world harmonic lines. The things that were done last night have upset the harmonies—not badly just yet, but the effects will increase and eventually threaten the balance of the planet unless we act now—"

She talked for some time in the same general vein, winging it, letting the sun go down. When it was nice and dark she nodded to Chuck, who took a burning stick from the fire and went along the line of initiates, lighting their candles. Red Hawk banged his drum each time a candle was lit, the hollow *boom* reverberating within the circular enclosing wall.

When the last candle had been lit and Chuck was back in position, Magda suddenly raised both arms again, this time high above shoulder level in a kind of two-handed Heil Hitler position. "Wait," she said, looking deliberately flustered, "he comes—"

Her head snapped back and forth a couple of times. "People of Terra," she intoned in a deep harsh rasping voice, "a time of danger is upon you. Concentrate all your inner power, now, to save your world."

Magda paused and passed a hand across her face, swaying faintly. "Thank you, Vaadu," she called in her normal voice. Then, to her audience, "You heard! Let us join together, now—"

She nodded to Red Hawk, who began to bang his drum and sing in a high-pitched nasal voice. It was an authentic Navajo *yebechai* night chant, and he was very proud of having gone to the trouble to learn it, though Magda suspected he was getting some of it wrong. As he started to go through it a second time Lenore turned to face the initiates and began to lead them in a slow chant, beating time with her hands, their voices forming a kind of plainsong between the boom of the drum and the descant of Red Hawk's wailing: *"Ommmm . . . ommmm . . . ommmm . . ."* The English rock singer's voice came through nicely, Magda noticed, clear and true; if his career ever went into the toilet she'd give him a job here any day.

"Concentrate, now," she cried above the chanting. "Purify your spirits of illusion and material distractions. Focus your inner power, as I have taught you. Feel it flow through you, as you become One with Mother Earth, with the cosmic harmonies—"

Which was precisely when the very strange thing happened.

The thing that reared up in the center of the circle, that burst through the earth in their midst and scattered the fire in all directions and stood huge and incredible above them, was of a shape not to be described, if indeed it had any true shape at all. The people who stood on the ceremonial ground saw only a great amorphous something against the stars, something so dark as to negate the reality of light itself. Simultaneous with the apparition came a bottomless roaring like all the tornadoes in the world. That was all any of them had time to register; it could not have been more than a couple of objective seconds before the horror descended upon them.

Chuck was the only one to come unstuck and try to run for it. He was almost to the gateway, hair flying, muscular legs pumping, when something that was not quite an arm and not quite a claw and not quite a tentacle and maybe not a material thing at all curled almost affectionately around his neck and clotheslined him off his feet.

None of the others even got that far.

IT WAS SOME time before anybody else came to find out what had happened. In fact it was some time before anybody else realized anything had happened. About half the regular guests were in the gym at a *t'ai chi* class, and heard nothing. The others, in their quarters or wandering about the grounds, listened enviously to the yelling and screaming coming up from the ceremonial area and thought enviously that those lucky bastards in Ninth Circle must be getting into something really heavy tonight; and a good many resolved there and then that somehow, whatever they had to do, they were going to come up with the money for Ninth Circle themselves.

The rest of the staff, more familiar with the routine, realized that something out of the ordinary must be going on, but they figured Magda had merely come up with some unusually spectacular special effects at the last minute. In the end it was Christie, the secretary, who talked half a dozen staffers and a couple of security guards into going down to check things out.

What they found would stay with them for the rest of their lives.

Chuck was the simplest case, and the messiest; he had literally been torn limb from limb, the major pieces of him scattered randomly about the circular enclosure, the minor bits decorating the ground and the wall and even the faces and robes of some of the initiates. The head lay in front of the altar. It was just barely recognizable as having been a head.

Lenore had become part of the wall artwork. Somehow—the county coroner would later come close to a nervous breakdown figuring out how, and never arrive at a scientifically possible answer—she had been slammed against the wall with such force that her body had stuck, fused with the adobe. Her arms were spread wide, her eyes and mouth were open in a look of intense surprise, and from in front she hardly looked damaged at all. She hung there in the middle of a copy of a Navajo sand painting, neatly centered between two *yei* figures, looking very much as if she had belonged there all along. Only the coagulating pool of blood beneath her dangling feet spoiled the artistic effect.

Red Hawk's body was the least mutilated. He lay beside the wall in his buckskins; it was not even clear at first that he was dead. The only thing obviously wrong with him was that his head had been shoved through the head of the cottonwood-log drum. That had been enough; Red Hawk, or Guido Caravello, was dead of a broken neck.

But it was Magda Simone who drew the immediate and total attention of the people who entered the enclosure. None of them had ever seen anything like it. Neither, probably, had anyone else in the history of the world.

She lay across the altar, face down and completely naked. She was not tied or shackled in any visible way, yet she seemed to be held in place by some unarguable force, against which she strained spasmodically with weak motions of arms and legs.

Huge quartz crystals, evidently wrenched from the altar, had been shoved into her major body orifices. Their exposed hexagonal ends glowed with a strange pulsing blue light. There was also a kind of singing hum, up close to the limits of human hearing, painful to listen to. Magda's body jerked and quivered helplessly in rhythm with the light pulses, her buttocks pumping, her thighs opening and closing with wet smacking sounds. Her eyes were closed and her face registered an obscene mixture of excruciating pain and orgasmic bliss. Muffled gobbling moans came from around the crystal in her mouth.

"God!" Christie cried, and the sound seemed to trigger some sort of release. Suddenly the pulsing light within the crystals died. And, with great and visible relief, so did Magda Simone.

When the staffers were able to function even minimally (one of the security guards had run away and the other, who somewhat resembled Jack Palance, lay curled up on the ground in a fetal position, sucking his thumb) they discovered one other fatality. The junk-bond hustler had simply fallen down dead, from what was later determined to have been a heart attack.

The rest of the Ninth Circle initiates were alive and unharmed, physically. The English rock singer had bloodied his hands trying to climb the wall, and when he tried to speak only tiny mewing sounds came from his mouth. The movie actress was all but unrecognizable, her hair dead white, her face that of an old woman. But then all the survivors' faces had aged cruelly, and all of them were at the moment hopelessly gibbering mad. Some psychiatrists and some cosmetic surgeons were going to make a lot of money out of this event.

It was some time before it occurred to Christie to go and call the sheriff's office. It was a good deal longer before she could get anybody to take her seriously enough to send out a car.

The next day's newspaper headlines read:

**FOUR MURDERED AT CELEBRITY GUEST RANCH
POLICE BAFFLED IN BIZARRE TORTURE SLAYINGS
SHERIFF SEES POSSIBLE DRUG CONNECTION**

And, on a sidebar:

HOUSE SPEAKER BLAMES DECLINE IN FAMILY VALUES

Coincidentally—insofar as the word has any real meaning—it was at almost exactly the same time that Billy Badwater decided to ride out to Nevada and see Janna again.

5.

THERE WAS NEVER any certain point at which Billy sat down and thought it out and reached a decision to go. He just went to bed one night knowing he was going to do it.

He went out in the yard next morning and stood awhile looking at the old bike, wondering whether he shouldn't do some work on it before setting out on a long run. The 1978 Honda 750K was possibly the best of the old single-cam four-cylinder Hondas, light and quick to handle, reliable as a tomahawk, and plenty quick for its day; but Billy had to admit this one was getting pretty long in the tooth.

He'd picked the old Honda up last fall, forking over most of his remaining savings to a white guy from the university who was getting married and whose new wife wouldn't let him keep the bike. It had needed a good deal of work, as you'd expect after being owned by a weenie like that, but Billy had done the necessary wrenching and fiddling himself in his uncle's garage, and he hadn't found any serious defects. Compression was down but still within specs, the brakes worked as well as could be expected on a bike of that era, and the transmission shifted through all the gears slick as K-Y Jelly.

The previous owner had fitted the bike out with a clear plastic windshield and a set of ugly but serviceable fiberglass luggage—topbox and saddlebags—plus an aftermarket exhaust system that improved power and reduced weight but also made the bike a lot noisier. Billy wished the silly bastard had spent the money on the suspension instead; the shocks were nearly worn out and the bike tended to pogo on rough or ripply pavement, of which there was sure to be a lot between Oklahoma and Nevada. The battery was also getting pretty geriatric, and when Billy pulled the drive chain away from the rear sprocket almost half a tooth showed, indicating imminent need of replacement.

The hell, though, with all of it. There was nothing bad enough wrong that the Honda couldn't make it to Vegas, and anything after that was farther than Billy felt like thinking. Besides, ordering and installing new parts would take time he didn't have.

He rode into town, bought four quarts of Castrol 10W-40 at Wal-Mart and a replacement oil filter at the struggling little bike shop, and on the way home stopped at the supermarket and picked up a jug of distilled water, a roll of paper towels, and a six-pack of beer.

Back at the trailer, he got out the cheap socket set and drained the oil and replaced it with fresh, changing the filter while he was at it. He dipped his hand into the bucket of used oil and rubbed his thumb and fingers together, holding his hand up in the sunlight, but he could find no glinting metal particles to suggest excessive engine wear. Raising the seat, he took out the battery and topped it up with distilled water.

He jerked the bike up onto its centerstand and spent a little short of an hour fiddling with drive chain tension, moving the back axle bit by bit in its slots until the chain showed the proper amount of slack. He got out the impact driver and removed the points cover and turned the engine over by hand, using the big socket, until the spring peg on the ignition advance unit lined up with the timing index mark, and loosened and then retightened the locknut to adjust the cam chain tensioner. A couple of tappets had been getting a little talkative, and he located his feeler gauge and started to remove the covers, but then he remembered you weren't supposed to do that with a hot engine and this one had already been to Tahlequah and back today. Well, screw that, then. Let them chatter, it wouldn't kill him.

When he had everything back together and the tools put up, he went back inside and washed the black oil and grease off his hands with dish soap and the paper towels. He opened a beer and did a little personal topping up before starting to pack.

He took only a couple of changes of clothing and a few basic personal-kit items, following Grandfather Ninekiller's often-repeated rule, "Travel light." His ratty old sleeping bag he rolled up and lashed with bungee cords to the seat behind him, to give his back a little support on the long miles.

Last of all, he stowed his hat in the topbox, placing it carefully so the eagle feather wouldn't be damaged.

In the morning, while the first light was still working its way down through the leaf canopy, he got up and put on jeans and a long-sleeved work shirt and his old G.I. boots—the Tony Lamas looked neat but were hopeless for a long run like this; with regret he had left them in the trailer—tied a fresh bandanna around his head, and sat at the table for a few minutes drinking a cup of coffee. Done, he picked up his old field jacket and his discount-store helmet, went outside, and straddled the Honda.

The starter whined for a couple of seconds, the engine taking its time like all Japanese fours on a cold start, and then fired. He let the mill warm up while he put on his helmet and zipped his jacket—wishing he had a good leather riding jacket, but they cost an arm and a nut these days—and then he put the bike in gear and rode slowly down the rutted dirt track to the blacktop.

As he swung onto the main highway down by the lake, an enormous hawk flew suddenly across his path, less than a dozen feet in front of him and no higher than his head. It wheeled and climbed steeply to hang for a moment above the road, the undersurfaces of its wings dazzling white in the morning sun. A single piercing scream came to him over the sound of the Honda's engine.

He grinned and made a palm-down gesture with his left hand, looking up at the hawk. *"Howa,"* he said, and gunned the engine, while the hawk climbed away and disappeared into the glare of the sun.

HE WAS ON the road for four days and part of a fifth. The ride turned out to be a tougher business than he had expected.

It was all right as far as Oklahoma City. The sky was clear and the trees and hills broke the force of the wind, and the only real problem was in staying alert over the long boring miles of Interstate 40. Even the truckers didn't seem quite as demented as usual. Getting through the Oklahoma City area without being killed presented something of a challenge, but he'd done that so many times he could have done it with his eyes shut—which, on the visual evidence, was how most of the local drivers *were* doing it, but he'd expected as much.

Out beyond El Reno (a bad town where they didn't like Indians; Billy rode on past, even though he was starting to feel hungry and the tank needed filling) and across the Canadian River, the land opened up and flattened out, becoming dry and John Ford-looking, with only a few scattered clumps of undersized trees to break the emptiness. Here the wind began to pick up in earnest. By the time he reached Elk City Billy was fighting just to keep the Honda somewhere on the road. At a McDonald's in Elk City he ate a quarter-pounder and washed it down with bad coffee and watched the signs along the road swinging and banging in the gusts, and realized that he was going to have to make some major readjustments to his plans. The daily mileages he'd estimated just weren't realistic, not if it kept blowing like this.

On west, the wind only got worse. The winds are brutal on the High Plains at the best of times, and early May isn't the best of times by any means. A dead-on headwind would have been bad enough, but here the wind came quartering across the Interstate from the northwest in great towering blasts, flattening the short sparse brush and grasses along the roadside, lobbing big balls of tumbleweed across the right of way and filling the air with grit. Billy had to ride for long stretches with the Honda canted way over like a tacking sailboat, leaning into the wind, just to maintain even half-assed control; and then when the wind did let up for a moment, or was broken briefly by a clump of trees or an underpass or a passing truck, the sudden change in lateral pressure made the bike go all over the road. His arms and shoulders hurt as if he'd been doing pushups, his neck ached from the wind's constant shoving against his helmet, his ass was getting raw, and his back muscles seemed to be trying to braid themselves. All in all it was not the most comfortable trip he'd ever taken.

And all the time there was the sound of the wind, an unceasing racket that his helmet could not shut out and the engine couldn't drown out. Sometimes it died down to a low disturbing moan; more often it rose to a teeth-aching screech of malevolent joy as it wrenched at his helmet and tried to slap the bike off the road, like a great invisible cat playing with an unlucky mouse. A witch wind, Billy thought uneasily, and it didn't want him there. . . .

He had planned to spend the night out in the open, making a free bivouac in some sheltered ravine or coulee or whatever they called them around here; the barbed-wire fences along the road were hung with prominent NO TRESPASSING signs, but he wasn't worried about that. But there was no way in hell he was going to sleep out on these Godforsaken plains, listening to that damn wind all night. On the outskirts of Amarillo he found a rundown old motel, run by a rather disagreeable family from India, and got himself a cheap room, knowing he couldn't afford it but too tired to care.

He lay on his back on the bed for a long time, watching the sky get dark outside the windows, trying to work up the energy to go get something to eat. At last he went over and switched on the television set, thinking he might get some useful information.

The set was typical cheap-motel garbage, the colors off and the picture out of focus and no way to make adjustments. Billy blinked dully as a familiar irritating voice came from the speaker and a familiar bespectacled face stared anxiously from the screen. He was about to flip to another channel when Jerry Springer said, "*'Siyo, chooch.*"

Billy was too tired even to be surprised. He sat down on the bed. "*'Siyo, eduda,*" he said. "Now you're on TV?"

"No animals handy," Grandfather pointed out. Billy noticed dully that the voice didn't match the lip movements, like on the old Japanese monster movies. "Figured this might be good for laughs anyway. Real interesting, you know, I never paid much attention to *yoneg* technology but inside this thing there's the damnedest mess of little—"

"Grandfather," Billy groaned. "I'm glad you're here, but I'm really tired, you know?"

The camera cut away to the stage, where a fat bald white man with a goofy goatee seemed to be talking about sleeping with his sister-in-law. "I'll never understand white people," Grandfather's voice commented.

Jerry Springer reappeared, waving one hand, and Grandfather said, "Tired, yeah, I bet you are. You looked like some kind of a big old bug out there on that road, all hunched over in the wind. *Whoa.*" Another woman, evidently the fat man's wife, had appeared on stage and was hitting the fat man and then her sister with some pretty solid-looking punches. A big scuffle erupted, with Jerry Springer in the middle of it. "Hell," Grandfather grumbled when the camera finally steadied down for another closeup, "this wasn't a good idea. This *yoneg* don't hold still long enough."

"Going with me all the way, *eduda?*" Billy asked.

"Figure on it, *chooch.*" The show had cut to a commercial; Grandfather's voice was now coming from a young woman in a white tennis outfit who was holding up a box of tampons.

"Damn," Grandfather said in wondering tones, "these *yonegs* talk about the damnedest things, right out in public. . . . "

"Why are you doing this?" Billy said. "You could just talk to me inside my head. Worn out as I am right now, it wouldn't make any difference."

"I know. But hell, even a dead man has to have a little fun now and then." The commercial changed and Orville Redenbacher added, "Hang in there, *chooch*. You're doing the right thing. A woman like that, she's worth a few hard miles. Now go get something to eat. You look like home-made hell."

The picture flickered for a second and the normal sound returned. Billy got up and went into the bathroom and splashed cold water on his face. When he got back the two sisters had the fat man down on the stage floor and were kicking him in the ribs. Billy shook his head and got his helmet and went out to see about dinner.

THE WIND WAS already coming down strong next morning as he rode out of Amarillo. On the outskirts of town he stopped at a small truckstop for a fillup and a cup of coffee. Coming out, starting across the gravel lot toward the bike, he was stopped by a Texas state cop car that pulled suddenly right into his path. A trooper with a red face stared at him through huge black shades. "Hey, chico," the trooper said, "you got some ID?"

The door on the far side opened and another cop got out. This one was tall and skinny and young, with nervous moves. "Don't even think about running for it," the second cop added, and then, "Compren-day you-stead, Pancho?"

Billy considered his options, but he had a long day ahead of him and no time to waste on confrontations with Panhandle goons. He reached for his wallet. The tall one said, "Careful, greaseball," and put his hand on his gun. Billy ignored him and flipped the wallet open and handed his driver's license to the cop behind the wheel.

"Shit," the red-faced cop said after a minute. "This for real, chief?"

"I'm not your chief," Billy said mildly.

"Don't get smart, chief," the red-faced cop said. "I can still find something to bust your redskin ass, if you piss me off." He turned his head. "You owe me that drink, Ray. He ain't a Meskin at all. He's a fucking Indian from Oklahoma."

He reached out the window and handed Billy back his license. "Here you go, chief," he said. "My partner had you figured for a wetback."

"Watch your ass on the highway, Tonto," the tall one said, getting back into the car. "We sure as hell will."

Billy watched as the cop car crunched off across the gravel lot and disappeared toward the Interstate ramp. When the troopers were out of sight he went over and began pounding both fists against the truckstop wall, tearing his hands on the rough concrete, until the pain cancelled out a little of the other. Then for a long time he leaned against the wall, shaking and sick.

You tell yourself they can't get to you, but they always do. . . .

THE WIND WAS if anything worse all the second day, but Billy was getting used to it, getting the hang of coping with it anyway. At day's end, an hour or so west of Albuquerque, he got off the Interstate and rode down a winding blacktop across a rough and apparently empty stretch of desert. It all looked about the same so Billy took the first dirt turnoff that wasn't closed by a gate, and a little later he was unrolling his old surplus-store sleeping bag in the shelter of a grove of stunted cedars. Big formations of black rock rose up all around and the ground was littered with boulders and smaller chunks of the same black stuff, volcanic he guessed. This must be the Badlands of New Mexico, like in the Marty Robbins song. He fell asleep trying to remember all the verses.

This was Indian country—well, hell, it was *all* Indian country, properly speaking, but here the Indians still hung onto some kind of possession—and, heading back toward the Interstate next day, Billy wondered if he should try to make contact with the local skins. But he knew almost nothing about the Pueblo people and their ways, or the equally but differently mysterious Navajos and Apaches, and the little he did know seemed to him as alien as the white world. Anyway, these western Indians, as he'd learned in the army, had little use for Cherokees or other Oklahoma tribes, regarding them as sellouts of dubious blood. He rode on.

At a truckstop in Gallup a beefy white man in a black Harley-Davidson T-shirt began making loud remarks about Japanese motorcycles and people who rode what he called "Jap crap." Finally, after Billy failed to rise to the bait, he declared in a loud voice that he personally would eat shit before he would ride a Japanese bike.

Billy told him politely that he was certainly right to stay with what he knew best from experience.

When the beefy man figured this out, he followed Billy out to the parking lot and wanted to get physical, whereupon Billy proceeded to beat the everlasting shit out of him. A short time later, clearing the city limits and jamming hard for the nearby state line in case of police pursuit, Billy reflected once again that you could indeed learn useful skills in the Berets.

He spent that night, probably illegally, in the Kaibab National Forest, up in the mountains near Williams. Stretched out on the ground in his sleeping bag, head pillowed on his rolled-up jacket, he looked up through the pines at the sky full of stars and remembered the night of the stomp dance. He halfway expected Grandfather to turn up in some form, but the night passed without a visit.

IN THE MIDDLE of the growing sprawl of Las Vegas, only a short way off the main Strip and virtually in the shadow of some of the fanciest hotels and casinos, lies an older, slightly seedy neighborhood known locally as Naked City. The nickname goes back to a time when a lot of showgirls lived in the area; they had a habit of sunbathing nude or nearly nude in their yards in the afternoons, resulting, among other things, in several near-collisions between private and military aircraft, cop helicopters, and the like.

The showgirls mostly moved out years ago, as the neighborhood started to run down, and later there came an influx of Asians and Spanish-speaking people, as well as a collection of low-level dopers and hustlers. (If the Las Vegas police have ever felt a sense of irony, rousting and busting nickel-and-dime drug dealers in a city built with Mob dope money, they have never given any indication.) People still call the area Naked City, though. Tradition dies hard in the American West.

Billy came to Naked City by accident, finding himself riding through the neighborhood after taking a wrong turn, trying to get back on the highway so he could find a gas station. The truth was, he had no clear idea where to go now he was here. Janna had mentioned that she was working somewhere in southernmost Nevada, not far from Las Vegas, but even before checking his tourist-information-center road map, he knew that took in one hell of a lot of territory.

It was midafternoon and damn hot, or at least it felt damn hot to Billy, who had spent the morning losing altitude and layers of clothing as I-40 curved down off the Coconino Plateau. The traffic had been remarkably heavy on 93 north from Kingman; it had taken forever to creep across the great hideous buttplug of Hoover Dam, everybody and his one-legged Uncle George apparently having decided to go take pictures (of a dam?) at the same time. Now, riding along the quiet Las Vegas street and seeing the CLOSED signs in doors and windows, Billy suddenly realized what was going on: it was Sunday. He'd completely lost track.

He pulled over to the curb at the next corner and killed the engine, looking up and down the street, wondering what he ought to do next. As the engine fell silent he became aware of the sound of music coming from somewhere nearby. From right across the street, in fact, good solid shitkicking honkytonk music with a heavy bass line and somebody flatpicking the ass off an electric guitar and over it all the whining *dew-dew-dewdy-yew-dew* of a pedal steel.

The music was coming from a one-story storefront building on the opposite corner, and Billy saw now that it was some kind of church. The windows had been covered with sheets of raw plywood and above the door hung a large painted sign:

THE LAST CHURCH OF NAKED CITY
LOSERS WELCOME

Without even thinking about it, Billy took off his helmet and swung his leg over the tank and headed across the street. The front door of the storefront church stood open and he walked in and paused, straining his eyes for a moment in the dimmer light. At the far end, up on a low stage, a flashily-dressed little man was singing into a microphone in front of a six-piece band.

Billy looked around. There were less than twenty people in the audience, mostly shabby-looking men sitting slumped on the wooden benches that served as pews, though there were also several astonishingly fine-looking young women. A couple of the men were obviously asleep, despite the noise the band was making. On the wall behind the stage, a big poster-board sign announced that GOD LOVES LOSERS – THAT'S WHY HE MADE SO MANY OF US.

Next to the door, on a battered table, was a large glass aquarium with a wooden cover. The wooden cover had a slot cut in it and Billy saw that the bottom of the tank held a small collection of bills, almost all ones, and a lot of loose change. He jumped slightly when he saw that the tank also contained a good-sized rattlesnake, obviously very much alive. Taped to the side of the aquarium was a marker-lettered card: PUT SOME IN OR TAKE SOME OUT–GOD DOESN'T CARE IF THE SNAKE DOESN'T.

Billy sat down on a back-row bench, listening to the music. The band was an odd-looking mixture of young kids and old-timers, yet they sounded good together. The singer was a skinny, sawed-off, wired-up character with whitish blond hair cut to less than half an inch and one of the biggest Adam's apples Billy had ever seen. He wore an electric-blue rhinestone-cowboy suit and strummed vaguely at a big Gibson Dove flattop guitar, his chord changes failing to match anything the band was doing. He had a high strong voice, though, and a good sense of phrasing. The band bridged into another verse and the little man sang:

> "Now it is just as easy as falling off a log
> To say the things that make your brother feel just like a dog
> Or start some gossip that will lead to bitterness and hate
> But when you try to take it back you'll find it's much too late."

The bass player, a tall Asian-looking kid with shoulder-length Rasta braids, stepped up to another mike and joined in the chorus, carrying the harmony:

> "Cause you can't put the shit back in the bird
> You can't take back the things you say, once they have been heard
> So just remember, friend, before you say that careless word
> You can't put the shit back in the bird."

The band slammed down a *boomp-boomp-boom-badda-da-baaa* finale amid a crash from the old black man on drums. The musicians began putting their instruments away and stepping down off the stage, to a scatter of applause, to take seats on the front row. Several people in the audience got up and left. One of the sleepers woke up, looked annoyed, and went back to sleep.

Now a big, dark, heavily-built man stepped up to the plywood lectern that stood beside the singer's microphone. He had bushy granite-gray hair and a wide big-boned face with the leathery lines of middle age, but the bright blue eyes behind the rimless glasses were lively as a child's. He wore black jeans and sandals and a black Meat Loaf T-shirt. In his right hand he held a closed Bible.

"Thank you, Jerry Dwayne," he said in a resonant baritone. He didn't use the mike; he didn't have to. "You can't, as you say, put the shit back in the bird. Too bad people can't seem to remember that. In fact I'm not sure your song shouldn't be our national anthem."

He laid the Bible on the lectern, not opening it. "Too bad you couldn't have sung it," he said, "to some people to the northwest of our not even marginally fair city, back when they were setting off all those bombs. Most of you still remember when we used to feel the shock from those underground explosions. Well, except for the band, they haven't felt anything in years." About half the audience laughed. "Now the Cold War is over," he went on, "and their last couple of ridiculous hot ones too, and they've finally stopped the testing—though it's no secret that plenty of the bastards in Washington, along with many of our own illustrious locals, are still pushing to start up again—but not one of them has a clue how to get their radioactive shit back into the bird."

He looked over the audience. "Why did the chicken cross the road? To show the turtle it was safe." Almost everybody groaned. "Sure, old, that's my point. Different places around the country, the punch line is an armadillo, a possum, or the like. So consider with me the implications of roadkill.

"Consider what animals you usually see flattened on the highway. You hardly ever see a run-over deer or antelope, do you? You might occasionally see a jackrabbit, but they get theirs at night because headlights do something to screw up their nervous systems. No, you take an animal whose built-in instincts tell it to respond to danger by hauling ass, he doesn't get hit very often."

He came from behind the lectern and began to pace slowly, almost to stroll, back and forth on the little stage. "But think about the ones you see all the time decorating the asphalt. Armadillos, skunks, possums, rattlesnakes, porcupines, they've all got one thing in common—they've got defensive responses that have worked for millions of years on their natural enemies, but that don't work worth squat against an oncoming eighteen-wheeler.

"Take the skunk. Millennia of evolutionary experience tell the skunk, 'Stand your ground and switch your tail, nothing's going to mess with you.' Except he does it in the middle of the road and the last thing he learns in his life is that trucks just don't care how bad you smell. Likewise the possum responds to threat situations by playing dead, only to find death imitating art under the steel-belted radials of a vanload of tourists from Dubuque. The rattlesnake *knows*, by God, that if he just buzzes that tail everything in the world will sheer off and leave him alone, and it probably surprises the shit out of him when that Toyota turns him into part of the pavement. And so on, and so on—the turtle and the armadillo assume their shells will protect them, the porcupine makes the same disastrous assumption about his quills, whatever."

He stopped pacing and took off his glasses and wiped his face with his hand. It was hot in the little church; there was no air conditioning, only a couple of big overworked fans.

"Now all this animal-behavior stuff," he resumed, "brings us back to our neighbors and benefactors of the nuclear test facility, and the kind of thinking they represent. Human beings," he said, putting his glasses back on, "started out, science tells us, as pretty half-assed physical specimens, considering they were trying to get into the predator business. I mean, you basically had this bunch of bald-all-over apes, no big teeth or heavy muscles, any chimp or baboon could easily whip three or four of them. And remember, they had to compete out there on the plains of Africa with some extremely serious customers—lions and hyenas and so on, all of them a damn sight bigger than anything alive today. Not to mention their own ape-shape cousins, members of other bands who claimed they saw that dead elephant first.

"So," the preacher said, "for a long time humans probably fell into the run-like-hell group, and they got pretty good at it; a first-class human runner can still outrun a horse over any distance. But then one day your X-million-great-grandpa and mine, and how we all miss him, suddenly figured out that if he picked up a stick or a rock he became a whole different animal. Now he could take on even a leopard, let alone some fellow-hominid who hadn't kept up in the arms technology race. And if he got together with a bunch of his buddies and they all had big enough sticks, they could just about knock the shit out of anything in their way. And this, my children, is when humans quit being an inferior breed of apes and became humans—to the subsequent detriment of the planet, some might say, but never mind that.

"Point is, over the next couple million years or so, while people got taller and prettier and, supposedly, smarter, the basic programming in their brain cells remained: *when danger threatens, grab the biggest weapon you can get*—and when in doubt, go ahead and start swinging, because you won't get a second chance."

He stepped behind the lectern and leaned his elbows on it. "And so you see where I've been going with this. Like the dead skunk in the middle of the road, that Jerry Dwayne likes to sing about, man—and I'm not being sexist in my language this time, sisters, this *is* pretty much a male-of-the-species thing and be glad you've got more sense—is responding to defensive reflexes that are no longer appropriate. We stand on the centerline of history, switching our tail, buzzing our rattles, flaring our quills at the oncoming headlights of the final eighteen-wheeler and shouting, 'Look out, I'm bad!'"

The big man shook his head. "We better smarten up, people. From the top-echelon idiots who want to set off some more atom bombs, clear down to Joe Numnutz blowing his foot off with the Magnum he bought to hold off the drug-crazed non-white hordes, we better smarten up. Or we're going to be just another smear on the Interstate of evolution."

He stepped back from the lectern. "This metaphor has gone on long enough. I will now shut up and ask everyone to do likewise for a moment. Use the time to pray if you like."

Billy bowed his head with the others. After a minute or two he heard the preacher say, "Amen."

"*Howa,*" Billy said without thinking. He hadn't meant to speak aloud, but nobody seemed to notice—except the preacher, who glanced sharply in his direction.

"On your way out," the preacher said, as the audience began to rise and head for the door, "you might drop some spare change on old Augustine, if you've got it. Try not to hit him with any coins, it pisses him off. Anybody in need of help, come see me. I probably can't do a damn thing about it but I'll give it my best shot."

He hurried down the aisle and stuck out his hand to Billy. "Cherokee?"

Billy nodded, taking the hand. "Thought I recognized that word," the big man said. "We had a Cherokee doctor at the Indian Health Service clinic back home. He used to say that a lot. *Hoe-wah*—what's it mean?"

Billy shrugged. "Different things. You can say it for 'yes,' 'you're welcome,' like that. Basically it means 'I agree, I'm with you.'"

He was looking at the blue eyes, thinking: IHS clinic back home? The preacher chuckled. "Mohawk," he said. "Eyes courtesy of an Irish grandfather. I thought you were a skin when you walked in. Want to try some authentically Godawful coffee?"

"Sure."

"Back this way." Starting up the aisle, the preacher glanced back over his shoulder. "Incidentally, my name's Mickey Wolf."

"Billy, uh, Badwater," Billy said, following him.

Mickey Wolf grinned. "And they call you Billy Badass, don't they? Well, you and our coffee ought to get along fine."

THE KITCHEN WAS large and surprisingly well-equipped. "This is the important part of the whole setup," Mickey Wolf explained. "We feed the homeless, and anybody else desperate enough to face our cooking. The bullshit out front, well, I have to put on some kind of regular services or they wouldn't recognize this as a church. Besides, I like to run off at the mouth. My Irish blood, I guess."

He handed Billy a plastic cup of coffee and got one for himself. "So we have our service on Sunday afternoon, which is a hell of a lot more realistic than Sunday morning in this town, where half the population doesn't even have a pulse before noon. I don't know why more local churches don't do it."

He gestured with his cup. "We're not quite as hard up as we look. For one thing, I do a lot of weddings—you'd be surprised, getting married at the Last Church of Naked City has gotten to be quite the in thing among certain celebrities. We've had several big rock stars and Hollywood names right here. And then some of the showgirls and strippers and hookers chip in, and a couple of big-time gamblers who think it brings them luck, and the musicians occasionally do a benefit show."

"Who's the singer?"

Mickey Wolf laughed. "Jerry Dwayne Austin. Still thinks of himself as the next Hank Williams, even though he's at least as old as I am—and I turned fifty last month—and never cut so much as a single, or appeared in any first-class places. Writes songs like the one you heard, and can't understand why nobody will record them. I met him while I was visiting the state pen. He was doing a one-year stretch on drug charges. After he got out he came to Vegas and put together his band. Jerry Dwayne Austin and the Piss-Cutters." He shook his head. "He's a piss-cutter, all right. Sort of reminds you of Ross Perot doing an imitation of George Jones."

The coffee was actually very good, despite the earlier disclaimer. Billy said, "What kind of a church is this, anyway?"

"As it says out front, this is the Last Church. I always used to see all these First Churches—First Baptist, First Methodist, whatever—and I wondered why there wasn't a Last Church for us people who come in last. Now there is."

He tapped himself on the chest with a thick finger. "As for my own affiliations, you see before you a former priest of the

Roman Catholic Church. Capuchin, if that means anything to you. Left the Church some years ago, for complicated reasons . . . but," he said, "to answer your question, I'm not affiliated with any denomination. The state of Nevada licenses me as a Non-Sectarian Minister. With all the quick-marriage operations here and in Reno, it's a common enough calling."

He looked about him with a proprietary air. "Kind of like being a dog that owns his own tree."

"Must have been a change." Billy knew nothing about the Catholic Church—Cherokee Catholics were rare—but he had an idea its churches were usually fancier than this.

But Mickey Wolf shrugged. "Hell, that's nothing. Before I went into the Church I was studying to be a medicine man. In fact that's how—never mind." Something dark passed across his eyes and was gone. "Tell me," he said briskly, "how do you happen to be in Vegas? Don't tell me the Cherokees have started holding conventions."

Billy told him the story. "No sweat," Mickey Wolf said at the end. "Let me make a few phone calls."

"You know where she is?" Billy asked eagerly.

"No," Mickey Wolf said, "but I bet I know somebody who does."

BUT HALF AN HOUR or so later, when Mickey Wolf emerged from the small church office, his face was not happy. The skin was very taut over his cheekbones.

"No luck?" Billy asked.

"What?" Mickey Wolf looked at him for a moment as if remembering who he was. "Oh, no, I found her all right. Took a few more phone calls than I expected." He wiped his sweaty forehead with the back of his hand. "Christ, it's hot in there, we've definitely got to spring for air conditioning . . . yeah, your Central Asian ladylove has been located. She's out at Blacktail Springs Reservation at the moment. Come on, I'll drive you there."

His voice sounded strained. Billy studied the big Mohawk for a moment. "What's going on?"

"I'm not sure," Mickey Wolf said, starting for the door. "The person I spoke to said that something terrible had happened. That's all she'd say, but she said it over and over: 'Something terrible has happened.' She was crying. I think we better get out there."

"Right behind you," Billy said.

6.

LEONARD HOZIA WATCHED the dust plume coming up the dirt road toward Blacktail Springs and hoped desperately that it was somebody, just about anybody, who would take charge of the situation.

He stood beside his semi-official pickup truck (it belonged to his uncle who was on the tribal council, but the BIA Law Enforcement people had paid for the installation of the radio and other cop-type accessories, and he got a small gas allowance from the tribe when they had any money) which was parked beside the big peeling warped-plywood sign that read:

> YOU ARE ENTERING
> BLACKTAIL SPRINGS INDIAN RESERVATION
> VISITORS PLEASE CHECK IN
> AT TRIBAL HEADQUARTERS
> NO PHOTOGRAPHY WITHOUT PERMISSION

The joke was frequently made, among the old men who had something sarcastic to say about everything, that the sign was bigger than the reservation, especially after that bunch of gangsters from Vegas had managed to steal the land on the other side of the ridge. The real joke, though, was that any visitors would have been lucky to find anybody at "tribal headquarters"—which consisted of a wind-battered double-wide trailer up on blocks, containing the office of the always-absent tribal chairman Marvin Tsequit, a few file cabinets, and the desk where a couple of Leonard's young female cousins put in a few hours each week doing BIA paperwork.

It was also, Leonard sometimes thought, a pretty comical idea that anybody would want to photograph anything around Blacktail Springs. It didn't matter, though, since there were never any visitors except official ones and damn few, thank God, of them. Although today he would have been more than glad of some help.

He was a tall rangy man in his mid-thirties, easily the biggest man on the reservation, which was one reason the council had given him the job of running—and, as it turned out, *being*—the tribal police force. That plus having family on the council, of course, and a general consensus among the older people that Leonard needed a job to keep him out of trouble.

Sometimes he drank too much and became hard to take, and everybody knew he wasn't very smart. He was also, on the whole, a big prick; but then the Blacktail Springs Indians, like most people of other races, pretty much expected that in a cop. All in all, Leonard Hozia had performed fairly well in his undemanding job, which mostly involved subduing obstreperous drunks and occasionally driving official visitors around the reservation.

Nothing, however, had prepared him for this day. For, specifically, what he had seen a few hours ago inside the peyote lodge. His stomach still turned over, the cold sweat still came to his skin, every time he let himself see the pictures in his mind.

He should never, he told himself bitterly, have gone in there in the first place. . . .

He had never belonged to the peyote church, though he'd attended a few meetings in his late teens out of curiosity. More than half the adult population of Blacktail Springs Reservation were at least occasional devotees; the peyote religion had come relatively late to the tribe, having been introduced in the 1920s by a Ute missionary named Sam Lone Bear, but it had caught on fast and grown steadily—especially in recent years, when some of the younger people had come to see it as an affirmation of Indian dignity.

Leonard Hozia, however, was supposed to be a Mormon. He *better* be; the half-dozen Mormon families who controlled the council had long made LDS membership a flat though never-stated requirement for any sort of employment with the tribe. Leonard could have kissed his badge goodbye if they'd ever heard of his taking part in a peyote service.

It wasn't just that, though. The truth was that he was scared shitless of peyote. His youthful experiments had yielded terrifying visions, and the spooky all-night ritual seemed uncomfortably close to witchcraft. The heavy peyote users he knew made him nervous, too; he always had the feeling they knew things he didn't.

Anyway, he had no desire to get involved with a religion that was even more opposed to drinking than the Mormons were.

So he had avoided last night's service, had stayed clear, as he always did, of the vicinity of the big canvas tipi from the time the worshipers started filing in. He had kept his windows closed all night, too, despite the heat, so he wouldn't hear the distant sounds of their singing and the relentless *ping-ping-ping* of the little water drum.

And wouldn't have gone near the place even today, even though he'd known by midmorning that something was screwy—nobody had yet emerged from the tipi, and usually they came trooping out right after sunrise—if he hadn't let some worried women, mothers and wives and sisters of men who should have been home by now, pressure him into going into the tipi to investigate.

Even then, he'd stood for a long time in front of the beatup old tipi (the Blacktail Springs congregation still kept to the tipi even though Indians elsewhere had begun meeting in permanent structures; this was less from traditionalism than from a hopeless lack of building funds) before he could make himself call out, hesitantly at first and then so loud he embarrassed himself.

But there had been no response to his repeated shouts, no sound at all but the dull booming of the tipi's canvas cover in the rising wind. So at last, very reluctantly and with a profound dread, he had approached the tipi's closed and silent doorway.

Covering the last few feet, he'd become aware of a powerful and very nasty smell, but he was too numb by now to think about it. Crouching down, he had pushed aside the door flap—the smell instantly much stronger, making him gag for a second—and stepped inside. And started to speak, but the apologetic words died in his mouth as his eyes adjusted to the dim light within the tipi.

Given too great an overload of shock and horror, the human mind will sometimes shunt the attention aside, deflecting the unbearable by focusing on irrelevant trivia. Leonard Hozia's first reaction, then, was one of simple and brainless surprise that the scene looked so familiar.

It had been at least fifteen years since he'd been inside a peyote lodge, yet he recognized almost all of the ritual arrangements and paraphernalia: the containers of food and water, the smoking remains of the fire in the center of the circle, the crescent-shaped altar of banked-up earth, the supplies of sage and cedar beside the roadman's place. The drum—a small iron pot, partly filled with water and covered with a hide head—lay, improperly, on its side beside the altar. Except for that and a couple of other details, everything was as he remembered it.

The worshipers sat in a circle around the perimeter of the tipi, their backs to the canvas. To the right of the door sat the fire-tender and the water-bearer woman. Next to the altar sat the roadman, the peyote church's equivalent of a presiding priest: old Dennis Saaba, a distant relative of Leonard's.

Not that Leonard actually recognized the old man; he just knew, as everybody did, who ran the local peyote services. Nobody would have recognized Dennis Saaba now, where he sat. His head was missing. That was one of the details.

His head, that was, was missing from its usual place on his neck. It hadn't disappeared or anything. It was, in fact, just about the most noticeable thing in the place. That was another detail that was wrong. On the earth altar, centered between the horns of the crescent, there should have been a single peyote button—the "Father Peyote"—on a bed of sage. Instead, in its place, the altar supported the staring-eyed head of Dennis Saaba. The Father Peyote was just visible through the smoke, sticking out from between the roadman's teeth.

The rest of the worshipers in the tipi merely had their heads in their laps. All the eyes were open. The heads seemed to be looking in the direction of the altar, as if waiting for directions from the roadman's head. That was the other detail. That and the blood all over everything; Leonard had never seen so much blood, never even imagined there could be so much blood in the whole world. That was what he had been smelling.

The people waiting outside the tipi heard a strange muffled cry, and then they saw Leonard Hozia burst through the doorway and begin vomiting on the ground. They watched patiently—it wasn't, after all, the first time they'd seen him dumping his guts, though he didn't often do it at this time of day—and when he seemed to be done they began asking questions. It was some time, though, before they got any answers.

NOW, LEANING AGAINST the fence and watching the dust plume coming up the road, Leonard tried again to push the terrible pictures out of his mind and concentrate on his own immediate problems. There was going to be hell to pay over this, that was sure, but how much of the paying was he going to get stuck with?

Reviewing his actions since the discovery, he couldn't see how anyone could find fault with his handling of the situation. He had, of course, immediately given orders that no one was to enter the tipi or come near it. He'd had to get a little rough with one hysterical woman who'd tried to force her way past him, insisting on seeing her husband's body, but finally her relatives had taken her home. He'd deputized a couple of strong young men to guard the door—he wasn't sure he had the authority to do that, but hell, this was an emergency—and headed for the headquarters trailer and the telephone.

Marvin Tsequit and the rest of the council were gone for the weekend, as usual, this time off in Utah at some kind of Mormon event and no way of reaching them. That left Leonard holding the ball and God help his ass if he ran the wrong way with it. Lose this job and there wouldn't be another one; the unemployment at Blacktail Springs was even worse than on most western reservations. One mistake today and Leonard could wind up sitting on his ass year in, year out, trying to survive on welfare and commodities, like everybody else around here. The possibility was so horrible that it almost pushed the grisly pictures out of his head.

He didn't think he'd made any mistakes, but who could be sure? Maybe he'd waited too long to investigate the matter. He could defend that on the grounds that he'd been showing respect for a religious ceremony, but that wouldn't cut any ice with the council members, who didn't recognize the peyote church as a real religion, or the BIA, which was only a tiny bit more tolerant.

Maybe he shouldn't have let that white woman doctor from the clinic go into the tipi. Somebody might say she'd disturbed the evidence or something. There had sure as hell been nothing any doctor could do for those poor bastards in there, but it had seemed reasonable to let her go have a look at them. If nothing else she could sign the certificates that they were dead, as if it took a doctor to tell that.

Anyway, he wasn't sure he could have stopped her, short of using force—which would *really* have been asking for trouble. Piss her off and she might go back where she came from, and then it might be a year or more, like last time, before they got another doctor out here.

At least he hadn't let that other woman go in there with her, that damn slanty-eyed Chinese or Russian or whatever the hell she was, the one who'd been staying at the doctor's place all week. He could just see himself explaining *that* to the FBI.

If, of course, the FBI ever got their overpaid white asses out here. He'd been waiting for them all afternoon, finally driving, for no reason but nervous impatience, down to the main gate to wait some more, though that hadn't been such a good idea what with the loneliness and the wind to get on his nerves. . . .

He knew he might have to wait quite a bit longer, too. The FBI had jurisdiction in a case like this—a major crime on an Indian reservation, especially a reservation with no real police organization of its own—but such cases, unless non-Indians were involved, took very low priority with the Bureau. Chances were they were still arguing and maneuvering over who was going to get stuck with driving all the way out here from Vegas just to look at a bunch of dead Indians and start the paperwork on a case that would probably never be solved. Leonard was not bitter as he thought of these things; in their place he'd have acted the same way.

It did occur to him, now it was too late, that he should have dropped some hints that this might be connected with some kind of militant Indian organization, AIM or something. That would have got the Feds out here plenty fast, all right.

Watching the approaching dust plume, he felt disappointment. He'd hoped this would be the Feds at last, but now he could see that the vehicle raising the dust was a Jeep; and he'd never, that he could recall, seen an FBI agent driving a Jeep.

Then the Jeep was close enough for him to see the faces of the driver and the passenger over the folded-down windshield, and as it slowed to a stop beside the sign Leonard Hozia said, "Oh, hey, Father Mickey," and walked over and stuck out his hand.

"Did you get the word, what happened?" he asked as Mickey Wolf shook his hand. "Or did you just happen to be out this way?"

The big Mohawk shrugged. "I heard something happened. No idea what."

Leonard was looking past Mickey Wolf at the young man in the passenger seat. Some kind of an Indian by the look of him, but not from around here. Kind of an attitude about him, hair way too long. But right now Leonard didn't care.

"Listen," he said, "there's some people could prob'ly use a visit from you, right now. I mean, maybe you can help calm everybody down, you know? You wanta follow me back up the road, I'll give you the whole story when we get there."

He turned away, but then after a couple of steps he turned back, remembering. "Say," he said, "you didn't see anybody else on the way here, did you? Anybody that looked like maybe FBI?"

"Nobody at all," Mickey Wolf said. "Nothing on the road between here and the Interstate."

"Son of a bitch," Leonard Hozia said, and then, "Sorry, Father." And started off again to get his pickup truck turned around.

BUMPING ALONG THE dirt road, following Leonard Hozia's pickup truck at a long distance and still getting choked and covered with dust, Mickey Wolf said, "Local law, such as he is."

Billy clutched for support as the Jeep hit a pothole. "Why the 'Father' business?" he asked through gritty teeth.

"Leonard's grasp of comparative theology isn't very extensive. As far as he knows there are Mormons, peyote people, and Catholics. Somehow he got it into his head I'm still a priest." Mickey Wolf grinned. "I haven't tried to explain. It makes him more co-operative."

Billy looked off to the right. The view was obscured by the dust, but what he could see of the country didn't look encouraging. They were rolling across a great flat stretch of the bleakest desert he'd ever seen, the bare whitish-yellow earth broken only by sparse clumps of low, desperate-looking bushes. The New Mexico Badlands had been the Garden of Eden compared to this. Jesus, what a dismal place; Billy couldn't imagine how anybody managed to live there. . . .

"Who lives here?" He turned to face Mickey Wolf. "I mean, what tribe are they?"

Mickey Wolf fought the wheel as the Jeep slammed over a stretch of washboard. "Paiutes, more or less," he said. "Separate bunch, though, not part of the Southern Paiutes. Hell, you've got these little bunches scattered all over Nevada and Utah, stuck off on dinky back-end-of-nowhere reservations like this, Paiutes and Gosiutes and plain Utes, not to mention Shoshones—the labels are mostly bullshit anyway. You know how it works."

Billy knew; it was the same with many Oklahoma tribes. "Tribe" was often as not a white invention; a lot of the officially-designated "tribes" represented little more than arbitrary groupings for political or administrative purposes, without real basis in history or tradition. From what Janna had told him, the Russians had played much the same game with their subject peoples.

Which brought Billy back to his main interest, and he said, "Where's Janna, then? And what the hell's she doing out here?"

Mickey Wolf pointed up the road with one finger, without taking a hand from the wheel. "She'll be at the clinic. That's the one thing Blacktail Springs has going for it," he said, "they've got considerably better health care than most of these small western reservations. Back a good many years ago, they got cheated out of a big parcel of land on the other side of those mountains—some Vegas hustlers pulled some strings—and because the deal was so raw, I guess somebody figured the Indians ought to get something in return, just for the sake of appearances. So part of the deal was that Blacktail Springs would get a modern clinic, and for once the bastards actually kept their word. True, I understand somebody got a really fat contract when they built it, but—"

There were a few houses along the road now, not much more than shacks, their unpainted board walls and tarpaper roofs warping in the desert sun. A couple of trailers sat on blocks, their wheels and tires long ago sold for spending money. Skinny, big-bellied children played listlessly in dusty, junk-littered yards. Half-derelict pickup trucks and old cars missing hoods lay next to outhouses with sagging doors. "God," Billy said.

"Pretty depressing," Mickey Wolf agreed. "Indians like us—you guys from Oklahoma, us Mohawks from upstate New York—we think we know how bad it is, but then we come to a place like this and we realize we didn't know shit."

"Third World, looks like," Billy mused, staring. "Poorest Arab villagers I saw lived better than this."

"Yeah, well, these people, you know, their life was kind of marginal even before the whites came. Took all they could do just to survive in this barren-ass country—Christ, just look at it, the fucking jackrabbits are on food stamps—so they really had it rough when the whites came around, stealing what little water there was and running them off the few bits of livable real estate. Especially the kind of white people who came to Nevada, silver miners and the kind of riffraff that always collected around mining towns, and then later on plain old mobsters. People who thought nothing of killing each other, let alone fucking over some bunch of scrubby-ass Indians."

"About Janna," Billy prompted.

"Oh, right. Well, as I say, she's at the clinic. Been working with the doctor here, it seems . . . there's the clinic now." A long, low, blocky building was just beginning to materialize through the billowing dust from Leonard Hozia's pickup truck. Various small houses and trailers were bunched together along both sides of the road, creating at least the semblance of a sort of village.

The pickup truck's brake lights came on—on one side, anyway—and Leonard Hozia pulled over and stopped in front of a big white double-wide trailer. A sign identified this as BLACKTAIL SPRINGS TRIBAL HEADQUARTERS. Mickey Wolf parked the Jeep beneath the pickup and said, "Welcome to beautiful downtown Blacktail Springs. *Lasciate ogni speranza, voi ch'entrate.*"

Billy didn't get the last part—he assumed the preacher was speaking Mohawk—but he was no longer really listening anyway. He was looking at the clinic, which he saw now was really quite a sizeable and solid-looking building, much bigger than anything else in sight. He saw no sign of Janna, but as he watched a woman came out the front door of the clinic and started across the road. "Mickey," she called. She was tall and good-looking, with long shiny black hair, and she wore a long white lab coat over T-shirt and jeans. "Thank God you're here," she said.

But instead of coming over to the Jeep she changed course and intercepted Leonard Hozia in the middle of the road. They stood for a minute talking, not loud enough for anyone else to hear. It looked as if they were arguing. Billy decided from her facial expression that she didn't much like the cop. Or maybe she just didn't like cops.

"Doctor Sarah Aronson," Mickey Wolf said. "Bless her round and marvelously firm behind."

"She works at the clinic?" Billy asked, still looking around for Janna.

"She runs it," Mickey Wolf said, gazing fondly at the tall woman, who was still arguing with Leonard Hozia. "Boy, does she ever run it."

Billy thought he picked up something in the preacher's voice. "Hey," he said, "you got something going with her?"

"Something." Mickey Wolf sighed deeply. "Not nearly as much as I wish."

The woman was walking toward them again, leaving a scowling Leonard Hozia in the road. "Mickey," she said again, reaching out to touch the preacher on the shoulder. They did not embrace or even shake hands, yet the intimacy between them was as tangible as the wind that whipped at her hair. "And you must be Billy," she went on. "I've been hearing a lot about you over the last few days."

She had large dark eyes and clear skin almost as dark as Billy's. He might have taken her for an Indian, but from the name he guessed she must be Jewish. He saw now that the long black hair was lightly streaked with gray; she had to be in her forties. He also saw that she had a really impressive chest.

"Janna will be right out," she said. "She's packing her things. I want you to take her back to the city." To Mickey she added, "Did Leonard tell you what happened?"

"Not yet."

"I'll give you the whole story, then, soon as we've gotten Janna away. This is no place for her right now—it's no place for anybody, but that's another story—and it's going to get even worse when the FBI arrives. I don't want her here when they start asking questions," Sarah Aronson said. "None of this business has anything at all to do with her, but they'd lean on her just on general principles. She's already having trouble about her status in this country—our work is starting to make some people nervous—and just being at the scene of a crime might be enough that they could use it against her."

"Crime?" Billy started to ask what was happening, but then he saw Janna coming out of the clinic. She had on the little blue-and-yellow dress he remembered, and she carried a small blue suitcase. For a second his throat tightened up and he could barely breathe, let alone speak.

"Deputy Dawg, there, doesn't like it that she's leaving," Sarah added. "He was saying nobody leaves the reservation till the Feds get here. Finally I told him if he tried to stop her I'd tell his relatives on the council about the time last year when I had to treat him for the clap."

Billy was already out of the Jeep and running across the road. Seeing him, Janna dropped the suitcase in the dust and ran to meet him. For a moment they stood in the middle of the road holding each other, not speaking. When they finally looked at each other's faces Billy saw that her eyes were red, as if she'd been crying. Her face was pale. "What's going on?" he asked. "Are you okay?"

She clung to him, pressing her face against his chest. "It's so terrible," she said, her voice muffled. "Oh, Billy, I'm so glad you've come."

He stroked her hair awkwardly. After a moment she pulled back with a ragged sigh. "I must get my things."

"Here." He walked over and picked up the blue suitcase. "Is this all you've got?"

"All I brought to this place. My other things are in Las Vegas, with some of Sarah's friends." She took his free hand and they walked across the road toward the Jeep, where Mickey Wolf and Sarah Aronson were talking in low tones. "Oh, Billy," Janna said again, so softly it was almost a whisper.

Mickey Wolf was getting out of the Jeep. "Billy, you can drive this thing, right? Take it and the two of you get out of here, right now."

"You're not going back to town?"

"Not yet. I seem to be needed here. Sarah and Leonard both think so, anyway, and my God, any time they agree on anything—"

Billy lifted Janna's suitcase into the back of the Jeep. "How will you get home?"

"Oh, I'll get a ride from somebody." He gave the doctor a grin. "Or maybe I'll just move in here."

"In your dreams, Your Horniness." Sarah Aronson looked at Janna, who was climbing into the Jeep. "If you've got a scarf in that bag, Janna, you'd better tie it over your head, or your hair will be ruined by the wind and the dust."

Mickey Wolf said, "Think you can remember the way back to the mission? There's a little room in back, next to my office, where transients sleep sometimes. Not very palatial, but it's clean anyway. You're welcome to move in for the time being. I doubt if your finances will cover a decent room at Vegas rates."

"Thanks."

"The long silvery key on the ring with the Jeep keys opens the mission," he added. "Help yourselves to anything in the kitchen. I'll be back tomorrow."

Billy got into the Jeep and started the engine. With some awkwardness—it had been some time since he had driven anything with four wheels—he got the Jeep backed up and turned around. A moment later they went rattling and banging off down the road toward the distant Interstate. Billy looked in the mirror for a glimpse of Mickey Wolf and Sarah Aronson, but the two of them had already been hidden by the pall of dust that rose behind the Jeep.

"NINETEEN PEOPLE," Mickey Wolf said, some time later. "With their heads cut off. I can't even imagine it."

"They weren't *cut* off, damn it," Sarah Aronson said impatiently. "That's just what I'm trying to explain. Leonard Hozia wouldn't listen, but he's an idiot."

They sat in her office in the clinic building. There were cups of coffee on the desk between them, but the contents had not been touched.

"Leonard isn't exactly your Tony Hillerman breed of Indian cop," Mickey Wolf admitted. "But okay, explain it again. What did I miss?"

She made an angry little noise. "Look, Mickey, a decapitation is basically an amputation, all right? A head, a leg, an arm, whatever, you can chop it off with one blow—which takes great strength and skill, which is why good headsmen used to make top pay—or you can do it with a lot of cutting and carving, very slow and messy." She paused, thinking. "Or I suppose you could do it with a saw, but I've never heard of anyone doing it . . . anyway, however you remove a head, you'd create certain distinctive patterns of tissue trauma. Any experienced butcher could tell you how the severing was done, never mind a doctor."

"And?"

She looked at him with terrible eyes. "And there's no way those heads were cut off, Mickey. As best I can describe it, they seem to have been *pulled* off—simply ripped from the bodies, the way a child might pull the head off a doll. There wasn't a clean cut in the lot, only torn flesh, things sticking out—ends of blood vessels, stretched-out ligaments and muscles—"

"God!"

"Yes, you don't want to hear the details. I thought I'd seen it all, but in two decades of medical practice, even in Bosnia, I've never seen anything like that. Never seen so much blood—do you have any idea how much blood nineteen human bodies contain?"

She shuddered violently. "And that's another thing. Whoever did the killings has to have gotten into the blood, has to have been fairly soaked. Careful as I was where I put my feet, careful as Leonard tried to be, both of us left bloody footprints outside the tipi. Yet there was no blood on the ground but what we tracked out, and no footprints around the tipi but ours."

"And they were all just sitting there? No signs anybody had tried to run or resist or anything?"

"Incredible, isn't it? Everything about this is incredible. Nobody heard anything, either, even though there were people passing nearby all night and at least five houses are within easy earshot of the tipi. Nobody heard a sound after the singing and the drumming stopped. Nineteen people," she said, "had their heads ripped off *in silence*."

"That's not possible."

"Of course it's not possible. Any more than it's possible for any human being to pull a head off by main force—do you have any idea how much strength that would require? That's what I've been telling you," she said. "Whatever happened last night wasn't just horrible, it was impossible."

While Mickey Wolf considered this, there was the sound of an automobile stopping in front of the clinic. Sarah got up and looked out the window.

"Speaking of the impossible," she said, "I think the FBI just arrived."

7.

IT DID NOT have a name. It did not know where it had come from and it did not know where it was.

None of these statements means anything.

It did not "know" anything at all in any humanly recognizable sense of the verb. It possessed an awareness—rough and chaotic, but rapidly developing—of itself and its surroundings, but this awareness had no resemblance whatever to the consciousness of man, beast, plant, or computer. There are no words in any human or electronic language to describe what it used for thought processes.

Where it had come from was an equally meaningless question. It had not "come from" anywhere, since it did not necessarily move through physical space and in any case its previous environment had not been, strictly speaking, a "where", being without spatial location or co-ordinates.

It was not, for that matter, an "it." It possessed neither form nor mass; its composition included nothing identifiable by the terms of this universe, or subject to any known or unknown laws of physical science.

Even the verb "to be" is inappropriate. By any rational and objective standard, *it did not exist.*

Knowing none of these things, (?it?) continued to (?be?) what (?it?) (?was?), and to do what (?it?) did.

This will not work. There is no way to describe the indescribable, and in the attempt lies madness. But let the words stand, without further quibble. If they have little or no real meaning, at least they will serve as the best available analogues.

Which, after all, is about all most words ever do.

WHEREVER IT HAD come from, there was no question of returning. The temporary discontinuity through which it had fallen—and for God's sake let's not get into *that*—had already vanished and had never been a two-way portal anyway. It did not really understand these facts, but at some level it had sensed and accepted them. After a period of confusion and disorientation, it had gradually stopped flailing about, so to speak, and settled down to investigate its new surroundings.

In this it was both aided and handicapped by the peculiar nature of its perceptions. It had none of the human senses, could not have used them if it had, because it was unaware of the material world they detected. Rather it perceived its environment in terms of interacting and changing fields of energy, including many levels and forms of energy unknown to human science and even parascience—just as a dog lives in a world of scent and sound beyond the limits of human experience.

And, for all its power, its perceptions were rather limited in range; it was still a very immature individual of its kind. Thus it recognized with ease the varying levels of residual radiation in earth and groundwater, and it fed happily on these, enjoying the sharp flavor of gamma rays and the tang of destabilized nuclear bonds, finding the beta maybe just a trifle cloying. Yet it had no inkling of the existence of the enormous riches of the nuclear-weapons test site, only ninety miles or so to the northwest, from which most of these goodies had come.

(Which was just as well, for if it had it would almost certainly have gone into a feeding frenzy, pigging out uncontrollably, and quite quickly and inevitably destroying both itself and the entire planet in an explosion visible from the nearer stars, to the great puzzlement of any astronomers living there.)

In any case, it was far more interested in the remarkable soft-energy entities that it found scattered about its new environment. They were such small, puny things, even by the standards of their own world—let alone the cosmos-ripping forces it was used to on its home grounds—and yet they produced the most wonderful range and subtle variety of energies, especially when stimulated in various ways. And, gathered in groups, they occasionally created combined fields of absolutely irresistible piquance.

Nothing in its experience had prepared it for its first encounters with humans. It had never known anything remotely like the wild mixture of their thoughts and emotions; its first taste of the raw pungent radiations of pain and terror filled it with a delight as intense as a pubescent human's first orgasm.

As for the concentrated psychic forces generated by Magda Simone's circle of initiates (yes, yes, the silly bastards had indeed stumbled blindly onto something bigger than all their fantasies, as silly bastards occasionally will), that had been almost too intoxicating. If the soft-energy fields hadn't turned out to be so unaccountably fragile, it might have been unable to make itself stop playing with them and move on.

After a period of inaction—its consciousness still adjusting to its strange new surroundings, its own energy field going through certain necessary changes; as has been said, it was still an immature individual of its kind—it set out again, more cautiously. Best to take novel experiences a little at a time.

It found a couple of the soft-energy entities in an isolated place, their fields highly excited and partly linked in some strange way; there was also a third entity whose field, though much simpler than theirs, seemed to surround them. Baffled, it probed clumsily, confused by the electrical circuitry of the parked pickup truck, the CD player and the CB radio, and the engine which the teenage driver had left running while his date masturbated him.

These two lasted an even shorter time than the others. At first they responded with very satisfying intensity—the combined aura was quite nice—but then their fields shut down and vanished, while the mysterious third entity suddenly enveloped the whole scene in a violent and tasteless eruption of the crudest sort.

Leaving the burning pickup by the roadside (the fire would conceal what had been done to the occupants; the coroner, examining the charred bodies, would notice certain strange things, but would put them down to the effects of the gas-tank explosion), it moved on once again.

And came at last to Blacktail Springs . . . where, to its delight, it found another gathering of soft-energy entities, even larger than the first, and giving off more of that almost unbearably exquisite force. The energy level was much higher here, in fact, more concentrated, the separate fields much more closely linked; and there was something else mixed in, an added savor of great subtlety and complexity.

Unfortunately, for all their splendid radiance, these entities weren't very durable either.

Heading back across the desert, passing through the mountains (not between or among them; it passed *through* the mountains, which it did not notice), it was filled with its equivalent of frustration and disappointment. These entities were able to produce the most marvelous energies, given just a little stimulation; yet almost immediately afterward, their fields went out and couldn't be persuaded to come back on. Clearly they would have to be treated with greater care.

These reflections were cut short by a sudden awareness of the presence of other fields, energies of humbler but welcome sorts. Still contemplating, it moved along the ridges and canyons above the darkened buildings of the New Age Enlightenment Center and Guest Ranch (now indefinitely closed), past the decades-old illicit toxic-waste dumpings, the acid-stained rocks and the patches of metal-poisoned earth, the bones of animals and the heavier bones of a couple of long-forgotten Mob figures dug up by coyotes. Till at last it came to the scattered collection of rusting, leaking drums of radioactive waste, where—with something almost resembling a sigh—it settled down for a little snack.

8.

It was dark by the time Billy and Janna arrived back in Las Vegas. The vivid lights of the casinos flashed and glared on either side as Billy steered the Jeep slowly down the Strip, but their garishness was lost on him, even though he had never been here before. He had not even meant to get onto the Strip at all; he had merely, once again, taken a wrong turn.

All he could think about was being with Janna again.

After some confused searching, they finally found their way to Naked City and the Last Church. The old Honda was still parked across the street, apparently unmolested. Billy got Janna's suitcase from the back of the Jeep and unlocked the storefront mission's door.

They spoke very little as they went back to the little room and began to undress. The bed was small and hard, single rather than double size, but for the moment they hardly noticed.

Billy reached for the light switch but Janna put her hand on his arm. "No," she said in English, standing naked beside the bed. He had already turned on the rattling old window fan against the heat and the blast of air was blowing her hair around her face. "No," she said again, "leave the light on. I want to see you. So that I know you are really here."

They piled onto the bed and went at it like a couple of hot coyotes. Some time later, they lay together and talked for a while, and then they went at it again. Eventually they drifted into the kitchen, still naked, and made peanut-butter sandwiches and ate them; then they went back to the room and went at it some more.

At last, very late, they fell into a warm exhausted sleep. Billy awoke only once that night, as she cried out in her sleep in Kazakh, clutching him in what felt like terror rather than passion. But the moment passed without her awakening, and they both slept again. And woke, finally, well into the next day, to the sounds of Mickey Wolf and Dr. Sarah Aronson coming in.

"*PULLED* OFF?" BILLY said incredulously, some time later. "Their heads were just *pulled* off?"

"Please don't use the word 'impossible,'" Sarah Aronson said, holding the bridge of her nose and closing her eyes. "I've heard it enough in the last twenty-four hours to last a lifetime. Said it myself, as much as anybody else."

Mickey Wolf shrugged. "I don't know. Indians been ripped off for everything else. Why not their heads too?"

"I studied some martial arts in the Berets," Billy said. "Knew some guys who could kill you fifty different ways with one finger, you know? But I don't believe there's anybody alive who could just tear a man's head clear off."

"Maybe an animal," Janna suggested. "A bear?"

Sarah Aronson shook her head decisively. "I'm sure a bear could do it, in terms of sheer strength—though I've never heard of a bear doing anything like that—but there aren't any bears, even small ones, anywhere near Blacktail Springs. There's nothing out there for an animal that size to eat. And a bear would have left tracks."

"Anyway," Mickey Wolf pointed out, "can you see nineteen people sitting there patiently waiting their turn while a bear—or a man, or the fucking Thing From Another World for that matter—yanks their heads off one by one? Much as I hate to say it, we're talking about something that can't be accounted for by any rational explanation. I speak," he added, "as one trained in theology, which consists in large measure of coming up with logical explanations of the logically absurd."

They were all sitting at one of the long tables in the mission's dining room, drinking coffee. It was midafternoon.

"Something else impossible—sorry—happened last week," Sarah said. "I don't see the connection, if there is any, but the Federal agent who questioned me brought it up. You remember, Mickey. That weird business at the New Age dude ranch."

"What's this?" Billy wanted to know.

They told him. That is, they told him what they had read in the newspapers and seen on television, though they knew little about the weirder details, which had not been announced. At the end Billy whistled. "Man," he said. "Sounds like Stone Man's back."

Now it was everyone else's turn to look baffled. So Billy told them the story of Stone Man, aka Stoneclad.

"It's one of the oldest Cherokee stories," he began. "This is how the Cherokees learned all the stuff they know. This is how we got so smart."

"This I've got to hear," Mickey Wolf muttered.

"See," Billy went on, "a long time ago, long before the whites came, there was this great big giant who lived up on top of this mountain. Either he was made out of stone or he just dressed in a kind of armor made of stone, depending on which story you hear. Anyway, now and then he'd come down and grab people and kill them, tear them up, even eat them."

Billy paused, trying to remember the story as Grandfather Ninekiller had told it to him. "Next part, I'm a little weak," he admitted. "I don't recall exactly how the people finally found the secret—probably somebody had a dream, that's how it usually goes in these stories—but anyway, they discovered Stone Man's weakness. The one thing he couldn't stand, the one thing that just drained him like Superman with Kryptonite," he said, "was a woman having her, you know, period."

"Sexism rears its ugly head," Mickey Wolf observed.

"Oh, I don't know," Sarah said. "I know what *I'm* like, three or four days out of the average month . . . anyway, go on. What then?"

"Well, so they went through the village, rounding up every woman they could find who was having her monthlies—which wouldn't have been hard, in those days, because there was a special house where women stayed during that time. And they stood these women all along the path that Stone Man used when he came down the mountain.

"So here comes Stone Man down the trail, boom boom boom, mountain shaking, birds screaming, leaves falling off the trees—make a good Disney cartoon, really—and then he comes to the first woman and it's like, *'Aaaaghhhh!'* like Dracula when they show him the cross. But he hustles on past, and then he sees another one, and another one, and now his strength's running out fast, he's all wasted, can't even make it back up the mountain, and finally he just loses it, falls on the ground and starts to croak, while everybody gathers around to watch.

"And so he says, like, 'Okay, you bastards, you got me, now listen up.' And while he's dying he tells them all these things about medicine and how to do various stuff, the whole nine yards. Which," Billy finished, "is how come Cherokees know so much."

"I always figured it had to be something like that," Mickey Wolf said. "Interesting story, though. Most of those tribal legends like that, there's a young guy who finally kills the creature. Every tribe I know has at least one Monster Slayer story."

"We do too," Billy said. "There's this one about this kind of a flying dragon, the *uk'tena*, and this young man who kills it with seven arrows. Come to think of it, this thing you're telling about sounds a little like the *uk'tena* too."

"Then maybe we need to buy you some arrows," Sarah said, grinning at him.

"Don't look at me," Billy told her. "I can't hit shit with a bow and arrow. Not bad with an M-16 or a pistol, but that arrow stuff, forget it. Afraid I'm just not Monster Slayer material. My heart ain't pure enough."

"Oh, I don't know," Mickey Wolf said. "Anybody for more coffee?"

"I'll take a refill," Sarah said. "I'm trying to figure out how you manage it. Making coffee, I mean, that's even worse than what we've got at the clinic."

Mickey Wolf got up and took her cup and his own and moved off toward the coffee machine. Billy said, "Speaking of the clinic, how long have you been with the Indian Health Service?"

Sarah stared at him for a moment. Then she said, "That's right, how would you know? I'm not IHS, Billy. I work with them to some extent—most of my staff do work for them, and the clinic gets its funds from them, along with various contributions from private organizations—but I'm strictly independent."

"Is she ever," Mickey Wolf said, coming back with the coffee. "They lost their resident doctor a couple of years ago, went through a long stretch with no full-time doc at Blacktail Springs. Sarah showed up and offered to work at her own expense, nothing in return but living quarters and the right to work on the studies she was doing. The IHS and the BIA weren't really thrilled about the arrangement, but since it got them off the hook about providing a doctor, they okayed it. The Indians, of course, were just damn glad to get anybody at all."

"You're the only doctor there?"

"A couple of young guys come over from the Mormon hospital in Cedar City, but they're just part-time volunteers. As a matter of fact they're minding the store right now, while I sit here in exciting Las Vegas drinking fossil coffee. My God, what died in this stuff?"

"So," Billy said, "what's this study you're doing?" He turned his head to look at Janna. "I guess it's got something to do with your business in this country too, huh? Radiation and like that?"

"Like that." Sarah's face went very tight and she sipped moodily at her coffee. "Oh, very much like that."

"Remember what I said, Billy?" Mickey Wolf asked him. "How us eastern Indians have no idea how bad it is for these poor bastards out here in the Basin? All they did to us was shoot a bunch of us, starve a bunch more, give nearly everybody fatal diseases, stick the survivors on reservations - and, in you guys' case, kill off a bunch more with mass deportations—and then mount a campaign to wipe out their language and identity. Just minor stuff like that . . . but these skins out here got all that and more," he said. "They got *nuked*."

"You mean fallout from the atom bomb tests? I think I heard something about that." Billy scratched his head. "But hell, that was a long time ago, wasn't it? Back in the fifties or so? I thought they went over to setting the damn things off underground, so that stuff wouldn't get in the air."

They were all looking at each other and then at him. "Number one," Mickey Wolf said, "those underground tests weren't nearly as harmless as the AEC's propaganda flacks led everybody to believe. Lots of times—maybe most times, I haven't seen any figures I'd trust—there was a certain amount of leakage, radioactive gases and particles escaping into the atmosphere, and a few times it was so bad even the AEC admitted it was serious. And, of course, guess who lives downwind—because," the big Mohawk added grimly, "even though they swore every time that this was one hundred percent safe, they always made damn sure the wind was blowing away from Vegas, toward the desert where there's nothing but a few reservations, before they set off the shot."

"Also," Sarah put in, "it's not just a question of direct harm from the later tests. The big problem—the one I'm working on, to answer your question—has to do with genetic damage from radiation exposure, effects carried into second and third generations."

She grimaced. "Which, as it happens, the AEC's tame scientists swear doesn't happen, or at least hasn't been proved. It's even in their official book on the effects of radiation on humans—no evidence of long-term genetic effects."

"Humans," Mickey Wolf grunted. "That's the key word. Indians aren't human, don't you know that? It's in the Constitution or something."

"Never mind that there are cases all over Utah and Nevada," Sarah told Billy. "I've got records and detailed studies of children and grandchildren—the effects seem to get worse in the third generation, nobody knows why—of Indian men and women who received radiation exposure. I can show you documents, hell, I can take you to hospitals and show you some of the cases. Leukemia, bone cancer, skeletal abnormalities, retardation—"

"I've seen some of this stuff," Mickey Wolf said, nodding. "Enough to make a marble statue sick."

"It's not just from fallout blowing across the reservations," Sarah added. "There were Indians who served with the military and were exposed to radiation as part of the big testing program in the fifties, sometimes in huge doses. White men, too, but I don't have any information on them. Needless to say, the Veterans' Administration never recognizes their claims."

"Jesus," Billy said.

"There's even a Shoshone man in Cedar City who worked as an extra in that dreadful movie in which John Wayne played Genghis Khan." Sarah mispronounced the name in the usual American way, with an initial hard *G* and sounding the *gh* like *J*. "There was a test shot during the filming and the whole area got a dose of fallout. The man is dying of cancer and most of his children and grandchildren have genetic defects. Of course, almost everybody else on that film crew died of cancer too. Including the Duke himself."

"Big fascist jackass," Mickey Wolf mumbled.

Billy thought it over. "But if there's all this radioactive stuff around, aren't you afraid to live out there on the rez?"

Sarah shook her head. "No, that's the strange thing. Blacktail Springs is well clear of the fallout zone. It's too far south—they'd never have set off a shot with the wind blowing toward Blacktail Springs, because that would be too near the Vegas area. No, Blacktail has always been about as safe from wind-borne fallout as any place in Nevada."

She sighed. "And that's the bitch of it. Because there *are* a lot of cases of the kind of thing I'm talking about—leukemia and other forms of cancer, birth defects—at Blacktail Springs. Not as many as at some of the reservations that took heavy fallout over the years, but more than at others that have no radiation-exposure history at all. Too many to be accounted for by any explanation I've been able to come up with."

She stared moodily into her coffee cup. "I've gone down a hundred blind streets on this one—had soil samples analyzed for possible metallic poisons, checked homes for sources of environmental toxins, you name it. Just another impossibility."

Her head came up and she looked at Billy. "And I wish to God I could solve the mystery, because this is exactly the kind of thing that can be used to discredit the study my organization is about to publish. See, no unusual radiation levels and still the same effects, obviously Indians are simply prone to certain disorders."

"I'll be God-damned," Billy said. "I never knew any of this."

Janna said suddenly, "You know nothing."

She had been quiet so long, everybody jumped slightly and turned to stare at her. "I am sorry," she continued in a high strained voice, "but you know nothing. None of you."

She stopped, seeming to search for words. Her face was very pale.

"In northeastern Kazakhstan," she said, "the Soviets tested their bombs since 1949. This was populated country, you must understand, not just empty desert. There were farms and villages and animals, even towns. And nobody moved the people, nobody warned them. They did not even know what was radiation, what was atomic bomb.

"After the explosions, the people were not told about risk to their health. Military medical teams went in and examined the villagers, but results were kept secret and no treatment given. Doctors in Kazakhstan were forbidden to—diagnose, yes?—diagnose things like cancer or leukemia, let alone give treatment."

"You mean," Billy said incredulously, "they used the people as guinea pigs?"

"That is laboratory animal? Yes, exactly so. And after the treaty, when tests were made underground, it was not so much better. The Soviets did not have technology to do the deep-down explosions as you have here. They just made, um, shallow holes. Plenty of radiation still got out. And I have told you about the radioactive lakes."

She looked at Sarah. "I said that none of you know. Nobody in the world truly knows. The information was all state secret. We are still learning how bad it was. We may never know the entire truth."

Billy saw that her hands were shaking. He wanted to put his arm around her but she was sitting on the other side of the table.

"The testing ended in 1989," she went on, "but there are so many dead—maybe two million in forty years, nobody can be sure. Also there was the big uranium mine at Karaganda, where the *gulag* prisoners worked without protection. And now we have national independence, we also have this national—*nasledstvo.*" She looked at Billy.

"Inheritance," he said after a minute's thought. "Heritage."

"Yes, inheritance. In Semipalatinsk region," she said, "this is where most tests were made, there is perhaps today no truly healthy person at all. One in five there has cancer. In some areas one child in three is born dead or with serious defects. Sometimes things are born that cannot be recognized as human beings. And all this is getting worse. As Sarah has said, third generation has more problems than second."

She pushed back her hair. "Every year, in America, in Japan, all over the world, people make fine talk of what a great crime was Hiroshima and Nagasaki. We Kazakhs received equivalent of over two thousand Hiroshimas and nobody ever speaks of it."

She stood up suddenly. "One moment. Something in my suitcase. I will show it to you."

As she disappeared through the hallway door Mickey Wolf said, "Jesus *Christ.*"

"What I don't get," Billy said, "is why we never heard about any of this in the United States. I mean, they were always telling us stuff about how bad the Russians were, you'd think they'd have jumped on a story like this."

"And bring up the whole subject of nuclear testing and the effects on nearby populations? Maybe cause some people in this country to ask questions about our own sacred test program? Forget it," Mickey Wolf said disgustedly. "Don't forget, a lot of extremely heavy individuals and organizations have bought pieces of the nuclear action—weapons and power plants too—and the U.S. government has for half a century maintained that radiation isn't really all that bad for you."

"As for the anti-nuclear organizations," Sarah added, "too many of them were dominated by left-leaning types who wouldn't hear any criticism of a Communist government."

Janna returned, bearing a yellow envelope. "Here." She took out a stack of photographs and tossed them onto the table. "Look. It is not beautiful, but you will look."

They picked up the prints and passed them around, in a silence broken only by small sharp sounds of incredulity and shock, and the occasional quiet curse. Billy had never seen anything so terrible. There were pictures of children missing arms and legs, misshapen dwarves, people with hideously deformed faces and massive scarring. What made it even worse was that so many of them looked Indian. Although, as Janna had said, there were some that didn't even look human at all. He felt his stomach do a slow roll.

"What about this one?" he asked, holding up a picture of a beautiful little girl with huge dark eyes. She was holding an adult's hand and she looked to be about five or so. "What's wrong with her?"

"She is fourteen years old," Janna said flatly. "She is one meter tall."

She leaned across the table and pulled a single eight-by-ten from the pile. It was an ordinary-looking group picture of perhaps twenty small children, lined up and looking serious in nice clothes, staring into the camera. Janna and another woman, wearing white uniforms, stood off to one side.

"Every child in this photograph," she said, "was dead within one year of the time it was taken."

She gathered up the prints and put them back in the envelope. The others all looked off in different directions. Sarah Aronson wiped her eyes with a quick angry motion. Mickey Wolf said softly, "Oh, the bastards. Oh, the bastards."

"Huh," Billy said. It was hard to get words up his throat. His vision seemed to be blurring a little, too. "I guess they really were as bad as everybody said. The Communists, I mean. I thought that was just propaganda."

Mickey Wolf made a spitting sound. "Communists my ass. Oh, sure, them too, but that's not the only bastards I mean. I'm older than any of you, and I've been hearing this shit all my life from our noble leaders, about how we could fight what they called a 'limited nuclear war' and it wouldn't be so bad. Acceptable losses and all that. Hell."

He waved a big hand at the envelope. "There's the results of a fucking limited nuclear war, right there. That's what the survivors and their children would look like. That's what the evil sons of bitches in Washington *and* Moscow were willing to do to all of us, just to prove whose ideological dick was longer. With apologies to the founder of my religion, God *damn* them, for they knew *exactly* what they did."

He slammed his hand down on the table. "Whoever or whatever is out there in the desert pulling off heads and the rest of it—nobody's had the guts to use the word 'monster' yet, but we've all been thinking it, haven't we?—it's no big deal, really. Compared to the two-legggged monsters who have been running the world for most of this century, our local creature isn't much more than a big playful puppy."

He stood up. "Let's have a drink."

Nobody dissented. As he headed back toward his office Janna came around and sat down beside Billy, who put his arm around her. She was trembling but her breathing began to grow less ragged as Billy held her. Sarah looked diplomatically toward the back wall.

Mickey Wolf reappeared, holding a large white-labelled bottle and several glasses. "Ice in the box, if anybody feels the need. Jim Beam," he said, setting the bottle on the table. "The cheap kind, not the seven-year-old stuff, but I say give youth a chance."

Billy thought the bourbon was pretty good; it was his usual brand, back home. Janna tasted hers cautiously. "I have not had much whisky, you know," she said self-consciously. "My family is Muslim."

"*Bismillah ir-rahman ir-rahim.*" Mickey Wolf said solemnly. "I speak in the ecumenical spirit."

"I'll drink to that," Sarah Aronson agreed. Her face was still tight and bad around the eyes, but she managed to smile. "And I'm Jewish."

They sat and drank and did not talk much. After a little while there came a series of noises from the main room, banging and trampling and muffled voices. "Jerry Dwayne and the Piss-Cutters," Mickey Wolf said. "They use the sanctuary for practice sessions."

The band began tuning up, a cacophonous mixture of twangs and thumps that went on and on. There was a series of squeals and grunts as somebody began fooling with an amplifier.

"At least," Billy said, "they finally stopped. You know, the testing."

"The Americans and the Russians, yeah," Mickey Wolf said. "They weren't the only ones doing it, though."

"The Chinese only stopped recently," Janna said, nodding. "And nobody is certain this is permanent. When I was at home they often set them off, big ones, just on the other side of the mountains from Almaty. Of course it is Kazakhs who live there, and a few Mongols."

"Don't forget the British in Australia," Sarah Aronson added. "They used the aborigines pretty much the same way the Russians used your people—had special Australian police detachments scouring the Outback after the tests, capturing natives and running tests on them. And then there were the French in the Pacific, only a few years ago. God knows what they thought *they* were trying to prove."

"National tradition," Mickey Wolf said, topping up his glass. "Acting like assholes just for the hell of it." He raised his drink. "To the Duke of Wellington. If it hadn't been for him, the whole world might be French."

He made a face. "But it's true the big powers have pretty much stopped, at least for the present. Now it's places like India and Pakistan. Progress," he said sourly. "No more nuking the little brown people out in the desert. Now the little brown people have started nuking themselves. Ain't it wonderful?"

"Don't be too sure it's over in this country," Sarah told Billy. "There's a small but powerful movement to resume testing again, and they nearly made it during the Bush administration. The way things have been going, who knows?"

Out in the sanctuary the Piss-Cutters broke into a lively intro. Jerry Dwayne Austin's voice came through the open doorway:

*"Oh darling since you left me, I feel so all alone,
I don't know how I'll ever find a reason to go on,
I sit here in this barroom with pain inside my head,
Feeling like a buzzard that can't find nothing dead."*

Somebody joined in on the harmony:

*"So until you come back to me I know just what I'll do,
I'm gonna sit right here and drink my beer
Till I'm missing the toilet as bad as I'm missing you."*

"I'll drink to that," Sarah said, doing so.
"Here is looking at you, kid," Janna said, raising her own glass. The color was coming back into her face now.
"*Dum vivimus, vivamus,*" Mickey Wolf pronounced.
"*Howa,*" Billy agreed.

IN THE EVENING Billy and Janna walked along the Strip, holding hands, looking at the lights this time, reading the names of over-the-hill singers and comedians off the huge marquees. What a Godawful town, Billy thought, what a perfect monument to everything that's wrong with this country. Come try to get something for nothing, it's as American as damming a river or fucking over an Indian. We'll even throw in a lot of naked tits and ass and out-of-gas entertainers. . . . But he couldn't get up any serious anger, or sustain the attitude. Just being with Janna made him feel so good, even the raw-colored lights of the Strip looked almost pretty.

In front of a medium-sized casino Janna said suddenly, "Let's go in." And when Billy started to object, "I have to use the, um, ladies' room."

They went through the front doors together and Janna hustled off to look for the facilities, leaving Billy to stand and gaze curiously about him. He had expected to look out of place among all these well-off white and black people, dressed as he was in his T-shirt and jeans and his black hat, but he saw now that plenty of them were looking just as scruffy as he was. For some reason that made him feel more out of place than ever.

He wandered over to a row of slot machines and watched an old lady slamming coins into a slot and yanking the lever with a vicious mechanical rhythm, cursing steadily under her breath. She wasn't, he noticed, looking down to see if she was winning anything.

Impulsively he stuck his hand in his pocket and found a quarter. Might as well blow twenty-five cents just to say he'd gone gambling in Vegas. . . . He chose an idle machine at random and pulled out a quarter.

A familiar dry voice said, "Not that one, *chooch*."

Billy jumped and looked around. There were no animals in sight, no people standing near, no possible source for the voice.

"I know," Grandfather Ninekiller said, "I said no disembodied voices, but there don't seem to be any other way to do this. Act calm, now. Go over to that machine down on the end."

Billy obeyed. The voice inside his head said, "Go on, feed that quarter in and give her a yank."

The quarter slipped into the slot and Billy pulled the handle. There was a great rattling noise and a cataract of quarters began to pour down the chute. "Two hundred and fifty bucks," the voice said cheerfully. "If I got it right."

Dazed, Billy took off his hat and began scooping up handfuls of quarters into it. Several people were looking at him and smiling. A man's voice said, "That Indian just hit the jackpot."

"How the hell," Billy muttered under his breath, and then, "Never mind. I just wish you wouldn't talk inside my head like this. It feels funny."

"Shut up," Grandfather's voice said, "or they'll see you talking to nobody, figure you're crazy, maybe throw you out. Take the money and go over to the roulette wheel."

"But—"

"Don't argue. Move, now. Oh, and go by the cashier's and get those two-bit pieces changed to chips. All of them."

A few minutes later Billy stood at the roulette table, glancing nervously about him. There was still no sign of Janna. The Mexican-looking guy who ran the table raised an eyebrow at Billy. "Place your bets."

Grandfather's voice said, "Put it all on thirty-three."

Billy took a deep breath and put the stack of chips on thirty-three. The wheel spun. The little ball went *bocketa-bocketa-bock-bock* and came to rest at last on 33. A moment later the dealer was giving Billy a pile of chips that represented more money than he'd ever had at one time in his life.

Grandfather's voice said, "Let it ride."

Billy gestured for the dealer to let it ride. The wheel spun again and the little ball bounced and rattled to a stop, once more on 33. There was a loud chorus of exclamations from around the table. A small audience was beginning to gather.

His mind reeling with visions of sudden riches, Billy reached for the chips. Grandfather Ninekiller's voice said urgently, "Now put the whole pile on seven."

With dry mouth and shaking hands, Billy obeyed.

The wheel blurred. The ball skittered around its orbit. The wheel slowed and the ball bounced into the 7, seemed to rest there for an instant, and then suddenly hopped crazily all the way over to the green zero.

Grandfather Ninekiller's voice said, *"Shit!"*

9.

That night Billy had a dream.

As with most dreams, there was no clear beginning. He was down in the warm darkness of deep sleep, and then without transition he was standing alone on a great open plain; and yet somehow it seemed that he had been there for a long time.

He looked around, curious but not particularly afraid. The ground was hard and smooth and featureless. The plain stretched off in all directions to a shadowy horizon. It was flat as a pool table, broken only by randomly scattered objects—rocks or boulders of some sort, the size of house trailers, but unnaturally, geometrically regular in shape, all corners and angles and flat planes. The sky was very dark blue and there was neither sun nor moon nor stars, yet the whole scene was lit by a kind of dim twilight.

He noticed that he was completely naked. Since there didn't seem to be anybody else around, this didn't embarrass him, but it was a little on the chilly side; he wished he had a blanket, at least.

With no conscious purpose, he began walking across the plain, heading toward the nearest of the big boulder-things, which he saw now was made of some glassy black substance. Swinging to the left, he walked around the object, and found that he was not alone in this place after all. A human figure sat on the ground on the far side of the object, cross-legged and leaning back against the shiny dark surface.

"*'Siyo, chooch,*" Grandfather Ninekiller said cheerfully. "Took you long enough. My ass was starting to go numb."

"*'Siyo, eduda,*" Billy said, not at all surprised.

He waited while the old man got to his feet. Grandfather looked pretty good for somebody who'd been dead for five years. He was as Billy remembered him: tall for an Indian, skinny as a snake, with a big bottle-opener nose and a toothless grinning slash of a mouth. Dark eyes glittered at Billy from a face as wrinkled as a sun-dried apple.

The old man was dressed to the nines tonight, or today or whenever this was. On his head he wore a neatly-wrapped turban in the old Cherokee style, decorated with a huge white egret feather. His feet were shod in pointy-toed center-seam moccasins without ornamentation. In between, he had on a really good-looking dark blue suit with a wide red tie. "Nice suit," Billy remarked.

"Well, I don't get that many occasions to dress up, nowadays. Glad you finally put some clothes on, though I can't say much for the outfit."

Billy looked down and saw that he was now wearing a patchwork Seminole shirt and bib overalls. "What the hell," he said.

"Hey," Grandfather said, "don't ask me. It's your subconscious."

"When did you start using words like subconscious?"

"Since I met this dead *yoneg* named Carl Jung. Plays good

dominoes, but you don't want to be around when he gets to arguing with this old Jew they call Siggy. I mean, they just go on and on."

Billy sighed. It was looking like a long dream.

"Anyway," Grandfather continued, "I've come to teach you some things you need to know—"

"These things," Billy interrupted with sudden feeling, "would they involve games of chance? Because I'd just as soon pass, thank you."

"Never mind that." The old man glared at him. "Just you never mind that. I don't want to talk about it."

"Easy for you to say," Billy grumbled. "It was me lost all that money."

"No," Grandfather said, "you lost exactly twenty-five cents. But never mind," he went on, raising his voice above Billy's protest. "We've got serious business to take care of."

He looked around at the endless dark plain. "Man, this place is too creepy. Let's get out of here."

Instantly the whole scene changed. Now they stood on the rocky summit of a high wooded mountain, overlooking a broad valley that was covered with unbroken forest. Other mountains rose in the distance. It was daytime and the sun rode high in a cloudless sky.

"More like it," the old man said, nodding and looking satisfied.

"Where are we now?" Billy wanted to know.

"Still inside your head, of course, like we've been all along. Just did some redecorating, you might say. Now be quiet and pay attention."

Grandfather Ninekiller slid a hand inside his suit jacket and pulled out a small leather bag. "You're about to step into some deep shit, *chooch*. I knew you were headed for some kind of trouble, but I didn't realize how fast things were going to happen. Or how big the trouble was going to be."

He shook his head. "There's something loose in your world, *chooch*, something so damn big and mean and dangerous it even scares me, and I'm already dead. I still don't understand what it is—and neither does anybody else in the spirit world—but it makes the *uk'tena* look like a little old toad-frog."

The *uk'tena*: the most terrible monster of Cherokee legend, worse even than the Stone Giant. A flying horned serpent that killed everyone and everything in its path, so powerful that even its breath—in some stories even its gaze—would destroy life; Billy remembered, now, mentioning it to Janna and the others earlier that day. He felt his bowels contract painfully.

"So—" Grandfather was undoing the thong that closed the little buckskin bag. "What I'm going to do, I'm going to give you a medicine to protect yourself. It won't destroy that thing, mind. It's just to keep it from getting you."

Upending the bag, he poured some of the contents out into his open right palm. "You know what this is."

It was a statement, not a question, but Billy nodded anyway. It had been a long time since he had seen the thin-leafed Cherokee tobacco—the real native leaf, descendant of seeds carried all the way from the eastern homeland by Trail of Tears refugees, and cultivated in secret places in the Oklahoma woods—but it was not something you forgot; he would have recognized it by the acrid scent alone.

"And you know basically what has to be done first," Grandfather went on, and Billy nodded again. For the tobacco to have any serious power, it had to be "remade" or "doctored"—programmed, so to speak, for the desired effect, by use of the appropriate *igawesdi* song.

"Listen close, then," Grandfather said.

Facing east, he held the tobacco up to the sun. "This really ought to be done at dawn," he said in an aside to Billy, "but that's all right, this is just a demonstration—"

Holding the tobacco up to the sun in one hand, he began to stir it with the forefinger of the other. As he did so, he sang in a soft but carrying voice, a song that was not much more than a chant—a single phrase repeated over and over, with one sudden high note in the middle and a drop to a near-grunt at the end. It was unlike any song Billy had ever heard, and the words were in no language he knew, which was a surprise; normally the words of an *igawesdi* were in clear Cherokee, though their meaning might be mysterious.

At the end of the song the old man paused and blew gently on the tobacco. Then he began again, the same strange monotonous song, his reedy old voice clear and true in the sweet mountain air. Billy was aware of the hairs rising up on the backs of his hands. The rocks and the trees seemed to shimmer.

Four times Grandfather Ninekiller sang the song over the tobacco, stirring steadily with his bony forefinger, blowing on the tobacco at the end of each repetition. "Now," he said, "you sing along with me. *Didihnogi.*"

Billy had made no conscious effort to memorize the song, yet he found himself repeating the unfamiliar syllables with complete and familiar ease. Well, this was a dream, after all. At the end Grandfather nodded approvingly. "You got it, *chooch*," he said, getting out the little bag again and pouring the tobacco carefully back in. "I wasn't sure you would."

"What language was that? Creek?"

Grandfather shook his head. "No language that anybody speaks any more. Very old song, goes back to the time when the people hunted elephants and horses had extra toes. You have to be careful and get the words just right, because it's the most powerful *igawesdi* I know and there's no telling what might happen if you screw it up. I had to get special permission to teach it to you, and I only got it because . . . somebody higher up, let's say, is worried about this thing that's turned up in your world."

He tied the bag carefully with the thong and held it up. "Now you know how to use the tobacco once it's doctored, right? Basically it's the same routine you saw me work two or three times when you were younger. Like the time I made that medicine to keep your cousin Minnie's worthless husband away from her house, remember? It ain't very complicated," Grandfather said. "The important thing is to do the *igawesdi* right. Oh, and it'll help if you mix a little cedar with the tobacco before you doctor it."

"Before *I* doctor it?" Billy looked at the little bag. "I thought—"

"Thought I was going to give it to you? Hell, boy, I can't do that." The old man snorted. "You ought to know better."

"Because it's too sacred? Or—"

"No, you young fool," Grandfather said scornfully, "because this is a God-damned *dream*. What did you think, you'd wake up clutching this bag? Boy, you got some weird ideas."

He began to sing again, this time a wordless high-pitched four-note phrase: "Doo-dee-doo-doo, doo-dee-doo-doo. Billy Badass doesn't know it but he has just entered the Twilight Zone."

"Being dead hasn't made you a bit easier to take," Billy said, while the old man cackled. "I think it's made you a bigger pain in the ass than ever."

"Well, you know, it's a hell of a job but somebody's got to do it." Grandfather folded his arms. "See you around, *sgilisi*."

There was a blinding flash of light and a loud boom, like a concussion grenade going off. A moment later Billy was sitting up in bed, shaking his head violently and fighting for breath, and Janna was holding his arm. "Billy, Billy," she said anxiously, "what's wrong?"

He rubbed his face with the back of his free hand. "Nothing," he said after a couple of seconds. "Just a dream."

And lay back on the pillow, staring wide-eyed up into the darkness, feeling Janna's body snuggling against him and hearing inside his head an old man's dry wispy laughter.

WHEN HE AWOKE again it was day and the sun was coming through the windows and flooding the little room. Janna was gone. So was the blue suitcase and, as far as he could discover, all her things.

Awkwardly, his head still a little fuzzed from a bad night's sleep, he dragged on his clothes and shuffled barefoot down the hall to the toilet. As he passed the open door of the office Mickey Wolf called out, "Billy!"

"Minute," Billy said indistinctly.

Several minutes later he came back up the hallway, checking his zipper and hitching at his jeans. Mickey Wolf was standing in the office doorway. "Hey," Billy said. "Seen Janna?"

"She went back to Blacktail Springs with Sarah, couple of hours ago. Said she didn't want to wake you up, since you'd had trouble sleeping during the night. You okay?"

Billy nodded jerkily. In fact he felt like hell, but mostly it was just sleepiness and general stiffness. That little bed really wasn't big enough for two people, however close their relationship.

"Coffee's ready," Mickey Wolf said. "You look like you could use some caffeine."

"Uh huh. Sure could." Billy thought of something. "Hang around, will you? I'll be right back."

He went and got himself a cup of coffee. It was so hot it burned his lips but he still managed to drink half of it on his way back to the office. "Listen," he said to Mickey Wolf, "have you got any tobacco?"

The Mohawk preacher frowned. "I quit smoking last year, don't have anything around the place. There's a store across the street—"

"No, no," Billy said. "I mean, you know, *tobacco*."

"What—" The heavy black eyebrows pulled momentarily together and then rose as the blue eyes widened. "Oh, I get it. You mean Indian tobacco."

"You said something about how you studied to be a medicine man," Billy said apologetically. This felt like a pretty touchy area; Mickey Wolf's face was already clouding up. "I thought you might have some stuff left."

Mickey Wolf turned his head and stared for several seconds at the wall, where there was nothing but a Madonna calendar. Billy stood and waited in silence.

"All right," Mickey Wolf said finally, turning back to face Billy. "I think you better tell me about it."

So Billy told him about the dream. At first the words came slowly and with difficulty—telling someone else about a dream was a serious and potentially dangerous business; no Indian was ever wholly comfortable doing it—but then the whole thing came tumbling out in a rush, as if under pressure from within.

"Hm," Mickey Wolf said at the end. "Your grandfather ever do this before? Speak to you, I mean?"

"Not in dreams." Billy hesitated, told himself he was talking to another Indian, blue eyes or not. "Sometimes he appears in the form of a bird. Or an animal." He couldn't make himself tell about the television set.

Mickey Wolf blew out his breath in what was almost a whistle. "How about that. Well—" The massive shoulders rose and sagged. "Why not? Let me see what I've got."

He turned and went into the office, moving with an odd reluctant slowness. While Billy watched from the doorway, he bent over and began clearing odds and ends—magazines, papers, coffee cups—off a big old-fashioned trunk that stood against the back wall. Taking a ring of keys from his pocket, he unlocked the trunk and lifted the lid. "Here," he said, reaching down into the trunk.

Straightening and turning, he placed an oblong wooden box on the desk. Behind him, in the shadowy interior of the trunk, Billy caught a glimpse of bright reds and golds and blues, but then Mickey Wolf's body blocked the view.

"Haven't had this open in a long time," he said in a far-off voice, not looking at Billy. "Not sure what's in here—"

His big hands moved with familiarity, though, as he raised the lid of the box—cedar, Billy was nearly sure—and handled its contents. Almost immediately he grunted softly and took out a little buckskin bag, very much like the one Grandfather had carried in the dream. "This do you any good?" he asked, passing the bag to Billy but still not looking at him.

Billy undid the thong drawstring and opened the bag. It was just big enough to let him get a thumb and forefinger in.

"Of course it's not Cherokee tobacco," Mickey Wolf remarked. He was staring down into the trunk, his face unreadable.

Billy took out a pinch of the tobacco and looked at it and then sniffed it. It was lighter in color and coarser than Cherokee leaf, but it was definitely Indian tobacco, with a good strong smell. "This is fine," he said.

Actually, in Cherokee medicine, the tobacco itself was not of absolute importance. In a pinch, even cigarette tobacco could be "remade" for ritual purposes with the proper *igawesdi*. Still, it was better to do things right.

"You got a pipe?" Mickey Wolf said abruptly. "Because I can't help you there."

"No problem." Billy started to explain, but then he realized Mickey Wolf didn't want to hear about it. "Thanks," he said instead.

Mickey Wolf made a wordless sound in his throat and turned to replace the box in the trunk. Again Billy saw a flash of color, some shiny fabric. It came to him then that he was looking at the vestments of a Catholic priest.

The Mohawk slammed the trunk lid down and locked it. Turning again, he looked at Billy. It wasn't a happy look.

"You're a nice young guy," he said. "I've enjoyed having you and Janna around, and all that."

He opened a desk drawer and fished out the bottle of Jim Beam. "But you've got a way of making me think about things I'd just as soon forget. . . . "

"Sorry," Billy said. It didn't feel like the right thing to say, but it was all he could think of. Maybe there wasn't any right thing to say, just now.

Mickey Wolf raised a hand in impatient dismissal. Billy turned and headed back toward the little bedroom to collect his things. A little later, on his way out, he glanced in through the office door. Mickey Wolf was sitting at his desk, back to the door, looking at the trunk. The bourbon bottle was in his hand and the cap lay on the floor.

10.

THE MIDDAY TRAFFIC was crazy all the way to the outskirts of Vegas, everybody jamming along at severely illegal speeds, changing lanes and coming off on-ramps with no apparent interest in what might be approaching from astern, bunching up in bumper-locking packs with great empty stretches of roadway in between.

He reminded himself that a lot of these people were here in the first place because they figured they had an exemption from the normal laws of probability, and a hell of a lot more had just lost their asses gambling or been cleaned out by whores and didn't particularly care whether they lived or died, let alone what happened to some Indian on a motorcycle. He ground his teeth and tried to give the most obvious maniacs a wide berth, and thought a bit more kindly of Oklahoma drivers.

Once clear of town, however, the Interstate stretched clear and smooth to the northeast, only a few cars and trucks and no cops in sight at all. Billy enjoyed the wind in his face and the feel of the old Honda winding up between his legs, and told himself this was the first time in days that he'd known what he was doing.

The pleasure quickly faded when he got onto the Blacktail Springs road. The 750 was no dirt bike; the weight, the gear ratios, the tires, even the basic frame geometry, all were totally wrong. And Billy had little experience of dirt riding, and the Blacktail Springs road wasn't even a very good dirt road. In fact "wretched" would have been the most optimistic possible description; and, as he fought his way through the ruts and potholes and washouts and patches of treacherous soft sand, there were many, many other adjectives that came to mind.

Before he had gone a mile he was coated all over, clothes and skin and hair, with fine white alkaline dust. He had no goggles and the dust and sand got into his eyes and stung painfully, as did the sweat that ran down his face in the oven-like heat. His arms and shoulders began to ache from the labor of keeping the bike upright and on course, and more than once he lost it and fell heavily, bike and all. One of the Honda's side plates cracked clear across and fell off, and several times he had to stop and let the overheated engine cool down to something like normal running temperatures.

Still he persevered, and at last he saw the main gate and the plywood sign announcing the reservation entrance. Today nobody was waiting by the gate; there was only a very large crow sitting perched on top of the sign, watching him.

"Having a hell of a day, ain't we, *chooch*?" the crow said, and flapped its night-black wings and flew away. Billy was too tired to feel interest, let alone surprise.

He labored on up the road, which had gotten even worse now, a thing he would have thought impossible. A big pickup truck appeared, coming the other way, and braked to a stop beside him. "Hold it right there," the driver said, and then after a second, "Oh, yeah, you were here the other day, weren't you? With the Father?"

Billy nodded and wiped uselessly at the mask of dust and sweat that caked his face. He wondered dully how anybody could recognize him right now.

"Better be glad you weren't here this morning," Leonard Hozia said. "Damn Feds were grabbing every outsider that showed up, even them Mormon doctors from Cedar City, dragging them off and asking a lot of questions. Strange Indian on a bike, man, they'd have eat you for lunch."

"FBI agents?" Billy asked, not really caring but glad enough of an excuse to take a breather.

Leonard Hozia scratched his head. "Damn if I know. Some kind of government agents, I guess FBI but I don't really know. Did that business, you know, flash the badge and the ID at you but so fast you never really get a look at what it says. Wouldn't even give *me* any answers," Leonard said aggrievedly, "and I'm the *law* around here."

He gave Billy a sudden gap-toothed grin. "Hey, if you're looking for that Russian girl, she's up at the clinic."

"Thanks," Billy said, and Leonard Hozia waved a hand and drove away, leaving a huge cloud of choking white dust. Too tired even to curse, Billy toed the Honda into gear and set out again.

WHEN AT LAST he pulled into the village and stopped the 750 in front of the clinic, he had acquired a considerable audience. Not that a crowd gathered around to stare at him—only half a dozen small children did that—but he was conscious of being watched from the windows of houses and trailers, and from tumbledown porches. It was all so silent, though; once he shut off the engine, the only noise was the hysterical barking of a couple of skinny dogs.

Somebody must have carried word inside; while he sat there, kicking the sidestand down and undoing his helmet strap, the clinic door opened and Janna and Sarah came out. They looked at him and immediately burst into laughter.

"My God," Sarah said when she could talk. "Look at you. Here." She tossed a ring of keys, which he caught with stiff clumsy hands. "Go on around back of the clinic and you'll find my trailer. The shower doesn't run very well but at least it ought to sluice a couple of inches of mineral deposits off your hide. Got a change of clothes?"

"In my saddlebags."

"Bring those to the clinic when you've changed, then. We've got a washer and dryer. Occasionally they even work."

Still laughing, she went back inside. Janna and Billy looked at each other. She wore a white uniform and her hair was tied back in a ponytail. He wanted to put his arms around her but then he remembered how dirty he was. "Hell," he said, and they both began laughing again.

"Go," she said, "clean yourself. I am busy now anyway. Later we can be together."

She glanced around and stepped closer. "I want to sleep with you," she said. "Tonight, in the desert. Is it possible?"

"We'll do it," Billy promised. And climbed stiffly off the Honda, while she vanished through the doorway, and bent to open his saddlebags, hoping he was right about having a clean change of clothes.

CONSIDERABLY LATER, cleansed of dust and sweat and engine oil and dressed in his last clean jeans and T-shirt, Billy strolled aimlessly up the dirt road and away from the little settlement of Blacktail Springs. There was nothing of interest in that direction, once he had passed the peyote tipi with the yellow crime-scene ribbons rigged all around it; just more desert exactly like that he had just crossed, but he was merely wandering now, letting the sun dry his hair, which was still wet from the shower.

A big black crow sat on a cactus by the roadside, looking at him. "*'Siyo, eduda,*" Billy said. "It's you, isn't it?"

"Fine damn fool you'd look if it wasn't," the bird said sarcastically. "And you know the old Cherokee saying: if you feel like a damn fool, think what you probably look like."

Billy looked around, but there was nobody anywhere nearby. He took off his hat and ran his hand over his wet hair. "Is that an old Cherokee saying?"

"Must be," the crow said. "I just said it, and I'm an old Cherokee. And a dead one at that. Put your hat back on, boy, this desert sun ain't no joke."

"Are you my grandfather or my mother?" Billy groused. But he put the hat back on. "You got something on your mind," he said to the bird, "or is this just a social call?"

"You got the tobacco," Grandfather said. "Like I told you in the dream."

"Yes. It's not Cherokee tobacco, but—"

"No, that's all right. You got it from that Mohawk preacher, it's good stuff. Good man there," Grandfather said, tilting his head to one side and looking pensive. Of course crows always looked pensive. "Too bad he's all tore up inside. Pulled in different directions, that's got to be hell. Wish I could help him."

"Why don't you talk to him?"

"Can't do that, *chooch*. If he was standing beside you right now, all he'd see would be you talking to a bird. Only reason you can hear me, you're my blood. Anyway," Grandfather said briskly, "you haven't doctored the tobacco yet, have you?"

Billy shook his head. "I was figuring to wait till tomorrow morning. Catch the rising sun."

"Yeah, well, usually that'd be the best way, all right. But I don't know if you got till tomorrow morning, boy." The mockery was altogether gone from Grandfather's voice now. "I think you better not wait."

"You want me to do it now?"

"That's what I been trying to tell you. Go over behind that patch of brush," Grandfather said. "Make sure nobody can see you. We don't want to shake these raggedy-ass Paiutes up."

Billy started toward the clump of bushes. Behind him there was a fluttering noise and then a weight settled onto his hat, pushing it down unpleasantly on his head. "Guess you don't mind giving your elder a lift," Grandfather's voice said.

"If you're going to sit up there," Billy said, walking around the bushes until he was out of sight of the road, "try not to shit on the hat. It cost me ninety-six bucks at the western store in Muskogee."

He took out the little buckskin tobacco pouch and undid the drawstring. He was about to pour the tobacco into his palm when Grandfather said, "Don't forget the cedar, *chooch*."

There was a small, scraggly-looking cedar—it would have been the last tree left on any Christmas lot—in the middle of the clump of brush. Billy broke off a few dark-green tips and crumbled them into the bag, shaking it to mix the cedar with the tobacco. "How about sage?" he asked. "Ought to be able to find some around here."

"Not for this." The crow shifted position slightly, tilting Billy's hat to one side. "Get on with it, now."

"Do I face east," Billy wanted to know, "or what?"

"Usually east, but then that would be at daybreak. Under the circumstances, you better face the sun."

Billy turned to face southwest. The sun hit him in the face with almost painful intensity. "All right," Grandfather said, "you're on your own."

The black wings flapped and the weight was gone from Billy's hat. Billy took a deep breath—this whole business was making him extremely nervous—and began.

Carefully he poured the tobacco into his left hand until there was a little brown mound, with a scattering of green flecks, covering his upturned palm. Shoving the empty bag into his pocket, he held the tobacco up to the sun and began to sing the *igawesdi* the old man had given him in the dream. The alien words came back to him without hesitancy; he might have known the song all his life.

He sang the *igawesdi* four times, all the while stirring the tobacco gently with his fingertip, and remembering to blow on the tobacco at the end of each repetition. It seemed to him that he could feel something happening, the tobacco coming alive in his hand; it felt warm now, with a warmth that was different from the warmth of the sun or his skin. When at last he poured it back in the bag—moving with great care; it would have been very bad to spill any now—the bag seemed to move slightly in his hand, as if it contained a breathing creature.

Grandfather Ninekiller's voice said, "All right, *chooch*. I got to admit it, you done that good."

Billy turned and saw the crow sitting on a bush a few feet away. "Of course," Grandfather went on, "like you said yourself, this ain't really the right time of day. Ought to be done at dawn, and you ought to have gone without food all night, better yet for four days and nights. Come to that, it ought to be done on the bank of a moving stream, but I bet you'd play hell finding one around here." The crow lifted a wing in what seemed meant as a shrug. "Well, hell, that's all details. *Iguhnedi* stuff. You know how it works."

Billy nodded. In Cherokee medicine, a ritual included both *igawesdi*—the words which were sung or spoken, or sometimes merely thought—and *iguhnedi*, the physical procedure which accompanied the incantation. Of these, the *igawesdi* was by far the more important, as it had the function of focussing the intent of the person working the medicine. An *igawesdi* had to be repeated with great precision or bad things might happen. The *iguhnedi*, on the other hand, was no more than a set of possibly useful aids, that might be modified or even dispensed with according to circumstances.

"Use it tonight," Grandfather said. "You and that girl—going to spend the night out in the desert, are you?"

"I think so."

"Well, wait till you're settled on where you're going to be, because the medicine won't follow you if you move. I don't know, boy." Grandfather's voice was soft now, sounding a little worried. "It might be really good, out under the sky like that, with somebody you love . . . but it's awful damn dangerous, too, right now. Use the medicine. It'll protect you if anything can."

"Maybe I ought to use it on this whole place," Billy suggested. "The village and the clinic and all."

"Nice thought, *chooch*, but it won't work. It's only good over a small space, and only for you and whoever's with you.

Only good for one night, too. Don't ask me why, that's just how it is."

The crow's beak opened slightly and Billy heard a kind of sigh. "Hell, *chooch*, if it don't protect you then there's no place in your whole world that's safe. For you or anybody else."

Billy nodded and pushed the little bag down into his jeans pocket. His throat felt very dry. *"Wado, eduda,"* he managed to say.

"Howa," Grandfather said, spreading his wings.

Billy watched as the crow flew away, circling on an updraft to vanish upward into the rising sun. After a minute or so he turned and began walking back toward Blacktail Springs.

IN THE EVENING Billy and Janna walked away from the settlement, up the dirt road for a mile or so and then out across the open desert. The bushes and the stunted trees cast long shadows on the desert floor. Behind them, the sky was aflame with a sunset so spectacular as to verge on the corny.

"Any special place?" Billy said finally, when they were well out of sight of Blacktail Springs.

"Anywhere," Janna said. "It is all so beautiful."

That wasn't the way Billy would have described the scene, but the bleak landscape did look considerably better in the dying light, the sunset tinting the dusty earth a faint rose. "Here, then," he said as they came to a little clear space.

They had already eaten in Sarah's trailer—Billy's stomach was still enjoying that; the doctor had turned out to be one hell of a cook—so they carried only a plastic thermos jug of cold water and a little bag of fruit and nuts for breakfast. Billy wished for a bottle of wine or maybe even some beer, but there was none to be had on the reservation and Sarah had told him there would be hell to pay if Leonard Hozia caught him with alcohol. Billy carried his old sleeping bag under one arm, while Janna lugged a nice new-looking goose-down bag borrowed from Sarah. They unrolled the bags and spread them on the dry sandy earth; and then they spent a few minutes just looking at each other.

"Uh, look," Billy said finally, remembering, "I've got something I've got to do. Take me just a few minutes—" He hesitated. "It's kind of a ceremony," he told her. "I really better not talk about it, okay?"

"*Harasho.*" She sat down on her sleeping bag and stretched her legs out in front of her. She was wearing a plain white T-shirt and red running shorts and her wooden-soled sandals. "I will sit here and wait for you."

Billy looked at her legs for a moment, feeling strong impulses that had nothing to do with Cherokee medicine. Or maybe they had everything to do with it, but this was no time to try to find out. Shaking his head and trying to focus, he strode off through the brush.

Twenty or thirty paces from the campsite—he wished he'd asked Grandfather about distances—he stopped and dug in his pockets for the little buckskin bag and the pipe he had bought at a discount store in North Las Vegas. The pipe was nothing but an ordinary cheap briar, selected at random from several on a card display, but it would do. Unlike many tribes, the Cherokees had no real tradition of the sacred medicine pipe; the power was in the tobacco, and the means by which it was prepared. The pipe itself was merely a tool; Billy could, if he had preferred, have simply rolled the tobacco in a cigarette and smoked it that way, and he would have done so except that people were getting very weird these days about selling rolling papers.

Carefully he filled the pipe with the remade tobacco, stowing the empty bag, with the little bit that was left, in his back pocket. For a moment, then, he stood there unmoving, facing the east, gathering himself.

There was a light breeze blowing across the desert and the cheap butane lighter kept trying to go out, but at last Billy got the pipe lit. The tobacco was very strong, hotter-burning than Cherokee leaf, and the cedar gave it an added bite and caused tiny crackling explosions in the bowl. Puffing vigorously, Billy blew a big cloud of smoke to the east, and then he turned and began to walk in a wide circle, around the campsite. At each of the cardinal compass points he stopped and blew smoke, though he did not offer the pipe to the four directions in the way of the plains tribes.

Four times he walked around the circle, puffing steadily all the while, stopping to blow smoke to the four directions. He did not sing or make any sound at all; the *igawesdi* was already contained in the tobacco, stored and now released by the act of smoking. He did not inhale the smoke, but his body responded all the same; the blood began to sing in his ears, and sweat appeared on his face even though the air was now growing cool.

When he had completed the fourth circle, he spat four times on the ground, dumped the ashes out of the pipe—the tobacco had lasted exactly long enough, a good sign—and went back to where Janna was sitting.

"Are you done?" she asked.

"Yes," he said, stowing the pipe in his jeans pocket.

"Then come," she said, lying back and holding her arms

out to him. "I want us to make love."

"Yeah," he said, "well, that's pretty much what I had in mind too—"

"No." She held up her hands, palms toward him. "I don't mean that. Well, all right, that *too*, but . . . Billy," she said, "there is something strange that people say in this country. They say 'make love' when all they mean is having sex. Why is this?"

Billy peeled off his T-shirt. The breeze was cool on his bare shoulders. "I don't know," he said, fumbling with his belt buckle. "Maybe they just think it sounds better."

"I don't want to just—*yebit*. What is English? Fuck," she said, surprising him; he hadn't known she knew the word. "I don't want to just fuck. I want to truly make love with you."

So they did, sliding and rolling naked together on top of the spread-out sleeping bags, slow and leisurely at first but then with an exponentially growing urgency, the last light from the setting sun washing their straining bodies with a warm pink glow. Till at last Billy hunched and bucked his way to a shuddering climax and then collapsed, boneless-limp, with Janna spread out beneath him like a pale soft star.

"Billy," she said, stroking his hair. *"Janim."*

There was nothing they did that they had not done before, with each other and for that matter with other people. Nothing, at least, in terms of mechanics and ergonomics . . . it did not matter. In this, too, the details of the *iguhnedi* counted for very little when the real magic was made.

THEY LAY ON the sleeping bags and watched the sky turn black and the stars come out, huge and jewel-like in the high dry night. The air was beginning to cool but neither of them made any move to cover themselves.

"Billy, *janim*," she said again. *"Kozlerini opiyorum."*

"Is that Kazakh?"

"Yes. It means I kiss your eyes." And did so, left and then right, while he blinked and smiled.

She rolled over and looked up at the sky. "Such a night. How many more nights will we have?"

Billy made a wordless vague sound in his throat. He didn't want to think about that just now. That or anything else.

"I will go to the city tomorrow," she said, "to the immigration office. I will try to get my visa—um—an extension, to get an extension, yes. To stay longer."

"Good."

"Don't expect anything, Billy. It will be very difficult." She propped herself up on one elbow and looked at him, her face serious in the starlight. "Already your government has made trouble—"

"Not my government."

"Hm. Yes. Anyway, they don't like it that I am here doing research so close to their atomic testing site. I think they don't want anybody learning too much about these things, you know? They have even tried to make trouble for Sarah," she said, "but her family has much money and influence."

She began toying with his hair. "The secret police were here this morning before you came."

"The FBI?"

"FBI, KGB, CIA, they are all the same, isn't it so? The secret police."

Billy thought it over and nodded. "Most Americans wouldn't agree, though."

"Then they know nothing. Believe me, I have been interrogated by KGB and your FBI, and now these men. There is American idiom I hear Mickey Wolf say: 'Six of one and half a dozen of the other.'" She made a face. "They asked many questions. I did not tell them much. Of course I knew nothing to tell them, but when does that mean anything to their kind, in any country?"

Billy remembered Leonard Hozia's remarks about mysterious government agents. "They were investigating the murders? At the peyote meeting?"

"So they said. But many questions had nothing to do with this," Janna said. "They wanted to know about Sarah's work, and mine, and things like whether I had ever belonged to Communist Party. Pfui." She ran her hand over his bare chest. "Enough about them. *Duraki.* I stop."

She put her arms around his neck. "Make love to me again, Billy."

"I don't know," he said as she began to wriggle against him. "I think Elvis has left the building."

"*Shto?*"

"Never mind," he said. "Evidently I was wrong."

LATER, THEY SLIPPED into the sleeping bags, leaving them unzipped so they could lie together and touch each other. By now the moon had risen, flooding the desert with cold silver light, transforming the harsh barren landscape of the day into a scene of weird and surpassing beauty.

"I could build a fire," Billy offered. "Plenty of dry brushwood here."

"No." She rolled over and put an arm over him. "No, don't. I love this as it is."

She raised her head slightly, looking past his shoulder. "I want to remember this forever," she said.

Billy closed his eyes and enjoyed the feel of her against him. "Me too," he agreed sleepily through a stray lock of her hair.

And felt, then, the violent leaping spasm that convulsed her entire body, a fraction of a second before she split the night open with the most terrible scream he had ever heard.

He rolled over and would have screamed too, in that first mind-blanking instant, except that he was unable to breathe. He saw a thing out of a madman's dreams, towering against the night, blotting out the stars, enormous and not to be believed. It was no more than a hundred yards away and it was coming directly toward them.

It was at least as big as a six-story office building; it might have been much bigger, for all he could tell. His eyes could get no grip on its size and shape. Parts of it seemed to shift in and out of visibility; he had the impression that it extended through dimensions beyond the normal three. All around it, the moonlight looked bent and twisted; things near to it appeared distorted, and even the stars beyond it shone with strange and disturbing colors. It flowed across the desert floor—not particularly fast, but inexorably—without quite seeming to touch the ground; and the only straight line on the scene was the course it was following in their direction.

And, with instant sickening certainty, Billy knew that this was no coincidence. There was an unmistakable purposefulness to the thing's movement; he could see nothing that remotely resembled eyes or other sensory organs, but there was no doubt in his mind that it knew where he and Janna were.

Janna had stopped screaming; now she was making only

tiny whimpering sounds. She was shaking uncontrollably and biting at the knuckles of one hand. Billy put his arm around her as the apparition bore down on them.

There was a terrible roaring now, growing louder and louder, so powerful it filled the whole world; and yet Billy had the feeling it was coming from inside his own head. He felt paralyzed, numb; he was far beyond anything as ordinary as simple fear.

Then, twenty or thirty yards away, the thing stopped. It was as if it had suddenly run into an invisible barbed-wire fence; it even recoiled physically. The roaring switched abruptly to a high, rising-pitch whistle.

It stood there for a few seconds—or minutes, or hours; time was not merely frozen but had ceased to have meaning—while the whistling ran up and down the scale and Billy's teeth began to hurt. Strange lights began to flicker within the black mass, following no apparent pattern, in colors that seemed to belong nowhere on the visible spectrum. A couple of freight-car-sized extrusions burst from the formless mass, waved briefly about in the crooked moonlight, and began to make groping, probing motions, pushing and drawing back, like a man testing drying paint.

Suddenly the thing began moving again, this time to its left, in a sort of slow sidling motion. The extrusions continued to poke and probe, and now they were joined by two more, lower down on the thing's body.

It circled them, whistling and hooting, keeping always at that same twenty or thirty yards' distance, while the huge pseudopods continued to press and paw at the unseen barrier. There was a weird hesitancy to the thing's movements; it seemed confused. Watching, Billy found himself remembering a bad street mime he had seen in Florida, pretending to feel his way along an imaginary wall.

When it had completed the circuit, it stood again at its starting point, flickering and whistling, and then it began to push forward with its entire mass. It was barely moving at all now, but there was an appearance of tremendous force being brought to bear; it was clearly straining against some unseen obstacle. The whistling stopped and the roaring began again, louder and louder, until Billy felt as if he had his head under a gigantic waterfall. The lights flickered faster and faster and the black mass seemed to grow even larger; there was a trembling in the ground.

Janna lost control and wet herself. A low moan escaped past the fist crammed in her mouth.

Billy moved, then. With quick efficient motions, and without an instant's pause to think about what he was doing and why, he grabbed his rolled-up jeans and dug into the pockets for the pipe and the lighter and the buckskin tobacco pouch. There was just barely enough tobacco left to fill the bowl and he almost spilled it in the crazy light, and then he had to thumb the cheap lighter repeatedly before the butane ignited.

Puffing, tamping the glowing tobacco down without even feeling the pain as he burned his thumb, he took a deep drag, held it, turned the pipe to point the stem like a pistol, and blew smoke straight at the thing. It seemed to him that the roaring faltered momentarily and then shifted to a higher pitch.

Seven times, deliberately and without a word, Billy blew smoke and pointed the pipe. Each time the roaring changed to a higher tone; the lights within the black mass flickered at near-stroboscopic speeds now, and in new and darker colors, while the armlike extrusions flailed about and then began to pull back and disappear within the great shifting bulk.

When he pointed the pipe and blew smoke for the seventh time, it was as if a switch had been thrown. All at once, the roaring stopped, the lights died, and the monstrous form ceased to press forward. A moment later Billy realized that it was moving away, heading back along its approach track, with that same unhurried sliding motion. Since it had neither eyes nor head, it could hardly be said that it did not look back; and yet that was the impression it gave.

When it was perhaps a third of a mile away, it disappeared. There were no special effects; it was just there and then it wasn't.

Billy turned the pipe up and knocked the ashes onto the sand. There had been exactly enough tobacco for the seven pointings.

Janna was weeping helplessly now, talking fast in Kazakh, her eyes wide and out of focus. Billy put his arms around her and held her tight until the sobbing and the trembling lessened. "Hey," he said then, "it's okay. It's gone."

"Gone?" She raised her head and looked around. Her eyes were still wild but the blank craziness was gone. "Where?"

"I don't know." Billy shrugged. "Maybe back to hell, or wherever it came from. Maybe not."

"Will it return?"

"Don't know that either." He stroked her hair. With a certain detached surprise he realized that his own hands were shaking now. In fact he seemed to be shaking all over. "I don't think it'll be back tonight," he said, "but we better stay inside that medicine circle until sunrise, anyway."

It occurred to him that there was absolutely no reason to assume the thing would object to coming out in the daytime. Still, they couldn't stay here forever.

"What was it, Billy?" Janna asked faintly.

"Another question I don't have an answer for." He looked out across the desert in the direction of Blacktail Springs village. With all the noise and spectacle, it seemed that somebody ought to be coming out to investigate; at least there ought to be lights coming on, sounds and signs of alarm. But nothing seemed to be happening in the village. Was it possible nobody had noticed? Or—even harder to believe—that only he and Janna had seen and heard the visitation?

"I don't think there's a word for it," he told her. "In any language."

SHAKING, THEY HUDDLED together for the rest of the night, holding each other tight, watching the desert with huge burning eyes. Sleep was never even a possibility; neither of them could conceive of sleeping, ever again.

The thing did not reappear.

And at last the sky grew light along the horizon, and the first rays burst into the empty sky; and as the sun began its climb, Billy and Janna staggered back across the desert and down the dirt road, back toward Blacktail Springs village, holding hands, stumbling over rocks and brush, red-eyed and sweat-sour, neither of them speaking at all.

11.

BILLY SAID, "I wish you wouldn't go. Not today, anyway."

"I wish I did not have to go," Janna said. "Not today, not any day. But it must be done, so why are we talking about it?"

"Wait till tomorrow, anyway," Billy suggested. "At least get a night's sleep."

It was going on nine in the morning. They stood in front of Sarah's trailer, behind the Blacktail Springs clinic. The day had already begun to grow hot. The sun shone in Janna's eyes, making her blink even though she wore dark sunglasses.

She said, "And if I cannot sleep tonight? That is possible, you know. Then tomorrow it will be even worse." She pushed back a strand of hair that was fluttering in the wind. "Right now I wonder if I will ever be able to sleep again."

She made an attempt at a smile. "Anyway, the immigration office is such a tiresome place, you know? I may as well go when I am already having bad day in advance."

He started to speak but she raised a hand. "Billy, there is little time left before my visa expires. I should have done this on Monday."

"Then let me go with you."

"It is impossible. You know this."

He did; he just didn't want to admit it because he was feeling cranky from lack of sleep and because he didn't like to see Janna going off without him today. She was getting a lift into Las Vegas with one of the clinic's nurses, who was driving an old woman to the University of Nevada Medical Center for some sort of treatment. They were taking a station wagon belonging to the tribe, and it was strictly against the rules to carry an unauthorized passenger, such as Billy, in an official vehicle. Sarah had already had to bend the regulations, and lean on a councilman, to get Janna the ride.

"I could follow on the Honda," he argued.

"No. You are too tired. Besides, what would you do? Sit there all day in a crowded waiting room full of Mexican laborers and their crying children, while I go from one stupid bureaucrat to another? Stay here and get some sleep," she said. "Sarah says you can rest on her couch. I will be back this evening."

There was a honk of an auto horn from out in front of the clinic. "They are waiting," Janna said. "I must go."

BUT AFTER SHE had gone, Billy discovered that he wasn't sleepy, didn't even feel particularly tired. On the contrary, he felt wired up, full of restless and unfocussed energy, as if he'd had too many cups of coffee. Which, come to think of it, he had, an hour or so ago at Sarah's table. His stomach lining was still sending up signals of protest, and there was a nasty faint singing in his ears.

Feeling a little out of it and a lot lonely, he drifted up the road to the outskirts of the settlement and stood staring out across the desert toward the place where they had spent the night. It still didn't seem possible that the night's events had gone undetected by the entire population of Blacktail Springs, and yet evidently that was the case. Sarah, who had been up most of the night working on a report for her sponsoring foundation, had heard nothing out of the ordinary; and Leonard Hozia, when Billy asked him if anyone had reported anything unusual during the night, had responded with a blank stare.

Billy wasn't at all surprised when the big black crow floated down and landed, with a noisy flapping of wings, on a nearby bush. "*'Siyo, eduda,*" he said, "*dohiju?*"

"*Caw!*" the crow said, and then as Billy glanced nervously around, "Oh, hell, *chooch*, it's me all right. Just having a little fun with you . . . but I guess you're not in much of a laughing mood right now."

"You got that right," Billy said morosely. "You know about last night, don't you? Since you seem to know everything."

"Well, not quite, but yeah. Hell of a business." The crow tilted its head to one side. "Listen, *chooch*, you feel up to doing some driving? Something not too far from here I think you need to see."

Billy rubbed his face, discovering that he needed a shave. Screw it for now. "I don't know, *eduda*. Been kind of a long night—" He pushed back his hat and scratched his head. "Oh, well, why not? Something to do, anyway. Let me go get the bike."

"Shit, boy, I'm not riding around on that damn roller skate of yours. Ain't there a car or a pickup or something you can borrow?" Grandfather sounded aggrieved. "I'm too damn old—hell, this *bird* seems to be pretty old—"

"You want to ride along?"

"What did you think, I was gonna fly ahead and point the

way? This ain't the Bible, son, and I ain't no dove." The black feathers ruffled briefly. "Go find that white woman doctor, tell her you need to borrow some wheels. Tell her it's got something to do with what she's been trying to find out, about what's making the people sick around here. Oh," Grandfather said, "and see if she's got one of those gadgets you use to measure radiation."

"I'll try," Billy said dubiously.

"You do that," Grandfather said. "I'll wait for you here. Try not to take too long, will you? The sun's getting hot."

"BILLY," SARAH SAID, "are you sure you don't just want to drive into town to be with Janna? Not that I'd mind, really, but—"

"It's not that," Billy said, though in fact the idea had occurred to him. "Just something I want to check out."

"A hunch? Hm." Sarah gave him a long cool look. "But you don't want to tell me about it."

Billy nodded, feeling stupid. When she put it that way, it did sound pretty thin. On the other hand, he wasn't anywhere near ready to tell her about Grandfather Ninekiller. "I, uh," he said, "I had this sort of a dream."

She leaned back against the white wall of the clinic's main corridor. He had caught her halfway through the morning's routine and she had a clipboard tucked under one arm and a stethoscope around her neck. She continued to give him that appraising look.

"This may surprise you," she said finally, "but I've been around Indians too long to dismiss that out of hand. If your dream told you something that might help solve this riddle—" She sighed. "Science and technology haven't done very well around here lately. Might as well let your dream have its shot."

From down the corridor came a strange wailing cry. Sarah Aronson looked in that direction and then back at Billy.

"Come with me for a minute, Billy," she said. "There's something I want you to see."

He followed her down the corridor and into a small, brightly-lit room. "Here," she said. "This is Sammy."

In the middle of the room was a child's-size hospital bed, rigged with metal side railings to form a kind of crib. In the bed lay a child, though it took Billy a second to realize what the grotesque shape was.

He could not guess at the child's age. The body under the thin hospital gown was that of a small boy, ten years old at most, but the head was as big as his own. The misshapen features gave no clue: an off-center lump for a nose, a shapeless sagging mouth, and tightly-closed eyes beneath startlingly heavy black eyebrows. The arms were those of a child of five or six, ending in stubby-fingered, baby-like hands. As best Billy could see, the boy had no legs or feet at all.

"We call him Sammy," Sarah Aronson was saying, "but we have no idea what name his parents gave him. Assuming, of course, they ever gave him one. The nurses chose the name for him, I have no idea why."

Sammy lay on his back, face toward the ceiling. From that and the closed eyes, Billy thought he must be asleep or unconscious, but then he saw that the little hands were making spasmodic motions and the shoulders were jerking back and forth. From the slack-lipped mouth came another weird high cry, like that Billy had heard in the corridor. It sounded like the cry of a cat, rather than anything human.

"We don't know how old he is," Sarah said, standing beside the bed. "Or anything else about his history. He was left here one night, on the ground in front of the clinic, in a cardboard box lined with a couple of old blankets. Nobody on the reservation seems to know anything about him—who his family might be, where he came from, anything at all. Leonard Hozia found a man who said he saw an old couple in a pickup truck heading up the road about sunrise that morning, people he didn't recognize, but they've never been identified or located."

Billy moved hesitantly toward the bed. He was trying not to stare but then he realized the child couldn't see him. The eyes were still shut.

"Besides what you can see," Sarah went on, "Sammy has a number of internal abnormalities. He appears to be severely retarded, too, but we don't really know because so far we haven't had much luck communicating with him. He may be autistic." She shrugged, looking down at the boy in the bed. "He can't talk, anyway, or doesn't, and we're not sure he hears anything. His eyes seem to be physically normal, but he keeps them closed all the time, so he may be blind. He doesn't seem to respond to anything, really. He has little or no motor control and can't feed himself."

She reached down and stroked Sammy's hair, which was thick and black. He gave no sign of awareness, let alone response.

"We're not set up to deal with a case like this," she said to Billy. "And I'm outside my sphere of competence in caring for him. Nobody at this clinic is even qualified to test and analyze, let alone work with, a child like Sammy—though Janna has more experience with such cases than the rest of us. He needs to be in a first-class institution under the care of specialists."

Billy nodded. He felt uncomfortable, standing there looking at Sammy and talking about him like that, yet he reminded himself that the boy couldn't possibly know or care. "Why's he here, then?"

Sarah's lips tightened. "Typical Indian-affairs bureaucratic mess. Nobody is willing to accept responsibility for him. There's no documentary proof that he's an Indian, by the BIA's definition—an enrolled member of a federally recognized tribe—so the Indian Health Service doesn't want him. I'm already getting heat for admitting him here. And the state of Nevada claims that since he turned up on a reservation and he obviously *is* an Indian, documents or not, he's the government's problem."

Sammy began to move his head from side to side on the pillow, a monotonous jerking motion without rhythm. Again he made that strange cat-like cry. Billy flinched and then felt guilty for it.

"You realize," Sarah said, "somebody took care of this child for a lot of years. He's got to be nine or ten—there are indications of approaching puberty—and that's a long time to care for a child who keeps growing but remains helpless. My God, he's only been here a couple of weeks, and already—" She sighed. "And the parents, or grandparents or whoever did care for Sammy, were almost certainly Indians from some Southwestern reservation, which means they were among the poorest people in the United States. Yet when we got him he was clean, well-fed, and, within his own limitations, healthy."

She shook her head. "Maybe they thought they were bringing him to people who could give him better care. So far I don't think we've justified their confidence."

She fell silent, still looking down at Sammy, who was now thrashing his arms in vague, apparently random movements. Billy kept quiet and waited for her to go on.

"Well," she said finally, making a quick impatient face, "you're probably wondering why I brought you in here."

Billy nodded. Sarah put her hands on her hips and looked him in the face.

"I don't know whether Sammy's problems are the result of radiation exposure," she said. "Everything about him fits the profile, but there are plenty of other possibilities. But there's nothing wrong with him that hasn't turned up in other cases, that *can* be definitely linked to radiation in one form or another, all over this part of the country. And he's the only one I've got here to show you. So—"

She raised a finger and pointed it at Billy. "If you actually think you may be onto something, however farfetched, that could help prevent horrors like this, then go for it with my blessings. If you're just screwing around, though, I don't have the time to waste."

She watched his face, seeming to wait for a reply. When he offered none, she sighed again, dug in the pocket of her white coat, and held out a set of keys. "Here," she said. "Take my car. It's parked by the trailer. There's an old but functional Geiger counter in the trunk. Try not to break anything."

SARAH'S CAR WAS a four-wheel-drive Subaru; not Billy's favorite vehicle, but good enough for a short haul, and the engine sounded clean when he started it. He backed out and turned around and drove up the road to the place where he had left Grandfather. The crow was still sitting on the bush. As he braked to a stop, the bird flew up and flapped toward the car. He opened the door and the crow flared its wings and sailed neatly in, to perch on the back of the seat beside him.

"Damn well took your time," Grandfather grumbled. "It's

hot out there, you know that? What were you doing, anyway, getting a little off the nurses?"

Not really listening, Billy glanced apprehensively around—if anyone had seen him stop to pick up a crow, things could get difficult; these Indians around here were probably as nervous about witchcraft as people back home—but saw no one. With a good deal of backing and wheel-twisting, he got the Subaru turned back around, while Grandfather muttered in Cherokee and made sarcastic remarks about Billy's driving.

"Head on south," Grandfather said, "the way you came when you rode out here. I'll tell you when to turn off."

Billy drove slowly through the settlement and down the rough dirt road, taking it easy since it wasn't his car. Nobody seemed to be paying him any attention. In fact there weren't many people around at all. A lot of the locals had taken off, gone to stay with relatives or friends in town or on other reservations, frightened off by the peyote-tipi killings.

"Been meaning to tell you," Grandfather said, when they were clear of the village. "You done good last night. Couldn't have done better myself."

Billy raised his shoulders in a shrug. He didn't want to talk about last night. He had just about managed to convince himself that the whole thing had been some kind of hallucination. Maybe he and Janna had seen nothing but a desert whirlwind with a lot of dust in it, and imagined the rest. But there was no stopping Grandfather and no point in trying.

"Tell the truth," Grandfather said, "I wasn't sure that medicine circle was going to stop that thing. Might not have, there at the end, the way it was pushing and straining. I kind of think you saved yourself when you did that business with the pipe." The beaked head turned; shiny black eyes stared at Billy.

"Now where the hell did that come from? You never learned it from me."

Billy thought about it. "Damned if I know. It just sort of came to me. Although I think I've heard you mention something like that—pointing a pipe at a witch to turn his power back on him?"

"Huh. You got the details wrong, but yeah, there's something like that, nobody much uses it any more. But seven times? Why seven, *chooch*? Four would be the usual number."

"I know. I guess I was thinking of the *uk'tena*," Billy said. "You know, in the story the young guy who finally kills the *uk'tena* does it by shooting it seven times in the same place with seven arrows."

"I'll be damned." Grandfather actually sounded impressed. "By God, that's pretty good. I didn't know you remembered those old stories I used to tell you."

The Subaru hit a pothole. The crow lurched and teetered, flapped briefly for balance. "*Watch* it, boy," Grandfather said irritably. "Anyway," he went on, "it worked, that's all that matters."

"How well, though?" Billy said, fighting the wheel as the tires hit a stretch of washboard. "I mean, is that thing gone for good now? Or is it going to come back?"

"We'll talk about that in a little while. First I want to show you something . . . *na*. See that side road off to the left?"

"Side road?" Billy said, braking. "I don't see any side road. You mean that old trail over there? Hell, that's nothing but a mule track."

"Take it, then," Grandfather said. "One more jackass can't hurt."

12.

FOR MOST OF AN hour Billy steered the Subaru down an unmarked, almost undetectable track that made the Blacktail Springs road look like the Indian Nations Turnpike. The Subaru was taking a hell of a pounding, bouncing and banging over rocks and ruts; he tried not to think what Sarah was going to say.

The road wandered confusingly across the desert flats, heading generally southward. In the distance Billy could see a line of steep, rough-looking hills that rose sharply out of the plain, in that strange abrupt way of Nevada mountains. A metal sign appeared beside the trail, blasted to illegibility by rifle bullets and shotgun pellets. "Reservation boundary marker," Grandfather remarked. "Now just a little way—ah."

The dirt track emerged suddenly from the brush, at the shoulder of a two-lane blacktop road. "What the hell," Billy said.

"Short cut," Grandfather explained. "Only other way to get onto this road, you'd have had to go all the way to the Interstate and then take the next exit. Worth a little cowpath driving to save that much time and gas. Hang a right."

Billy maneuvered the Subaru up the steep shoulder and onto the pavement, glad at least to be back on a real road. He wasn't sure where they were now. Somewhere south of Blacktail Springs Reservation, that was as close as he could figure.

The paved road ran for several miles across the desert until it reached the chain of hills, then swung southward to wind along at their feet. The slopes looked old, heavily eroded, strewn with rocks and clumps of brush. There were no houses in sight and no other cars on the road.

"Watch for a dirt road off to the right," Grandfather said as they sped along. "I checked all this out from the air, but I ain't sure how it looks on the ground."

The line of hills ended suddenly and rather arbitrarily, without tapering off or petering out, as if someone had simply decided that was enough mountains for now. Almost immediately after that, Billy saw the turnoff. It was a wide, well-graded gravel road, and as he slowed the Subaru and started to make the turn he saw a big sign on steel posts:

NEW AGE ENLIGHTENMENT CENTER
AND
GUEST RANCH

The borders of the sign were decorated with odd-looking figures that Billy thought must represent the signs of the Zodiac. To his surprise, there was no gate or fence.

The gravel road ran for several miles across the floor of a broad desert valley that was walled off on three sides by those jagged brown hills. In the distance Billy could see a considerable collection of buildings.

"Don't worry," Grandfather said, "nobody lives there now. All closed down."

Remembering the story he had heard in town, Billy said, "This is where the killings happened, isn't it?"

"Killings among other things. Some *yoneg* fools got to dabbling around in things they didn't understand, wound up paying some almighty heavy penalties for it. I kind of think they may have had a part in whistling up that booger you saw last night."

"You think it's the same thing that got them?"

"Lord God, boy, I hope so. If there's two of them around, I'm outta here. But we can talk about that later," Grandfather said. "Take that road off to the right."

The road, if you could call it that, was almost as bad as the short cut they had taken across the reservation. It was deeply rutted in places—Billy had the impression it had once been in regular use, by heavy vehicles—and covered here and there with clumps of brush. It ran at right angles to the main entrance road, almost due north across the valley floor, toward the line of hills. Out in the middle of the valley it forked again, in three directions this time. "Left fork," Grandfather said. "Go slow, it gets pretty rough from here on."

It did that. The valley floor turned out to be crisscrossed by a network of disused tracks and trails that split and rejoined and wandered aimlessly through the brush in the most confusing way. Billy gave up trying to understand and simply settled for following Grandfather's directions. At times it took an act of faith to believe there was any road at all beneath the blowing dust. Now and then Billy had to stop and get out and move rocks, or pile brush in little gullies, before he could proceed. By now it was impossible to tell what color the Subaru had originally been.

The trail ended at last at the foot of a hill that very nearly qualified as a full-sized mountain. A pile of big boulders blocked the way; Billy couldn't tell whether they had been piled there or just happened to roll down the hillside. Beyond, there appeared to be the washed-out vestiges of a road that climbed the hillside and vanished among the rocks.

Billy shut off the engine and said, "Well, what now?"

"Now," Grandfather said, "we get out and walk. Fetch that radiation dingus."

Billy opened the door and climbed stiffly out. He wasn't overjoyed at the prospect of hiking in this heat, but it would be a change from all this dirt-track driving. He went back and opened the trunk, while Grandfather fluttered out and landed on the Subaru's roof.

The Geiger counter was in a foam-lined aluminum case in the Subaru's trunk. Billy had used one in the army, during a training session on atomic warfare; this one didn't look all that different from the G.I. model. He plugged in the earphones and hung them around his neck and switched on the device. The needle bounced and a series of sharp clicks, slow and evenly spaced, began to sound in the earphones. Grandfather flew over and lit on his shoulder, cocking his head to listen. "Picking up something already, *chooch*?"

"There's always a certain level of background radiation," Billy explained. "From the sun or something." He wondered if he knew what he was talking about. It seemed to him that the clicks were coming a bit faster than he remembered from that long-ago training exercise, but he decided it was just his imagination. He switched the Geiger counter off, wishing he had gotten Sarah to give him a little instruction.

"This way," Grandfather said, taking off and soaring up the rocky gullied slope. A hundred feet up or so, he perched on a protruding spur of rock and watched as Billy began to struggle up the steep hillside. "Let's go, *chooch*," he called cheerfully. "*Nula*. We ain't got all day."

BILLY SPENT THE next hour or so scrambling and slipping and most of all sweating, following the flapping, mocking crow across the slopes of those barren brown hills, which were much bigger than they had looked from the desert floor. At first Grandfather led him along the course of the abandoned road, and that wasn't so bad; but then they left the road and set off upward, angling sharply on up almost to the skyline.

"What the hell," Billy panted as he caught up to the bird once more. He could barely talk for the dryness in his throat. "Why'd we leave the trail?"

"Wait till we get where we're going," Grandfather said. "You'll be damn glad you stayed clear of that old road." And flew away again, easy and graceful, riding the wind without apparent effort, leaving Billy to curse through dry-swollen lips and stumble after.

The going became a little easier, though, once they were up over the shoulder of the first hill, and there were sketchy but usable trails left by wild animals. Billy could see the whole valley now, spread out below, with the hills around it like an enormous horseshoe—he wondered what freak geological event had caused that; nothing in the local geography seemed to make any sense—and, way off in the distance, the buildings of the New Age Enlightenment Center shining in the sun.

Crossing a high saddle to the next hill, he paused and looked northward. He saw nothing in that direction but empty desert, but the crow flew up and lit on a rock and pointed with its beak. "Blacktail Springs up that way," Grandfather said.
"Probably there's some way to get here from there without going all that long way around like we did. Probably a lot of ways, and I'd guess those Paiutes know all of them. But I couldn't see anything from the air that looked possible without a horse, or maybe a Jeep."

Billy followed the crow around the shoulder of the next hill. Down the slope, perhaps fifty feet below, he could see the course of the abandoned track, the deep-worn ruts of heavy tires still easy to make out. A landslide had wiped out part of the trail, but then it reappeared a short way along, swinging up the hillside to go around the head of a big ravine.

Grandfather appeared ahead, sitting atop a Volkswagen-sized boulder. "Look down there," he said.

Billy looked, and saw nothing in particular at first. Then he spotted them, the half-dozen cylindrical shapes at the bottom of the ravine, partly buried by rocks and sand and scree.

"Barrels?" he said after a minute. "You dragged me all over hell and half of Nevada to show me some rusty old barrels?" Then it came to him. "Oh. Oh, you think this is one of those toxic waste dumps, like they talk about on the news? What's in those drums?"

"Got no idea, *chooch*. Or what used to be in them, since it's sure as hell leaked out by now. But I think we can rule out any chance it might of been strawberry sody pop." Grandfather looked at Billy. "Now you see why I made you stay uphill. But come on, you ain't seen shit yet."

For the next mile or more along the hillside, Billy looked

down on scenes that made his stomach hurt. Almost every gully and ravine contained evidence of dumping: rusting drums and cans and cylinders, rocks stained unnatural colors, evil-looking black deposits in rock pockets. Most of the containers had been buried and later exposed by erosion, but quite a few loads appeared to have been simply tipped out, to roll down the slopes and come to rest wherever they might.

"This is old," Grandfather said. He was riding on Billy's shoulder now, providing a running commentary on the sights below. "You can tell by the way the ground's been washed away from the buried items—takes time to do that, in an area that gets so little rain—and by the rust. Some of this shit has to have been here twenty, thirty years. I'd guess most of the poison is long gone, washed down into the valley, soaked into the ground—and the ground water, there's a nice damn thought—but you better stay clear, all the same. Keep going."

"You mean there's more?"

"Oh, hell, boy, there's junk like this all over these hills here. There's places so bad you can see animal bones around the waterholes, and others where there's nothing worse than a pile of old tires. This is just one piece of it." Grandfather shifted his weight on Billy's shoulder, digging his claws in. "But it's where they dumped the really hot stuff. Just a little farther, you'll see."

And, a little farther on—though it didn't feel like a little; nothing would have felt like a little on that south-wall-of-hell slope—Billy did see; but at first he couldn't tell what he was supposed to be seeing. The big metal cylinders down in the dry wash didn't look all that special to him. Larger than any of the other containers he'd seen on the hillside, and giving the impression of unusually solid construction, but that was all. Of course, they were still partly buried under earth and rocks; it was hard to tell much about them, even to be sure how many there were. And the sun and wind-driven sand had long ago removed painted markings.... Billy said, "I don't get it."

Grandfather cackled in his ear, a dry harsh combination of an old man's laugh and a crow's caw. "Switch on that little box you been dragging around, *chooch*. You'll get it right away."

Billy looked down in momentary surprise at the Geiger counter in his hand. He'd been carrying it so long he'd all but forgotten about it. He flipped the switch and held one earphone up to his ear.

The string of clicks that poured from the headset made him jump slightly and look again at the Geiger counter to see if he had somehow damaged it. This time there was no way it was his imagination; the counter wasn't clicking off the scale but it was definitely registering well above normal environmental levels of radiation. He said, "Holy shit."

"Is it really hot here?" Grandfather asked anxiously. "If you need to run like hell, don't wait for me—"

"Oh, no." Billy shook his head, holding the earphone with one hand and swinging the Geiger counter through a slow arc with the other. "I don't think there's any danger right here, not over a short time anyway. I don't know that I'd want to camp on this spot for a year, or bring a pregnant woman up here, but we're safe enough for now. Aha." The Geiger counter was now pointing toward the collection of half-buried cylinders down the hillside. The frequency of clicks from the earphones had increased, not spectacularly but measurably. "Okay, *eduda*, you were right. That's what you think it is, down there."

He reached up and fitted the earphones over his head,

wishing the Geiger counter had a shoulder strap. "Excuse me, Grandfather, but would you mind hopping down for a minute?"

Very slowly and cautiously, placing his feet with extreme care and hanging onto shrubs and rock outcrops with his free hand, he began to work his way down the slope toward the dry wash where the cylinders lay. From his perch atop a boulder, Grandfather called, *"Jagasesdesdi, chooch,"* but it was wasted advice. Billy had absolutely no desire to go sliding and tumbling down the hillside into the middle of the radioactive dump site. The chatter from the earphones was already growing ominously rapid, even at this distance.

When he was halfway down from where he had left Grandfather, Billy stopped. By now the earphones were making sounds like popcorn in a popper, yet the cylinders were still a long pistol shot away. Christ, Billy thought, talk about hot. He called, "I'm coming back up," and began to clamber back the way he had come.

"Damn, *chooch*, don't take chances like that," Grandfather said as Billy flopped down beside the boulder and switched off the Geiger counter. "Didn't know you'd go that close. You ain't going to start glowing in the dark or anything, are you?"

Billy shook his head, staring down at the cylinders in the dry wash. "It's all right. I wasn't close enough for long enough."

"Well, don't do it again, will you? So," Grandfather said, "how bad is it?"

"Can't say. I just don't have the training to take readings and analyze levels. Pretty bad, though, I think."

"What I thought. Bad enough to mess people up if they did come around here? Like people from the reservation, hunting rabbits or something?"

"I don't know." Billy wiped sweat from his eyes. "Could be. It'll be worse on downhill, of course. If these things are leaking—and they have to be, for the readings to be this high at this range—then every rainstorm and flash flood will have carried radioactive material downstairs." He gestured with one hand. "The valley floor ought to have some real hot spots, if the leakage has been going on very long."

"How about that." Grandfather didn't seem particularly surprised. "Well, that explains something else, maybe."

Billy took off his hat and began slapping dust off it. "What's that?"

"Your friend from last night. The local monster," Grandfather said. "It's been here. I mean, this is where it went when you chased it off."

Billy sat up with a violent jerk, all fatigue and thirst forgotten. "Here? You mean that thing's around here somewhere?"

"Relax. It ain't around right now. Last I saw, it was way to hell north of here, killing some cows and sheep. Gonna have another of those animal-mutilation stories in the paper tomorrow, I expect."

Billy leaned back against the boulder, still uneasy. "What was it doing here?"

"Damn if I could tell," Grandfather admitted. "I sort of got the impression this is its regular hangout, though. Looked like it was getting strength from something around here. Maybe it feeds off radiation, some way. Nobody on my side of the line is sure yet, and there's some damn heavy people working on the problem, I guarantee you. Should have heard the big argument last night, Enrico and Albert and Ike all talking at once—"

Billy didn't want to hear another of Grandfather's spirit-world stories right now. He wanted to get the hell out of here. "Listen," he said, "are we done with this business? For now, at least?"

"Don't see why not," Grandfather said. "Let's go back and see what's happening on the rez. Give that lady doctor her car back."

"I think I ought to wash it for her," Billy said, getting to his feet. "At the very least."

"I wouldn't worry none," Grandfather said, and hopped up onto Billy's shoulder. "You tell her what you've found here, she'll be ready to give you that Japanese heap. See if I ain't right."

"Hell," Billy said, "I'd settle for a cold beer. Seems like I'm having the longest days, lately."

BUT A LITTLE while later, as he steered the Subaru up the last stretch of gravel road toward the paved highway, Billy had a feeling that the day was about to get even longer.

Parked across the road, blocking the way, was a medium-sized white car without markings or distinguishing features. The ground on either side of the road was open and level and fairly solid-looking, so it would have been easy enough to go around the white car and make for the highway; but somehow Billy had the feeling this wouldn't be a good idea. As he braked the Subaru to a gravel-grinding stop, the white car's front doors opened, almost in unison, and two men in light gray suits got out and began walking toward him. Their suit jackets were unbuttoned and their right hands hung close to waist level.

Grandfather said, "Oh, shit. Cops."

"Yeah," Billy said, watching the two suits approach. They were doing it very professionally, keeping a good distance apart so as not to present a single target, each in a position to cover the other, yet not being obvious about it. "Not regular cops, though," he added after a moment. "Maybe some kind of spooks."

"I didn't think they were the local Mormon missionaries, *chooch*." Grandfather hopped up onto the back of the seat and ruffled his feathers. "Well, from here on I'm just a dumb-ass bird. Good luck."

Billy rolled down the window as one of the suits came up alongside the car, bending down to check the interior without getting too close. The other suit stayed back a few paces, looking watchful but not particularly tense. Billy kept his hands in sight on the wheel.

"Afternoon," the first suit said. He was a big husky white man, maybe thirty, with curly hair and a snub nose and a lot of big white teeth that he showed in a wide phony smile. He looked a good deal like Joe Piscopo. "Mind answering a few questions?"

"Depends on who's asking," Billy said in a neutral voice. "You got some ID?"

"Sure." The suit reached into his breast pocket and took out a little leather folder and flipped it open, just long enough for Billy to see some sort of card with a picture, but not nearly long enough for him to read a single word. "U.S. government," the suit said briskly, snapping the little folder shut and putting it back in his pocket. "Special agents. Now I'm going to ask you to return the favor, all right, guy?"

Billy reached for his own wallet with deliberate and careful movements. The suit who looked like Joe Piscopo had taken an unobtrusive step back from the car, right hand casually near his belt buckle. The other one, maybe less inclined to worry about impressions, had his hand inside his jacket and his knees slightly bent. He had on shades but Billy didn't need to see his eyes to know what he was looking at.

The one who looked like Joe Piscopo took the driver's license from Billy's outstretched hand and studied it for a moment, while his partner continued to watch Billy. Partner was tall and skinny, with lumpy features and a bad haircut that Billy guessed was supposed to make him look like Eastwood. It didn't.

"From Oklahoma, eh?" The suit tapped Billy's license against his palm. "Long way from home, aren't we?"

"Visiting my girl friend," Billy said in his best stupid-Indian voice. "Up at Blacktail Springs Reservation."

"Oh?" The suit glanced over the dusty Subaru. "This your car?"

Billy shook his head. "Belongs to the lady doctor at the Blacktail Springs clinic. She gave me permission to borrow it. You can call and ask."

"Hm. Wait here a minute, would you, guy?"

The suit walked over to where his partner stood, taking Billy's ID with him. They conferred briefly, glancing over at Billy a couple of times. Partner walked around and looked at the Subaru's license plate and took out a little notebook and wrote in it. The one who looked like Joe Piscopo held Billy's license up and his partner wrote some more.

Neither of them made any move toward the white car, which answered any lingering doubts Billy might have had; whoever these two were, they weren't cops. Cops would have handled the whole thing differently. They'd have made him step out of the car, and they certainly would have gotten on the radio by now to ask if the Subaru had been reported stolen. They might have made him wait while somebody contacted Sarah Aronson and verified his story about having permission to drive her car.

These two didn't even seem interested in that part of his story. He wondered who the hell they were, then. FBI? Drug agents? CIA, even? As Janna said, they were all pretty much the same.

The first suit came back and handed Billy back his driver's license. "Thanks," he said, flashing that phony smile again. "What are you doing in this area? Just driving around?"

"Uh-huh." Billy decided on a bit of selective truth. "Saw the sign there, heard on the news how some people got killed here. Just curious."

One of the agent's eyebrows went up. "That so?" He leaned on the car, giving Billy a serious stare. "Well, you know, you shouldn't go poking around near the scene of a major crime. Besides, this is private property."

"I didn't know."

"Yeah, you'd think there'd be some no-trespassing signs. Maybe the late owner was afraid they'd spoil the atmosphere." Once more the standup-comic smile. "I'd suggest you stay on the public highways if you're going to drive around these parts. Never know," he said pointedly, the smile gone now, "what might happen to you, out in the desert alone."

He peered suddenly into the car, past Billy. "Hey, is that a crow you've got there?"

Billy said, "No, it's my grandfather," and the suit laughed and stepped back.

"Nobody loves a smart-ass Indian, guy," he said. "All right, you can go. Just a minute and we'll be out of your way."

SARAH ARONSON SAID, "For God's sake," and took off her glasses and threw them down on her desk so hard Billy was surprised they didn't break. "Mickey always says Cherokees are crazy, but my *God*."

"Hey," Billy said, "I just thought this was something you'd want to know about. Might answer some questions, like you were talking about back in town."

She sighed and collapsed into the chair behind her desk. "Oh, it could answer some questions, all right. It's not that I don't appreciate your efforts." She put her elbows on the desk and rested her chin in her hands, staring at him. "But don't you realize how dangerous it was, prowling around a place like that? God knows what you might have been exposed to."

"Yeah, I know." More than you do, Billy thought; he hadn't told her about Grandfather seeing the thing there. He hadn't told her about the thing at all. He and Janna still hadn't decided whether or not to tell anyone what they'd seen last night. As for talking to any white person about Grandfather—

"I had the Geiger counter," he said defensively. "I stayed uphill and I didn't get too close. I was real careful."

"Careful? I'm a doctor, Billy. Do you have any idea how many of the patients I've treated in my professional life have been people who were being *careful*?" She sat back and sighed again. "All right, you did it, you probably got away with it, too late to chew you out now. And you're sure about what you saw."

"I'm sure about what I've told you. What it all means, that's another story. You figure people from the reservation could have wandered off over those hills and got dosed? Enough to cause those cases you couldn't figure out?"

"It's certainly possible. People do go down that way from time to time, I know that. Hunting for rabbits—that's about the only game animal in the area, though now and then somebody gets a skinny little deer—or gathering herbs and edible roots, anything to supplement the government commodities most of them live on. So you've got the possibility of food-chain contamination too."

She paused and thought for a moment. "I've heard of people going there for other reasons, too. The young people have been known to sneak down and try to get a look at the weird goings-on among the crazy whites at the ranch, and years ago, when the place was a whorehouse, I imagine the curiosity element was even stronger. Then, too, quite a few of these people have worked there as groundskeepers or kitchen help or in other menial jobs. No shortage of opportunities for exposure, is what I'm saying."

"You think there's enough radiation from that one site to do that much damage?"

"From your description, that's not impossible. But radiation isn't necessarily the only explanation. There are plenty of ordinary chemical toxins capable of causing cancer, birth defects, and the rest of the list." Sarah was looking past Billy now, seeing something that wasn't in the room. "I'll have to get down there myself, of course, and then we'll bring in a proper investigative team . . . you can find the place again, can't you?"

Billy nodded. Actually he wasn't so sure, but he figured Grandfather would help if necessary.

"Good." Sarah stood up. "All right, I want you to go change out of those clothes and run them through the washer, and shower and wash your hair, just in case you weren't as careful as you think. Don't forget to wash those boots off."

She came around the desk and put a hand on his shoulder. "Sorry I gave you a hard time this morning, Billy. Thanks for the help."

"Sure."

"I wasn't sure about you. Ever since Janna came to this country, she's had men coming on to her—"

"I can imagine."

"No, I don't think you can. You see, she's spoken at so many meetings and rallies, been the guest of honor at so many receptions and dinners, among these environmental and social activist types—and don't misunderstand, most of them are good people, but the movement does include some of the phoniest bastards you ever saw. And," Sarah added, "there are quite a few otherwise admirable fellows whose high principles seem to go out the window when they get a look at her."

"I bet," Billy said. "They try to get into her pants, huh?"

"I've seen some of our most dedicated enviro-yuppies sniffing around her like so many well-dressed dogs. And not just the men, either. It's not just simple horniness, you understand. She's the honored international visitor. Nailing her would be a major coup."

"Assholes."

"I won't argue with that characterization. At any rate," Sarah said, "I wondered about you—who you were, what your real angle was. But I don't wonder any more. I've seen the look on your face when she comes into a room. Or just when her name comes up, like now."

"It shows that much?"

"It's only slightly less noticeable than the Grand Canyon. Go wash up now," Sarah said. "She'll be back any time now."

13.

BUT WHEN JANNA did return from the city—riding up the dirt road in the Jeep with Mickey Wolf, in the last hour of daylight—her face was clouded with anger and frustration, and she carried bad news.

"They will not extend my visa," she said as Billy helped her down from the Jeep. "I have tried all day. It is impossible."

"Son of a bitch," Billy said. "Can they do that?"

Mickey Wolf got out and came around the Jeep. "They can do anything they want," he told Billy. "The Immigration and Naturalization Service pretty much operates as a law unto itself, even worse than the drug cops. They don't even have to have a reason for a decision."

"It is more than that," Janna declared as they walked toward Sarah's trailer. "There is some . . . influence?"

"Pressure," Mickey Wolf suggested.

"Yes, pressure from somewhere. Believe me, I can tell these things. I have been dealing with such people for many years." She snorted angrily. "They made many reasons, of course. I have waited too long to apply, I have no proof I am doing necessary scientific research. Pfui. The stupid little man read my name, then he talked to someone on telephone, then finish. *Govno.* It is too ridiculous."

"I suspect she's right," Mickey Wolf said to Billy. "I went in and talked to the bastards—even got out the old dog-collar and wore it, thought that might add a little weight—but it was obvious they had their orders."

"I am not surprised," Janna said. "Already, many times, there have been threats of deportation. Because I am involved in controversial movement, working with foundation which makes trouble for big corporations and government agencies."

She put her arm around Billy's waist. "I am sorry," she said. "I tried."

SARAH ARONSON WAS white-faced with anger. "They can't do that," she said through her teeth. "I'll get the foundation's lawyers on it. They can't pull this shit."

"I hate to say it," Mickey Wolf said, "but yes they can, too. You know that better than any of us."

"Fuck. You're right. They've done everything else—harassed us over our tax status, sent spooks to follow our people around, blackbagged our offices, the works." She glanced around the trailer's little dining space. "I wouldn't be surprised if this tin can is bugged."

"The government's been on your case?" Billy asked.

"Sometimes it's hard to know whether you're dealing with government agencies or the private sector. At a certain level the distinction is blurry at best." Sarah ran her fingers through her graying hair. "So far there's been no direct violence or physical intimidation. Even so, there's been trouble in some areas—towns where a nuclear installation provides a lot of jobs, for example—where local goons have taken it upon themselves to beat our people up, or torch offices or homes. I've always wondered how much behind-the-scenes encouragement the perpetrators had. Certainly the police never seem to be able to catch them, and prosecutors don't show much interest."

Billy thought of the two spooks who had stopped him over by the ranch entrance. He decided not to bring it up just now. Everybody was upset enough as it was.

"I don't care about any of that," Janna said. "Not just now. All I care is, what will we do?" She looked at Billy with red-rimmed eyes. "Two more weeks and I must fly back to Kazakhstan. And what then?"

Sarah patted Janna's shoulder. "I'll get the foundation's lawyers on it," she said. "They ought to be able to do something. Get a temporary restraining order, anyway."

Mickey Wolf made a scornful noise. "Don't start giving these kids false hopes. Most of your lawyers have been trying to put the make on Janna ever since they met her. They're not going to knock themselves out so she can spend more time with some Indian who doesn't even own a BMW."

Sarah said something Billy didn't catch. Clearly an old anger had flared up, some ongoing beef between her and Mickey Wolf; but Billy was thinking of something else now.

"Listen," he said suddenly, "we'll get married."

Everybody stopped talking and stared at him. *"Bozhe moi,"* Janna breathed.

"No, really," he said, feeling a little self-conscious but excited too. "If we get married they'll have to let you stay, right?"

"Billy," Mickey Wolf said. "Billy, old son. Old Native American bro. Have you thought this out?"

"I hate to tell you this," Sarah said, "but it wouldn't necessarily work. The INS has gotten very suspicious over the last decade or so, when it comes to foreigners marrying Americans. Too many Green Card marriages taking place. They could very well refuse to recognize it."

"She's right," Mickey Wolf agreed. "I've been involved in these cases myself, performed some of the weddings, and I know. La Migra can be very chickenshit."

"I don't care." Billy was talking fast now, catching fire, the whole thing coming together in his mind. "I want to do it anyway. If they make her leave then I'll leave too. I don't know how much a ticket to Kazakhstan costs, but I'll raise it some way. Sell the bike or something. Hell," he said, "it'll only be one-way."

"You would do that?" Janna's eyes were almost round. "Leave your own country to be with me?"

"Why not? They've stolen most of it anyway, working on ruining the rest. I'd like to stay here, sure, I won't deny that, it's my country and I'd miss it bad. But fuck taking this kind of shit. Who the hell do they think they are, anyway? They're all foreigners just as much as you are."

Janna continued to stare at him. "You are insane. *Sovershenno bezumniy.*"

"*Howa,*" Mickey Wolf said.

Billy grinned. He felt energized and goofy-happy, like the first time he'd smoked grass. "Hey," he said, "this is the best idea I've had in years."

Then, sobered by a sudden thought, he said to Janna, "That's if you want to do it. If you'll have me."

"Oh, don't worry about that." She grabbed him around the waist again, this time with both arms. "I will have you, yes. Always."

* * *

THE WEDDING OF William E. Badwater and Janna Turanova took place the following Friday night, at the Last Church of Naked City, Las Vegas, Nevada, Rev. Michael A. Wolf presiding. The bride wore a simple powder-blue creation from Wal-Mart of North Las Vegas, with necklace of Navajo ghost beads and bouquet of Hare Krishna carnations. The groom wore an ensemble of T-shirt by Jerome Tiger of Muskogee and jeans by Family Dollar Store of Tahlequah, and carried a black hat tastefully decorated with an eagle feather.

The storefront church was nearly full, only a few empty seats remaining. Very few of the people present knew Billy or Janna or even had any clear idea what was going on, but they all liked Mickey Wolf and anyway it was something to do. Several were under the impression that Billy was some kind of music or movie star. Quite a few simply came hoping there would be something to eat or, better yet, drink.

Mickey Wolf cleared his throat loudly and looked out over the congregation and waited until the place was as quiet as it was ever likely to get.

"Dearly beloved," he boomed, "we are gathered together—as we ministers like to say, in our redundant way—to join this man and this woman in marriage. Which is an honorable institution, best defined as a long-term relationship between two mutually resenting adults. If there be any here who knows why these two should not be joined, keep quiet, they'll find out soon enough."

There was a little obbligato of sniffles and sobs throughout the crowd. Almost all the hookers and strippers and showgirls were crying. Down front, a pair of spectacularly constructed identical twins, known professionally as Hanky and Panky, were getting downright noisy with their blubbering.

"Janna," Mickey Wolf said, "will you take this crazy Indian here, to love and cherish, for drunk and for sober, for poor or for broke? Will you pick up his rancid socks and tell him when he's forgot to zip his fly? Will you put up with his moods and pretend to listen to his half-assed ideas? Of course you will, why else are you standing there? Billy, will you take this lovely young woman to love and to cherish, sure you will, who wouldn't, Christ, just look at her. Join hands."

Billy took Janna's hand. To his surprise she was trembling, just the least bit.

"Now by the extremely dubious authority of the state of Nevada," Mickey Wolf proclaimed, "I pronounce you man and woman and legally entitled to go prove it. You have the right to remain silent. Anything you say can and will be used against you. May God have mercy on your souls. Kiss her, stupid."

A SHORT TIME LATER, the mission's dining hall became the scene of a quiet and unpretentious reception that rapidly evolved into a pretty damn good party, with music by Jerry Dwayne Austin and the Piss-Cutters and various refreshments in circulation, not all officially sanctioned.

"Christ," Billy said, "I haven't seen so many brown bags since I was a kid working in a supermarket."

"*Shto?*"

"Never mind." He accepted a plastic cup of bright red liquid from Hanky, or maybe Panky, who was moving through the crowd with a tray. "Thanks," he said, trying not to stare at the front of her silk blouse, which was open to the waist, exposing a black leather bra and enough white slopes to hold the Winter Olympics. He took a sip of the punch and discovered it was not merely spiked but loaded. "*Woof,*" he said when he could get his breath.

"You must not get drunk," Janna said. "I will not have you pass out on our wedding night. If I wanted that I would have stayed home and married a Russian."

"You're sounding like a wife already."

"Why not? It is what I am." Janna's cheeks were flushed and her eyes shone. He thought he had never seen her look so happy. Or so beautiful. Damn, he thought, I'm like a teenage boy with a crush. He wondered what Grandfather was going to say about his getting married. Probably something sarcastic.

Jerry Dwayne Austin came out of the crowd, his guitar slung across his back. "Howdy," he said. "Can I kiss the bride?"

"Of course." Janna tilted her head and Jerry Dwayne kissed her on the cheek with courtly formality. He was the only man present who hadn't had to bend down to kiss her.

"Congratulations," he said. "This come on so sudden, I didn't have a chance to get y'all kids a present. So I'm writing a song for you instead. That all right?"

"We are honored," Janna told him. "May we hear it?"

Jerry Dwayne unslung his guitar and dug a flat pick out of the pocket of his fancy Western shirt. Several people gathered around to listen. Mickey Wolf and Sarah Aronson materialized beside Billy and Janna. Billy noticed the preacher had his arm around the doctor's waist.

"I just got a little bit wrote," Jerry Dwayne explained apologetically. "I call it 'The Ballad of Billy Badass and the Rose of Turkestan.'"

He struck a pose and then a chord, and began to sing:

*"Billy Badass was a warrior
From Oklahoma way
A hero of his nation
Who had wore the Green Beret.
He met the purtiest lady
She was from a fur-off land
And Billy Badass fell in love
With the Rose of Turkestan."*

Jerry Dwayne lowered his pick and added in his speaking voice, "That's all I got so far. But she's coming along good."

"It is a beautiful song," Janna assured him. "When it is finished you must sing it all for us."

"It's got a good beat," Mickey Wolf observed. "You could dance to it."

"I've never seen you dance to anything," Sarah said, and then to Janna, "Congratulations, many happy returns or whatever they say. *Mazel tov,* since we all seem to be padding our ethnic parts around here. Boy." She shook her head slowly. Billy realized she was a little drunk. "Always a bridesmaid and never a bride, that's me."

"Something could be done about that," Mickey Wolf murmured.

She turned her head and gave him a long look. "Don't say it unless you mean it, Reverend."

"Hm. Maybe I'll make you an offer."

"I'm in the book," Sarah said. "Well, actually not, but you know where to find me. Out in lovely, romantic Blacktail Springs, population rapidly decreasing. Come up and see me some time."

Mickey Wolf said, "I've got a couple of presents for you two. Come into the office for a minute."

In the office, after closing the door, Mickey Wolf opened a desk drawer and took out a paper bag containing some sort of long cylindrical object. "Don't open this here, or you'll be doing well to reach the door alive. Laphroiag," he said, rolling the word on his tongue as if savoring its taste. "Fifteen-year-old single-malt Scotch, the finest whisky in the world. I speak as a minister of the Gospel and therefore as one with authority to pronounce judgments."

"Thanks," Billy said. "I'll take it back to the room—"

"No, no. Can't have you spending your nuptial evening in that stuffy little broom closet, for God's sake. Here." He held out a key, attached to a large plastic tag. "Arrangements have been made, my children. Hanky and Panky have called in certain personal or perhaps professional favors. The name and address of the establishment is on the tag. The room has already been reserved for you, for the entire weekend. Use it with the blessings of our little flock."

"Thanks," Billy said again.

"Don't thank me. Thank Hanky and Panky."

"I will thank them," Janna said pointedly. "You will stay away from those two. Or rather those four."

A little before eleven, everybody went out onto the sidewalk and stood watching and calling out assorted remarks as Billy and Janna prepared to ride off. Billy stowed his hat carefully in the topbox while Janna put various mysterious bags and bundles into the saddlebags until they would barely close.

"Your helmet," she said as he straddled the bike. "Why do you not wear it? This is dangerous for you."

"Don't have one for you yet," he said. "If we go, we go together."

"You are crazy." She climbed on behind him. He had expected her to turn and sit sidesaddle, but she hiked that blue dress up around her hips, giving everybody a nice flash of stockinged thighs and a few square inches of white panty bottom, and mounted in the regular way, hooking her high heels over the Honda's footpegs. There was a loud cheer from the crowd on the sidewalk.

Billy thumbed the starter button and the 750 mill bumped over and fired. When he put it in gear and let out the clutch there was a sudden horrible clatter and he hit the brakes and looked down, fearing the worst, but it was only a couple of cans some damn fool had tied to the Honda's back fender. At least, Billy thought as he accelerated away, nobody threw any rice.

IT TOOK A CERTAIN amount of riding around and asking questions before Billy located the address on the room-key tag. For some reason the people he asked tended to laugh, or give him funny looks, when he told them the name of the place he was looking for.

When they finally found the motel and opened the door of their room, they saw nothing immediately strange about the place. It was just an ordinary motel room, maybe a little on the small side, not luxury class but not a dump either. The bed struck Billy as pretty large, but then he was used to living in a trailer.

"This is very nice," Janna said.

He went over and set the bottle of Laphroiag on the nightstand. Janna moved toward the bathroom door, her arms full of this and that.

"Some of the women gave me some things," she said. "You wait for me. I think you will like this."

As the bathroom door closed behind her he stretched out on the bed, folding his hands behind his head. And got a serious shock: a man was suspended from the ceiling, looking down at him. He jumped, the man jumped, and then his brain caught up with the information his eyes were transmitting. He said, "Holy shit."

From the bathroom Janna called, *"Ne var?"* The door opened a little way and she stuck her head out. "You said?"

Billy pointed. "There's a mirror above the bed."

"My God, it is." She began laughing. "What kind of place is this?"

Still laughing, not waiting for an answer, she closed the door again. Billy looked up at the mirror, not sure he liked the idea. Well, he could always turn off the lights if it bothered him.

Curious now, he examined his surroundings more closely. There was a gadget on the nightstand that, as best he could figure, would cause the bed to vibrate. He wondered why anybody would want the bed vibrating while they were getting laid. Or any other time, unless they had a sore back or something. Takes all kinds, he reflected.

Janna was taking her time in the bathroom, something he had a feeling he was going to have to get used to. He sat up, swinging his legs over the side of the bed, and switched on the television set.

The screen brightened and filled with the images of a man and a woman lying on a bed. They were both naked, except that the woman had on red high-heeled pumps. The man was penetrating her from behind at an awkward-looking angle.

The sound track consisted of moans and groans and heavy breathing.

Billy turned the sound down hastily, glancing toward the bathroom door. He was about to switch the set off, but he paused, fascinated, as the couple changed to a position that didn't look possible.

Then, catching himself, he reached guiltily for the controls. Hell of a thing if Janna came out now—

The man on the screen said, "Don't turn it off yet, *chooch*. Been a lot of years since I did anything like this."

Billy stared. "Boy," the man said in Grandfather's voice, "I never knew white people were so *limber*. No wonder there's so many of them."

"Why now, *eduda*?" Billy said plaintively. "Give me a break. I just got married."

"I know. My only grandson, goes off and gets married without even asking his grandfather's advice."

"You weren't around."

"Been busy, *chooch*. Finding out some things, doing some studying on matters, tell you all about it some other time. Right now I just wanted to give you my blessing, wish you two all the best. Tell you I'm proud of you."

"*Wado, eduji.*" It was all Billy could think to say.

"Even if I do catch you watching dirty movies. Now what's this?" A second woman had appeared on screen and was climbing into bed with the couple. "Hold on there, boy, this is something I got to see—"

Billy turned the knob firmly to *off* and lay back on the bed, while the TV set made its little crinkly shutting-down noises. After a moment he got up and turned on the bedside lamp and switched off the main room lights, leaving the room nice and dim but not dark.

The bathroom door opened. Janna stood in the doorway, posing. "Well? How do you like it?"

She wore a snug-fitting white lace teddy, cut high at the bottom to show a lot of hip and low at the top to show a lot of bosom. Narrow white garter straps held up patterned white stockings. White lace gloves covered her hands and came up past her elbows. Her skin glowed in the dim light, its apricot tones warm against the white lace. Her thick black hair hung loose over her bare shoulders.

Billy opened his mouth. Nothing came out.

Janna laughed. "I thought you would like. Now." She ran toward the bed, smiling, her face flushed. "Take your clothes off, Billy," she said, "let me look at you too. Look at my husband." She laughed excitedly. "My husband, that sounds so strange. I have never had a husband before. What does one do with a husband?"

Skinning off his T-shirt, Billy said, "You'll think of something," and, sure enough, she did.

14.

IT DID NOT SLEEP, as organic beings understand sleep. It had no need.

Being without corporeal existence, it did not experience fatigue or have any requirement for rest. There were times when there was nothing it wanted or needed to do, and during those periods it did nothing—did literally nothing, since it had no body processes to sustain—but it felt neither relief nor boredom in repose, because it did not perceive the passage of time in the human way.

All this was in the normal course of things. Now, however, was a special time, bringing special requirements.

For all its apparent size and power, it was still—as has already been remarked—an immature individual of its kind, not yet fully developed in any sense. This was the chief reason for its random and, relatively speaking, ineffective behavior since its arrival in this world. A full-grown specimen would by now have killed everything on the Earth and then begun dismantling the planet, merely as a warming-up exercise before getting down to serious business.

But then a mature individual would have known enough to stay clear of the momentary dimensional discontinuity that had trapped this one. Not that its race never used such rifts to travel between incompossible realities, but they tried to avoid doing so inadvertently.

Unready in every respect for its new situation, it had had great difficulty in adjusting to this weird new world, which seemed to contain no end of surprises. It had been particularly confused by the recent encounter with the two soft-energy entities, or rather with the strange and incomprehensible force-field that had surrounded them. It had never encountered such a barrier, in this world or its own, nor could it conceive of how such a thing could exist. And nastier by far had been the sudden blast of violent force—apparently the same mysterious energy that made up the force-field, but focussed in a staggering concentration—which one of the soft-energy entities had somehow fired just as the barrier was starting to give way.

Clearly these entities had unsuspected powers, might even be dangerous. Badly shaken, it had avoided human contact for the next few days, experimenting instead with other life forms, which had proved disappointing in the crudeness of their energy fields.

These things no longer mattered very much. Its attention had begun to turn inward, in response to disturbing new pressures and tensions. It had only a vague idea what was happening; it had no more understanding of the changes taking place than a tadpole on the verge of growing legs and crawling up onto a mudbank. It only knew that everything felt very strange.

It was, in fact, on the verge of the final metamorphosis that would transform it into (for want of a better word) an adult. The process was a complex one, involving a series of stages rather than a single transformation; but, once begun, the process was inexorable.

Metamorphosis brought certain requirements, chief of which, in the initial phase, was immobility. The developing being fell gradually into a dormant state, barely conscious and incapable of movement, and remained so until the first stage was complete. It was better, though not absolutely essential, for this to take place away from such distracting stimuli as atomic radiation.

The time at last came when the compulsion could not be ignored. Then (about the time Mickey Wolf got the last of the wedding-party guests to go home; about the time Billy was figuring out how the snaps worked on that white lace teddy) it began to move, driven by instincts it did not even try to understand. It traveled roughly northeast, away from the hills and the reservation, into a remote part of the desert, where only coyotes and jackrabbits and burrowing owls saw the great dark mass flow past.

As the sun rose, the need to move was replaced by an equally irresistible lassitude. Now it wanted only to be perfectly still, to shut itself off almost to the point of oblivion.

And so it came to pass that, on the seventh day, it rested.

MEANWHILE, IN ANOTHER place—or rather in other places, some not so far away—another formless entity was beginning to stir. Like the one in the desert, it had no name, no face, and no very clear understanding of what was going on; it too violated, by its very existence, a number of supposedly inviolable laws, for which reason there was no word for what it was.

This one, however, was very much of this world. It, and its kind, had been here for a long time.

It was a strange composite creature, manifold rather than unitary in structure. It manifested itself in seemingly diverse components: government offices and agencies, military and paramilitary forces, business corporations, the families of so-called organized crime, groups of religious and/or ideological axe-grinders . . . the list could be extended much farther, but to no good purpose. All these divisions, after all, were basically meaningless.

Its true nature could best be understood in the terms of Hindu theology: numerous separate entities which, to one in the know, were seen to be in fact mere aspects of a single Power, their individual identities mere illusions to keep the ignorant masses quiet.

At the lowest levels, however, the parts of this beast did function with some degree of independence. Not all the players, at the lowest levels, realized the nature of the charade; after all, does the average policeman understand that his relationship with the criminal is not adversarial but symbiotic? The whole worldwide body was too vast for complete integration; one tentacle-tip might have little or no idea what the others were doing.

And so sometimes this monster moved reflexively, the limbs jerking and twitching without proper direction from the higher nerve centers; and then, sometimes, stupid things happened.

In the present case, the reaction was triggered by the grotesque events at the New Age Enlightenment Center and Guest Ranch. Not, of course, that anybody at any level had the faintest idea what had taken place; the only ones who came close were a few religious fundamentalists who muttered darkly that the devil-worshipers had brought on their own destruction by calling up Satanic forces. Certainly nobody cared what happened to a bunch of rich weirdos, though some of the local mobsters did have fond memories of Magda Simone from when she was Eddie Caravello's old lady.

It was just that the place had associations. Someone or something had rattled the door of a long-closed closet, one that contained a number of skeletons. Memories had been jogged; there were those who suddenly recalled that things had been done on that particular piece of Nevada real estate, things that needed to stay locked away.

The literal skeletons, the Mob-hit victims buried in the hills, were probably too old to be identified—though you never knew, these days—and the other crimes involved were mostly on the safe side of the statute of limitations. But there were other kinds of trouble that could come down if the area got too much attention.

For one thing, there was the original deal by which the Blacktail Springs Indians had been ripped off for the land itself. Some smart Indian-activist lawyer could drag that business into court, causing serious political embarrassment for certain official persons—some quite highly placed by now—who had been part of the fraud. Other officials had been in on, or at least looked the other way for, some of the toxic-waste-disposal arrangements; they too had risen in the hierarchy in the intervening years, and this was no time for a scandal.

There were also the underworld types who had been directly involved in the dumping racket. Most were dead by now, or retired or doing time; some, however, were still around and in business, one way or another. Several had gone more or less legitimate, becoming respected members of society. A few even held public office. None cared to have people taking an interest in the site of the old Putty Tat Ranch.

And one thing had a way of leading to another. Let some inquisitive journalist or ambitious investigator start tugging at dangling threads, and there was no telling what might unravel before it was over.

NOTHING HAPPENED AT first. There was only a mild flickering of uneasy interest; various people heard the news and said, "Hey, wasn't that where. . . ?"

But then there were the equally bizarre deaths, only a short time later, at Blacktail Springs. The official scenario was that the beheadings had been the work of a person or persons crazed by peyote. Certainly there seemed to be no evidence of any connection with the events at the ranch. Yet the juxtaposition was enough to bother a few people, and phone calls were made.

A sort of ripple ran through the beast's extremities.

AT THIS POINT a new element entered the picture. Besides those with personal stakes in the history of the ranch, there were those for whom it was simply a matter of overriding policy to keep this closet door, and all others like it, firmly shut.

The whole atomic-energy thing was touchy as hell. Despite half a century of unremitting propaganda, the American public remained nervous about radiation. It was necessary to prevent irresponsible persons from spreading alarm and despondency. Sometimes extreme measures had to be taken. (As in the case of one Karen Silkwood, but that was another story.)

Sarah Aronson had not been giving in to paranoia. The foundation she represented *was* under covert scrutiny, both by government agents and the hirelings of concerned corporations. Its ranks had been infiltrated from bottom to top—its Board of Directors included two government informants, one also reporting to a private concern—its phones tapped, its mail read, and all the other routine violations.

Naturally, then, when the FBI investigation of the Blacktail Springs killings turned up the name of Dr. Sarah Aronson, certain alarm signals went off.

The blinking and beeping intensified sharply when it was learned that a citizen of the late Soviet Union had also been on the scene. The Cold War might be over, but to any right-thinking national-security linebacker, Janna Turanova was still an enemy alien and always would be. An enemy alien, moreover, who was working with an important member of a radical environmental organization with international ties, and not all that far from the nation's nuclear testing site, as well as other secret installations. . . .

Nothing really added up to anything, yet the overall picture was becoming vaguely disturbing. There were more phone calls and electronic conferences, and clandestine meetings between people who weren't supposed to know each other. Information went into computers and came out at other places, including places it was not meant to go.

That was how the people who were interested in Sarah and Janna learned for the first time about the radioactive waste in the hills.

At this point the alarm system went to red-alert. This was hot in every sense. The disposal of radioactive wastes formed one of the touchiest points in the whole nuclear-policy controversy. Even though this particular site was two or three decades old, the tree-huggers and the Chicken Littles would jump on this as proof of all their damn loony anti-nuclear, anti-growth, anti-American propaganda. They could do more damage with it than they could with a couple of real atom bombs; they might even be able to use it to force an investigation into present-day standards and practices in the transportation and disposal of nuclear wastes.

Which—nobody even had to say it—wouldn't do at all.

So, in accordance with standard procedure, a couple of good reliable field agents were sent to check things out.

ONE OF THE first things they found was a strange man—another Indian, but not a local—screwing around in the area of the New Age Enlightenment Center, driving Dr. Aronson's car. He told a plausible story about checking out the ranch from idle curiosity, but the dust plume that stretched off across the valley showed that he'd just come from the direction of the hills.

Nobody knew much about him. A quick check by computer turned up his military service record, which was impressive—and included a couple of highly secret and sensitive missions, for which he had held a top-level security clearance—but there was nothing following his discharge but a single arrest in Florida, charges later dropped, for what appeared to have been a fist fight.

Sources reported, however, that he was involved with the alien woman, Janna Turanova, and also with a local store-front preacher who had a record of subversive activities and arrests going back to the sixties.

It was too much. Something was going on and something would have to be done about it.

At this point the whole thing should have been referred to higher authority. But too many different people were involved now, with too many different angles on the matter. Especially since some of those people were starting to panic a little. So instead there developed a hasty local consensus: handle this thing fast and get it buried, never mind the procedural bullshit.

From that point on, it was inevitable that something bad was going to happen, and soon.

15.

THE MAN BEHIND the desk at the Las Vegas office of the Immigration and Naturalization Service was typical of a certain class of government employee. Which is to say he was a petty, arbitrary, supercilious little shithead.

"This isn't automatic, you know," he said to Billy and Janna. He tilted his head, apparently the better to look down his snubby nose at them. "You people all come in here and produce a marriage certificate, and you think that's that."

He picked up the handful of forms and documents that lay in front of him, as if weighing them in his hand, and dropped them back on the desk with an air of bored disdain.

"It's not that simple," he continued in a lecturing tone. "We don't just hand out the Green Card to everyone who asks. There are criteria to be met, guidelines to be followed—do you have any idea how many people want to come to America to live?"

"Some of us already ran into that problem," Billy remarked.

The man gave Billy a look of mixed annoyance and suspicion. He leaned back in his chair and picked up a pencil from his desk and began doing pointless little things with it. "You realize," he said, "in a case like this, there's always a question as to the legitimacy of the marriage. Especially in view of the timing."

He pointed the pencil at Janna. "You come here on a regular visa, supposedly to do medical research under the auspices of an international foundation. Then, just as your visa is about to expire—*and* right after your request for an extension is denied—you suddenly marry this . . . man."

He riffled through the stack of papers and produced the copy of the marriage certificate. "I happen to have heard of the presiding minister. We've gotten several of his alleged marriages in here—Central American illegals who had been refused political asylum, for example. Even in this city, which admittedly is notorious for dubious marriages, the man has a certain reputation."

"He is licensed minister," Janna pointed out. "This marriage is completely legal."

"What the state of Nevada chooses to recognize is one thing. What the INS recognizes may be something else. We are not bound by any state or local laws." The man tossed the certificate on top of the other papers. "We have the right, in any case we consider questionable, to require further proof that this is a genuine marriage and not a subterfuge. Do you have any supporting material? Letters, for example, between the two of you, dating back some appreciable time? Especially letters discussing or proposing marriage?"

Billy said, "I wouldn't let you read them if we did," and Janna kicked his ankle.

The man sighed and blew out his cheeks, like Dizzy Gillespie going for a high one. "It would be much simpler if you had come to this country under a K visa. That is, as the fianceé of an American citizen. You wouldn't want to do it that way?" he asked hopefully. "Return to, ah, Kazakhstan," he mispronounced the word, "and apply for a K visa, then remarry after you return to the United States? Approval would be virtually automatic, then."

And of course, Billy thought, you bastards would come up with some excuse and *never* let her back into the country. He was getting very tired of this snotty little *yoneg* pissant. Hours of waiting in an overcrowded reception room, now this chickenshit. Worse than the army.

He said, "We're already married. I don't see where you've got any right to question it."

"Oh, I've got the right, Mr., ah, Badwater." The prissy mouth pulled itself into a smirk trying to pass as a smile. "I've got the right, for example, to order an interview session. That means you and this young woman will be taken to separate rooms and asked questions about the details of your marriage—how you met, the present sleeping arrangements, that sort of thing—and also personal questions about each other. Then we compare the answers and see if they match up."

Billy felt the blood drain from his face. "You can go straight to hell," he said, and was about to say more but Janna was kicking him again.

"Be quiet," she said in Russian. "If you make him angry we have no chance. He is just a little bureaucrat making himself feel big."

Billy subsided, forcing himself to keep his mouth shut and his hands still, even though, down in his DNA chains, generations of Cherokee ancestors were screaming for blood.

The man was shuffling through the papers again. "Of course all this may be irrelevant. Let's make sure there are no other problems . . . well, Form I-130 appears to be in order, if we leave aside the question of the marriage itself. Form I-485—" He peered at Janna suspiciously. "You have never been a member of the Communist Party?"

Janna shook her head. "No." It was a lie but let them prove it. The way things were these days, even Gorbachev would have trouble confirming his own membership history.

"Hm. Form ER-531, what's this? We have to have an address, your permanent place of residence, in order to mail your Green Card when it is finally issued. Assuming it *is* approved." His face and voice said that this was an extremely remote possibility. "You seem to have no permanent address."

"General Delivery, Tahlequah, Oklahoma," Billy said. "They don't deliver the mail where I live. Or at least I don't have a mailbox."

"Oklahoma?" The pinched face brightened at the possibility of getting to turn something over to somebody else. "Then you should have applied at the INS office in Oklahoma City."

"I don't know when we'll be going back to Oklahoma." Billy realized suddenly that this was true. They hadn't even discussed where they would live.

The man shook his head again. "Everything about this . . . arrangement, and this application, is irregular." He looked at Billy. "And I must say your attitude isn't helping."

"Listen, you pencil-necked little sack of shit," Billy said, starting to stand up. Janna was kicking furiously at his ankle and trying to drag him back down in his chair. "You want attitude, I'll show you attitude—"

A new voice said, "What's going on here, Harold?"

Everybody looked up. A heavy-set, gray-haired black woman was standing just behind the INS man's chair. Even Billy hadn't heard her arrive.

Without waiting for an answer, she reached past Harold and scooped up the documents from the desk. "My name is Catherine Ledbetter," she said to Billy and Janna. "I'm the supervisor of this department. I think you'd better come to my office and let me work this out."

The little man started to speak but she gave him a look that would have frozen helium. "That's all right, Harold, I'll take it from here. I'm sure," she said pointedly, "you've got other things to do. If not, I can certainly make some suggestions."

To Billy and Janna she said, "This way, please."

MICKEY WOLF STARED down at Sarah Aronson's desk, at the crude map Billy had drawn. "I think I can find it," he said at last. "No guarantees, but I think I can get you there. Assuming this so-called map bears any relationship to reality."

"Leonard Hozia looked it over," Sarah Aronson said. "He knows the area, says he used to hunt down that way. He said the map looked all right to him."

They were in her office at the Blacktail Springs clinic. Outside, the waiting room still held a number of people, mostly women with children, though it was getting on toward midday. The two young doctors from Cedar City were helping work through the morning's intake, but it had been a long day so far.

"I can find the ranch itself easily enough," Mickey Wolf said. "I had to go there once when it was still a whorehouse. One of the girls had a chance to get married and go straight," he added quickly as Sarah gave him a baleful stare. "Wanted my advice."

"Oh, sure. I'll just bet she did." Sarah looked through the open office door as a nurse hustled past, holding a urine-specimen cup. In the waiting room a voice called, "Mildred Saaba. Mildred Saaba, you're next."

"It'll be a little while before I can get free," Sarah said to Mickey. "If you'd like to practice your own trade while you're waiting, I imagine there are people here who'd like to talk with you."

"Sure," he said.

CATHERINE LEDBETTER FINISHED looking through the forms and documents and gave Billy and Janna a long unsmiling look. "My, my," she said. "I suppose you're waiting for me to say that I can't see any reason for denying this application."

They made wordless sounds of hopeful agreement. Catherine Ledbetter snorted. "Forget it. Just at first glance, I can see half a dozen absolutely unassailable reasons for tossing this into the vertical file. If Harold really knew his job, he'd have nailed you on a lot of points he completely missed."

She plopped the papers onto her desk and leaned back, while their hearts sank. "You two," she said, and shook her head, and then suddenly she laughed. "For a couple of people who've seen so much of the world, you're a pair of innocents. Don't you realize what you're up against? Even if you had the best documentation in the history of the INS, even if you had the marriage performed by the Pope, it wouldn't matter. You were in the army, Badwater, don't you know what it means when the Word comes down? Well, the Word has come down on your wife here."

She looked at Janna. "You were in here the other day, I remember. For God's sake, girl, didn't you see it then? The part of the world you're from, I know you've had to learn to read between the lines. Oh, there's no straight-out orders in writing anywhere," she said. "All the official asses are covered. But the message that came down, loud and clear as an elephant letting a fart, was to make damn sure you were on that plane back to where you came from by the end of next week."

She gave them a sudden speculative look. "Of course you may be way ahead of me. If the innocence is just an act, then you do it well."

They watched her face and did not respond. When it became obvious that they weren't going to speak she snorted again, more softly, and held out a large strong-looking hand. "Give me your passport, girl."

Janna handed the passport over. Catherine Ledbetter opened it one-handed while fumbling with the other hand in a desk drawer. "You understand," she said, "we don't actually issue the Green Card at this office. Used to, but not any more. Supposedly, it'll be mailed to you in six months to a year. In practice, there's a good chance it won't arrive at all. If it hasn't turned up by this time next year, you'll have to go down to the nearest INS office and go through all this routine again. Don't worry, though." She was busy affixing a stamp to Janna's passport. "This stamp gives you the same status as the Green Card itself. In effect, it says you've been approved, that you've got permanent-resident status. If you have to reapply, you won't be challenged again. It'll be a pain in the ass, but they can't revoke your status. Unless you shoot the President or something."

She handed the passport back to Janna. "Keep this with you, though, until you do get your Green Card. All right?"

Billy was too amazed to say anything. Janna managed to say, "Thank you. Thank you very much," and, after swallowing a couple of times, "Why?"

"Huh. Don't ask me. I sure as hell bought myself some trouble just now. Not that they can actually do anything to me. I've got seniority up to my natural African-American ass." She looked at Billy. "Maybe because my mama's daddy was full-blood Seminole. From Oklahoma, in fact. His name was Billy too," she said. "Billy Wildcat."

"I'm a son of a bitch," Billy said without thinking.

"If you're anything like him, I wouldn't be surprised. Well, maybe it was because I saw you were about to knock the shit out of Harold. Of course, my own inclinations, I'd watch you do it and cheer and then buy you dinner, but he's just enough of a little prick to have you arrested."

She stood up. "And maybe," she said, "I just don't like being told how to do my job. Get out of here, children. Girl, make this man get a job. And a haircut."

MICKEY WOLF WAS just done saying a prayer for a Paiute woman with a sick baby when Sarah Aronson came back into the waiting room. "Almost through," she said. "Come on. I'll finish up on the way and we can go out the back door."

She led the way down the main corridor, toward the rear of the building. At the last door she turned and he followed her into the room where the child called Sammy lay in his high-sided bed. At the foot of the bed the two young doctors from Cedar City stood side by side, studying some papers on a clipboard. It was the first time Mickey Wolf had seen them together and he noted that they looked a lot alike: curly reddish hair, pale skin, freckles, babyish faces. Maybe they were brothers, or otherwise related. They both looked up at him and smiled and the nearer one said, "Hello, Father Mickey."

Sarah took the clipboard and looked at it. She asked a question, using medical terms that Mickey Wolf didn't understand, and they gave her answers that he didn't understand either. He looked down at the grotesquely misshapen body on the bed and thought: I try, I try, but sometimes You make it very hard to believe in You. . . .

One of the doctors said, "I can't believe he's still here, Sarah. Still no luck getting someone to take responsibility for him?"

Sarah shook her head. "It just goes on and on."

"Want us to see if we can interest someone in LDS?" the other doctor asked.

"Anyone at all. He just can't go on this way." She looked at Sammy, who was making his spasmodic hand movements and rolling his oversized head from side to side. "I'm not even supposed to have in-patients here at all, you know. I'm only supposed to admit patients on an immediate-need basis and get them out of here within twenty-four hours, either discharge them or send them to the med center in Vegas. We're just in over our heads with a case like this."

Sammy made one of his catlike screams. Mickey Wolf felt his stomach tighten. Sarah stroked Sammy's rich black hair for a moment and turned to the doctors. "I'll be gone for the rest of the day," she said. "If I don't see you—"

"We'll be back Wednesday."

"Great. I don't know how I'd get by without you two. Mickey—?"

Going out the back door of the clinic, Sarah said suddenly, "I shouldn't have rushed you out like that. Did you want to say a prayer in there?"

"For Sammy?" She nodded. "I probably should have," he said. "But what is there to say about something like that, even to God? I wouldn't even know what to pray for."

He hesitated. "I'll tell you, though," he said, "I had the craziest thought, just for a second, while we were in that room. I had the strangest feeling that somehow I needed to ask Sammy to pray for me."

COMING OUT OF the INS building into the bright sun, Janna said, "*Nu, slavo Bogu.* Finished at last." She grabbed Billy's arm and leaned against him. "Now we are free of these people. We can get on with our lives."

When Billy did not respond she said, "Billy?" And turned and stepped in front of him, making him stop in the middle of the sidewalk, while she studied his face. "Something is the matter?"

"I'm okay." His face had closed up, in a way she was beginning to recognize. "We better go get something to eat, huh?"

"No. You will talk to me." She took both his hands. "Is it that you are sorry we are married?"

"Oh, no. Hell, no." He looked off over her head, his eyes very dark. "I mean, I'm not sorry we're together. You're the best thing that ever happened to me. But oh, hell." His voice held a note of uncertainty that she had never heard before. "What happens now? You know, that little punk in there was right. We don't even know where we're going to live. Or *how*," he added. "I don't have a job, no experience or training—been in the army since I got out of school, except for a little hardhat work right after I got out. Not much demand for the kind of stuff I learned in the Berets, that's for sure."

He sighed heavily. "I don't know, Janna. You didn't get much of a bargain in the husband department."

"Pfui. I will not listen to such talk about my man. You must stop this worrying. I am trained medical technician. You are strong and intelligent. We will find things to do."

She tugged at his hands. "But you are right about one thing. Come, we will get something to eat. This is low blood sugar making you feel depressed."

They walked down the street toward where the Honda was parked. It was hot and the air smelled of exhaust fumes. Billy took off his hat and ran his fingers through his hair. Maybe he ought to get it cut if he was going to look for a job. On the other hand who wanted to work for the kind of assholes who would think it mattered? Maybe he could get a job with the Cherokee Nation, back home. The eagle feather in his hatband fluttered in the wind as he replaced the black hat on his head.

"You really think I'm intelligent?" he asked Janna.

"Of course. Crazy, but intelligent. You are a good man, Billy Badwater." She reached out suddenly and patted his bottom. "Also your buttocks look very fine in tight jeans. Now come, I must have double cheeseburger with lettuce and tomato or I die."

STANDING ON THE hillside in the bright afternoon sun, Sarah Aronson took off the earphones and hung them around her neck and switched off the Geiger counter. "My God," she said, and then again, "My God." Her voice might have come from an open grave.

Mickey Wolf said, "It's as bad as Billy thought?"

"I only wish it were." She wiped sweat from her forehead with the back of her hand. "It's worse. I don't know how to explain just how bad it is."

She waved an arm in a gesture that took in the whole area. "I don't even know how bad it is, myself. I'm not going to try to find out, either. This is a job for a team of specialists with proper equipment and protective clothing. Billy shouldn't have come here. *We* shouldn't be here, right now."

She turned and began working her way up the slope, moving slowly, her lug-soled boots slipping in the loose scree before finding holds. She had changed into a lightweight bush jacket and khaki shorts. Following her up the hill, Mickey Wolf admired her legs. Not a very appropriate subject for attention under the circumstances, but hell, there they were, right in front of him. Without asking permission, his memory put up a couple of scenes from Friday night at his apartment, after the wedding. Looking at her now, all dusty and sweaty and dressed like Indiana Jones, you'd never guess. . . .

He said, "How do you plan to handle this? Call the EPA, the press, what?"

"That's going to bear some thinking. We need to move as quickly as possible, but we don't want to give anyone a chance to bury this—in any sense." She stopped and leaned against a rock outcrop. "I'll have to turn this over to the foundation. They've got people who know how to handle cases like this."

She looked at the Geiger counter in her hand. "You realize this thing is almost irrelevant? The radioactive material is the most spectacular item out here, but there are any number of other toxins in the area, many just as dangerous. I've never seen anything like it."

"Think this is what you've been after? The explanation for all the cancers and birth defects?"

"As sure as I can be without detailed case-by-case studies. And I did manage to talk with a few people in the last couple of days—most of the cancer cases are in hospitals or dead, but Leonard Hozia helped me find the families of several children with birth defects. Sure enough, one or more parents admitted to having been in these hills years ago. I'm sure it's going to check out." She smiled without looking very happy. "This may be the breakthrough. I could kiss Billy."

"If you're in the mood for kissing Indians—" Looking at her face, Mickey Wolf realized she wasn't in the mood for much of anything right now. "Sorry," he said.

"Let's get out of here," she said. "This place isn't just dangerous, it's depressing. I want to go back to the trailer and stand under the shower for about eight hours."

BILLY AND JANNA came out of the Burger King clutching big white paper bags, which they loaded carefully into the Honda's saddlebags, packing them so the drinks wouldn't fall over and spill. They rode out of Las Vegas on a secondary road, in the general direction of Pahrump Valley. Billy was struck once again by the abruptness of the transitions in these parts: one minute you were in town and the next you were out in the desert. What a small town Vegas was, for everybody to make such a big deal about it.

He found a little rest area, just a couple of concrete picnic tables with sheet-metal sunshades overhead, and parked the Honda. "This okay?"

She nodded, looking around at the desert. He wondered as always what she saw in this dry dusty country. Personally he felt the need for trees and running streams. Maybe it reminded her of home.

"It's fine," she said. "Which is my double cheeseburger?"

Some time later, Billy wadded up a greasy paper bag and went over to toss it at the trash barrel. "Badwater runs down the court," he said under his breath. "He jumps, he shoots, and it is . . . *in*, just as the buzzer sounds, winning the game for Sequoyah High School."

"Hm?" Janna said around a mouthful of fries.

"Nothing. *Nichevo.*" Billy sipped at his slushy Coke and looked around. The rest area was without facilities but there was nobody around. "Be right back."

He went off behind some chest-high bushes and turned his back to the road. A few minutes later, as he zipped up, he heard Janna's voice behind him. She didn't seem to be calling to him; it sounded as if she must be talking to somebody. He turned and hurried back to the picnic area, where he stopped as if he had stepped in a bear trap.

A large crow, of familiar appearance, was sitting on the picnic table in front of Janna, who was feeding it French fries. She turned as Billy arrived. "Look," she said delightedly. "Look who has come."

Billy approached the table slowly, not sure how to play this. "Tame bird," he said finally. "Somebody's pet, I guess."

"Of course not," she said indignantly. "Do you not know your own grandfather?"

"Yeah, *chooch*," the crow said, "what's your problem all of a sudden?"

Billy sat down on the concrete bench, staring at the bird

and then at Janna. "You, uh," he said, "you can hear him?"

"*Konyechno.* He even speaks a little Russian."

"Picked it up playing dominoes with Leon Trotsky," Grandfather added.

Billy took off his hat and scratched his head, though it didn't itch. "I thought I was the only one who could hear you."

"She can now," Grandfather said. "Now she's family."

Billy picked up his Coke and drank the rest of it, wishing it were something stronger. He wasn't at all ready for this. Look at Janna, too, taking it so calmly. You'd think ancestors appeared as talking birds all the time. Come to think of it, she was from Asia. Maybe people where she was from were into reincarnation or something. Then again, compared to the other things she'd seen lately, a talking bird might not seem particularly weird.

"Reason I'm here," Grandfather said, "besides wanting to meet the bride, and don't think that hasn't been a pleasure—"

"*Spasibo.*"

"*Nye za shto.* Reason I'm here," Grandfather repeated, "I wanted to fill you in on the situation. Been learning some things, and I'm afraid they're not good. Hate to spring this kind of stuff on you kids just now, but—" The black wings fluttered briefly. "Let me have another bite of those fries, child. Been a long day, lots of flying, and there ain't a lot to eat in this damn desert."

They watched as the bird finished off Janna's fries. Billy said, "Seems like you're sticking with this crow now. Instead of switching around like you did back home."

"Well, I ain't all that familiar with most of the birds out this way. Old *koga* seemed like a safe bet. Good-sized brain, big enough not to have to worry about cats or snakes, plenty of range and speed for getting around. And nobody pays any attention to a crow, even in town." Grandfather pecked up the last of the fries. "Now then—"

He looked at Billy. "You remember that place I showed you? And I told you that thing had been hanging around there?"

Billy nodded. Grandfather said, "Well, it showed up again that night. Went off again next day, chewed up a couple of horses at a dude ranch, came back and fooled around some—I'm pretty sure, now, it's feeding off that stuff you saw, some way. Anyway," he went on, "it took off again Friday evening, disappeared for the whole weekend. I missed what happened next, on account of your wedding and all."

"And now?" Billy asked, knowing he wasn't going to like the next part.

"Now," Grandfather said, "it's back. On the move again, out in the desert. Last I saw, it was headed toward that same place again—maybe it worked up an appetite, whatever it was doing, wherever it was, or maybe it just likes it there—but no telling where it'll go next."

Grandfather looked back and forth, from Billy to Janna and back. "This is the bad part," he said. "It's different now. Bigger, for one thing, a lot bigger. And—it's kind of hard to explain this—it moves different. Like it's got more of a purpose."

"Jesus," Billy said.

"Yeah. Life just got a lot more dangerous. And I got a feeling this is just the start. Things are moving, children, toward something big and scary. Somehow both of you figure, in a big way, into what's getting ready to happen, but I don't know any more than that. To start with, though," Grandfather said, "you need to get back to that reservation and warn people.

That woman doctor's got a wild hair about that place, liable to go looking around there herself. If she runs into that thing—"

Billy and Janna stood up simultaneously. "We will go now," Janna said.

"Be careful," Grandfather said. "Billy, you got any of that tobacco left? No? Well, it don't much matter." He sounded somber. "I don't think it would stop that critter now. I'm not sure anything would."

COMING UP THE gravel road toward the highway, Mickey Wolf saw the white car blocking the way and knew immediately that there was going to be trouble. He braked the Jeep, wondering what to do. Before he could decide, a second car appeared, pulling out from behind the white car, swinging out and around to stop beside the Jeep in a swirl of white dust. Doors opened and men leaped out, holding nasty-looking pieces of hardware. A voice called, "You in the Jeep! Get out and keep your hands up!"

For a second Mickey Wolf considered making a break for it. Maybe he would have tried, if Sarah hadn't been along. But he looked at the automatic weapons, and at the cars that could easily overtake the old Jeep if they did make it to the highway, and with a very bad sinking feeling he said, "Better do it, Sarah," and raised his hands and climbed awkwardly to the ground.

There were four men from the second car, all of them armed with some sort of machine pistols, all of them dressed in ordinary street clothes. There were also two men in the white car, but they did not get out; they only seemed to be watching. The nearer one looked remarkably like Joe Piscopo.

Whoever these bastards were, they had done this sort of thing before. There was a rough but practiced efficiency in the way they moved, two of them standing back with weapons ready, the other two grabbing Mickey Wolf and Sarah Aronson and hustling them toward the car, pushing them into the back seat. A voice—it seemed to come from the white car—said, "Somebody bring that Jeep. Don't leave it here."

As she was being shoved into the car Sarah Aronson said, "You have no right to do this. You haven't even identified yourselves," and a couple of the men laughed.

"You think we're some kind of cops, lady?" the nearest gunman said. "You should be so lucky. You should only be so fucking lucky."

16.

THEY GOT BILLY and Janna not long afterward. There was nothing fancy in the way they did it. Billy had the Honda bumping along the dirt road, a few minutes after taking the Blacktail Springs turnoff, when a black van came up from behind and simply ran the motorcycle off the road.

It happened fast. Billy saw the van in his mirror and pulled right to let it pass; the van came alongside and started drifting to the right, crowding but not making contact. The van had smoke-dark windows and it was impossible to see who was inside. Billy moved over, cursing, but the van kept coming at him. He wondered if the driver was drunk.

Then the Honda was off the road, banging over stones, while Billy fought for control and Janna screamed. He hadn't been going very fast and he got the speed down, using the gears and the back brake; and he almost made it, almost had the Honda stopped, when the front tire hit a deep pocket of soft sand and the bike slewed violently and went down. The grips wrenched themselves from his hands and he went flying and tumbling through the air, to land with a heavy thud on the hot dry earth.

The impact knocked the wind out of him and he lay there for a moment dazed and unable to move. He didn't seem to be seriously hurt, though. He hadn't been wearing a helmet, but his head had struck nothing harder than loose dirt. He rolled over and pushed himself up into a sitting position, wincing at the pain in his scraped-raw palms.

Janna was lying a few feet away, sprawled on the ground, not moving. His heart went up his throat and out the back of his head, but then she said, "*Govno*," and sat up. Her hair was full of dust and there was a rip in her jeans but she looked all right.

There was a rattling roar from the road and the van reappeared, coming the other way. It stopped amid clouds of dust and doors banged. A moment later two men came running through the dust toward Billy and Janna.

"You stupid son of a bitch," Billy said, getting to his feet, ready to kick some ass. "You could have killed us."

The man in the lead stopped a couple of paces away and pulled out what Billy immediately recognized as a .45 automatic. "Yeah," he said, "well, since we didn't, I guess you two better come with us."

Billy shifted his weight and the .45 came up. The other man was pointing some sort of automatic weapon. "Don't," the man with the pistol said conversationally. "We'll shoot her first."

He gestured with the .45. "Let's go, now. Some friends of yours been waiting for you to join them."

THE BUILDING WAS a big flat-roofed affair, vaguely Mexican in style, with a kind of low porch running along the front. Once it had been white, but the windblown sand had eroded most of the finish away, leaving a rough grayish-brown that appeared to be some sort of adobe. Out front, a cracked concrete pedestal held bits of rusted plumbing for long-gone gas pumps.

There had been big picture windows in the front of the main room, but these were now covered by large sheets of warping, graying plywood, pierced here and there by random bullet holes and decorated with fading graffiti. The place had been abandoned so long even the vandalism had a look of age.

There were no other buildings around except a crumbling concrete-block structure out back with two doors on which the words MEN and LADIES were just barely readable. The desert stretched off in all directions, with only a few lines of distant nondescript hills to break the monotony of the view. The road that ran past was still blacktopped, but the surface was gnarled and pitted from years of neglect. There were no signs to indicate that this was anywhere in particular.

Mickey Wolf couldn't figure out where the hell they were. Or rather he couldn't figure out where this place was in geographical terms, though he had an idea it was somewhere not far from the state line and might just possibly even be in California. In terms of his own immediate surroundings, he knew exactly where he was.

He and Sarah were sitting on the floor in the big main room of the abandoned building, their backs to the rear wall. Their position didn't represent any particular malice on the part of the gunmen who had brought them to this place; there was simply nothing to sit on but the floor. Obviously this room had once functioned as a restaurant and/or tavern, but the tables and chairs had long been removed, leaving the floor bare except for a thick layer of dust and the droppings of animals and birds.

A couple of the kidnappers, though, had found themselves somewhere to sit; the stools were gone, but the long wooden-topped counter was still in place, and the two men had climbed up and seated themselves there, where they could cover the room with their weapons. One was a skinny, hatchet-faced, pale-skinned man with graying streaks in his slicked-back, comb-tracked hair; the others called him Sonny, even though he was obviously the oldest of the group. He was clearly in charge of the operation and taking his duties very seriously.

At the other end of the counter, placed to watch both the prisoners and the back door, sat a husky young man with blond hair and a great tan. Amazing muscles bulged from the armholes of his sleeveless T-shirt, which bore the cryptic legend DO IT. He looked as if he hardly needed the machine pistol on his lap, but when he handled the weapon it was with practiced ease.

Neither man spoke to the prisoners; neither even seemed to be paying much attention to Mickey Wolf and Sarah Aronson, though this illusion instantly vanished whenever either of the captives made the slightest movement. Shift to a different position to relieve the fatigue, or stifle a sneeze in the dust-filled air, and two gun barrels snapped up and locked onto the target with frightening speed. Neither man had spoken at all since Sonny had told the other two to go move the car and the Jeep around back and then watch the road.

It was very hot in the low-ceilinged room. From the light that came through the broken rear windows, though, Mickey Wolf judged that the sun would be going down soon. He wondered what these people meant to do for light. The electricity couldn't possibly be working here. Of course, he reflected, they might not expect to be here after dark. They might intend to do whatever they meant to do before night fell. Somehow that wasn't an encouraging thought.

There was a banging of feet along the porch. Sonny said, "Watch them," and pointed his submachine gun at the front entrance, while DO IT raised his own weapon to cover the prisoners.

But it was one of the men who had been sent outside, a chunky Hispanic type with a Viva Villa mustache. "They're here," he told Sonny. "Just coming up the road."

Sonny nodded, a very tight economical nod. "So get your ass back out there," he said. "In case you're full of shit and it's somebody else, okay? Case you ain't noticed, there's more than one black van in the world."

A few minutes later, though, tires crunched in the dirt in front of the old building and doors opened and shut, and Viva Villa came back in and said, "It's them, all right." And almost immediately afterward there were more footsteps on the porch and more men with guns came through the entrance, herding Billy and Janna ahead of them.

"*All right,*" Sonny said, sounding pleased. "Now we got everybody together. Track, go back out and run that van around back. Don't seem to be any traffic on this road, but we may as well be careful."

When Track had left the room Sonny said, "Over there with the others," and waited while Billy and Janna were prodded across the room and made to sit next to Mickey and Sarah. Billy had some nasty-looking abrasions and Janna's clothes were torn, and Mickey wondered if there had been a fight.

"Listen up," Sonny said, "because I'm only gonna say this one time. The only reason any of you are still alive is because some people still ain't decided how to handle this. Seems there's those who think maybe somebody ought to ask you some questions, find out who you are and what you're up to, shit like that. I don't know anything about that part of it and it ain't my job to think about it. So shut the fuck up," he added as Sarah opened her mouth to speak.

"What I'm saying," he continued, "right now you're alive because some people want you that way. But they ain't the people me and these boys work for, so—" He tapped the machine pistol on his lap. "Give us any trouble, any reason at all, you all get dead—and if we have to burn one of you, we'll go on and do the other three, right then, you better believe it. Then our boss gets to tell some people hey, too fucking bad, these things happen."

He spat on the floor. "Personally I'd just as soon go ahead and do it right now. Don't none of us get paid overtime . . . but if you all hold still and don't fuck with us, you might get to see the sun come up tomorrow."

THE DAY TURNED into evening and the evening turned into night and the night turned into a very long one.

The gunmen seemed to have expected this. There were a few muttered curses and glances in the direction of the road, and fragmentary remarks that "they" (or various nouns implying illegitimacy or first-degree incest) were sure taking their fucking time, but the general feeling seemed to be one of routine annoyance rather than real surprise. They sounded and acted, Billy thought, like a squad of experienced infantrymen sitting out another hurry-up-and-wait, bitching mostly to kill time until the brass decided what to do next.

They had come prepared, anyway. At Sonny's orders, a couple of men went out to the van and came back lugging a plastic ice chest and a paper bag of sandwiches. The ice chest held only soda pop and two or three men grumbled that there should have been beer, but Sonny shut that off as quickly as it began.

"We're gonna be here late, maybe all night," he said. "Gonna be hard enough keeping everybody awake. Beer just makes you sleepy. What I shoulda done, I shoulda brought a thermos of hot coffee."

One of the men, a curly-haired young guy with impressive tattoos down both arms, jerked a thumb toward the prisoners. "We feed them too?"

Sonny considered this. "Hell, why not? We got plenty. Give them something to keep them busy." He looked at the captives, who still sat against the back wall. "Make sure they go easy on that soda, though. I don't wanta have to fuck around taking them outside to piss every few minutes."

"Hell," the tattooed kid said, "let them go in their pants."

"Yeah, right, Spider, you wanta smell it all night? I sure as fuck don't." Sonny laughed shortly. "Hey, assholes. Anybody has to go, speak up—don't raise your fucking hand, this ain't school, just speak up—and somebody'll take you out back. I ain't gonna bother telling you not to try to run for it," he said, "because I kind of hope you will. First one of you makes a break, we waste the others. *All* the others. So go for it. Then I can go back to Vegas and hunt for pussy."

He took a bite out of his own sandwich and made a face. "Mayonnaise. I fucking hate mayonnaise."

* * *

AS THE DAY died, a man went out and brought in a Coleman pressure lantern. The too-bright glare threw the big room into stark lights and darks, like a high-contrast photograph. Sonny had the man set the lantern on the counter, where its dazzling light blinded the prisoners if they looked in that direction. Billy figured that was no coincidence. Having some training in the handling of prisoners—and some practical experience, in Iraq—he had to give these people high marks in planning and technique. This was no pickup group of street punks; whoever they worked for, they were pros.

The night wore on. Sonny seemed immune to fatigue, but the others started to look a little ragged. Spider and DO IT had a long monotonous discussion about whether wrestling was faked. A couple of men stretched out on the floor and slept, or tried to. An owl hooted outside and half the gunmen jumped, confirming Billy's guess that they were city types, not comfortable about spending the night out here in the desert.

The four prisoners sat and endured. None of them had any interest in sleep, which would have been difficult anyway, since Sonny would not let them stretch out or lean on each other; Billy started to put an arm around Janna and was told flatly that there would be no touching. The floor was hard and so was the wall they leaned against; the air was so stale and full of dust that it was hard to breathe. Their dusty clothing had begun to itch but they did not dare scratch.

A little after midnight, Billy asked to go outside. Sonny said, "Sure, chief. Just take off the boots first."

Billy undid the laces and worked his old combat boots off. One of the men said something and Sonny laughed. "Even an

Indian isn't gonna take off across that desert barefooted in the dark. Okay, chief, go take your leak."

Billy's muscles and joints were stiff from hours of sitting in one place. He moved awkwardly and painfully out the back door, followed by Viva Villa and watched by the single unblinking eye of a machine pistol which looked like a MAC-10. A piece of shit, in Billy's ex-professional opinion, but perfectly capable of cutting a man nearly in half at short range.

He stood in the open area between the main building and the derelict outhouse and unzipped his fly and, with considerable relief, let fly. The stars were huge and bright in the clear sky; there was almost enough light to read by, let alone shoot. Even so, he considered his chances. He was fairly sure he could take Viva Villa, who had already gotten too close a couple of times, and who didn't seem very alert. Probably he could do it without any noise. Then he'd have a weapon.

Then what? That would leave five men, but the odds weren't a problem; they were what they were and he was what he was, and in the desert, after dark, he could take them out one by one. Bare feet didn't bother him; he had been ten years old before he'd worn shoes in warm weather except to school and church.

But Janna and Sarah and Mickey were still inside, and he had no doubt whatever that Sonny would carry out his promise to kill them all at the first sign of trouble. Billy sighed to himself, tucked in and zipped up, and turned and walked back toward the brightly-lit doorway, followed by Viva Villa and his MAC-10.

THE MORNING LIGHT was coming through the ruined windows, and the grumbling among the gunmen was turning into a muttered chorus, when at last there was the sound of a car turning off the road. Everybody stood up, readying weapons, and the man who had been keeping watch came in off the porch and said, "They're here."

Sonny slid down off the counter and went to the front door. After a minute or so he said, "Well, shit. Talk about taking your fucking time."

He stood in the doorway, seemingly speaking to someone on the porch. A voice responded, but Billy couldn't make out the words.

"Yeah, yeah," Sonny said impatiently, and slung his MAC-10 over his right shoulder, leaving it ready to hand. "Sorry I forgot my fucking violin. So what's the word?"

Billy saw movement now, a man standing on the porch beyond Sonny. Sonny's body blocked most of the view but Billy thought the new arrival looked like the suit who had rousted him back at the ranch road the other day.

Sonny's voice came back through the room, loud and harsh: "You're shitting me, right? After all this fucking around, that's it? That's what we been sitting around all night to hear?"

The man spoke again, his words still indistinct. Billy could see him better now; it was definitely the spook who looked like Joe Piscopo. Either that or it *was* Joe Piscopo. He wondered if the other one, the Eastwood wantabee, was along.

"Well, I'm a son of a bitch." Sonny's voice had taken on a very ugly edge. "So what you're telling me, we spent this last fucking night out here in the middle of fucking nowhere for no reason at all, right? Waited all this God-damned time for something we coulda took care of yesterday and been back in town for dinner. Jesus H. fucking Christ."

The other man seemed to be protesting. Sonny said, "Hey, asshole, don't get salty with me. I don't give a shit, you're some kind of government spook. You guys do the fingering and we do the dirty work, okay, that's the way it goes sometimes, I follow orders just like you do. But don't step back and wash your hands and then try to give me a buncha shit, cause I don't hafta take it."

He raised his voice as the man on the porch started to reply. "Hey, you delivered your fucking message, okay? Now you better get your ass outta here. You ain't supposed to see what happens next. That's the whole fucking *idea*, for Christ sake."

Janna said very softly in Russian, "They are going to kill us."

"I think so," Billy murmured, also in Russian. "Be ready—"

"Hey, you." The one called Spider pointed his machine pistol at Billy. "No talking in Indian. No talking at all."

Sonny came back into the room, looking seriously pissed off. Out front a car door slammed and an engine fired. "On your feet," Sonny said to the prisoners. "Move, God damn it."

They all stood up, moving stiffly, shuffling their feet to get the circulation going. "Stand still," Sonny said irritably. "Just stand still for a minute, okay?"

He stood for a moment, listening. Out front car tires crackled across the washed-out gravel and then there was a sudden roar as the car accelerated off down the old blacktop. Sonny waited until the engine sound had died away. "All right," he said. "Spider, you and Track go out and start the van and the Jeep—I'll drive the car myself, when we're ready for it—and bring them around front. Check and make sure the road's clear before you do."

"What're we gonna do with the Jeep?" Spider asked. "Ditch it, torch it, give it to Ramon's guys to chop, what?"

"Leave the fucker here," Ramon suggested. "Who's gonna—"

"For Christ sake," Sonny said furiously, "what is this, everybody's giving me all this shit? Just go do what I fucking *told* you to do. You'll find out what we're gonna do with the Jeep when it's time to do it."

Spider and Track nodded and disappeared out the back door. Sonny looked at Viva Villa. "Start gathering up that stuff we brought in. Or are you figuring to argue about that too?"

The man in the Viva Villa mustache shook his head. "Lighten up, Sonny," he said, almost gently. He slung his machine pistol across his back and bent to pick up the big plastic ice chest. "Just dump the ice out here, huh? It's all melted."

"Jesus, who *cares*?" Sonny rolled his eyes back briefly. "I swear I shoulda become a priest like my grandma wanted . . . Reno."

"Yo." The man who had driven the van yesterday stepped forward. Unlike the others, who wore a variety of sport or work clothing, he was dressed in a fairly decent lightweight suit, though he had taken off the tie and unbuttoned the collar during the night. Billy noticed that he still carried the .45 auto, rather than the buzzguns all the others were packing.

"Get all the stuff they got on them," Sonny said. "Wallets, personal jewelry, anything that could be used to ID them. You know what I mean."

"Sure." Reno stuck the .45 into the waistband of his trousers and took a step forward. Sonny made a gesture and DO IT hopped down off the counter and took up a stance, covering the four prisoners with his machine pistol.

Reno said, "Okay, how we're gonna do this, I want you to—"

There was a sudden noisy banging at the front door. It didn't sound like a man knocking; it was more of a rattling, pecking sound, like somebody rapping at the boarded-up window with a stick. Sonny said, "What the fuck?" and, loudly, "Who's that? What's going on out there?"

There was no reply, but the rapping continued. Sonny said through his teeth, "I don't *believe* this shit," and strode toward the door, cursing under his breath. Reno paused, a few feet from Billy, and turned his head to watch. Viva Villa stopped screwing around with the ice chest and turned his head too. Only DO IT continued to watch the prisoners, his face blank, the MAC-10 steady in his huge hands, as Sonny yanked open the door.

The crow was a big one, and coming through the door into that low-ceilinged room it looked bigger than a 747. It flew straight at Sonny's face, wings beating, beak stabbing, making a horrible croaking sound like something from a prehistoric swamp. Sonny yelled and stepped back, raising both hands to protect his eyes. The crow kept coming and Sonny took another step backward, caught his heel on the warped wooden floor, and fell heavily, arms flailing, the crow battering his face all the way down. As he hit the floor Sonny screamed.

Even DO IT had turned to watch by now, the machine pistol in his hands apparently forgotten, pointing at the floor. Reno was staring, mouth open, and Viva Villa was pouring water and slush ice over his own feet without noticing.

That was as good as it was likely to get.

Billy hit Reno just under the sternum with the second knuckles of his folded and stiffened right hand, crushing his larynx with a slashing left to the throat just for insurance. As Reno's face went dying-on-his-feet blank, Billy snatched the .45 from his waistband and shot DO IT three times through the chest, the .45 making an enormous boom in the enclosed space. The MAC-10 went off as DO IT's muscles contracted on the trigger, but the burst went into the floor.

Viva Villa was starting to come unstuck now, dropping the ice chest and trying to unsling his weapon, but he didn't have a chance. Billy dropped him with two rounds through the heart and then swung the .45 to cover Sonny, who was still lying on the floor by the entrance. The crow was nowhere to be seen.

"No," Sonny said. His eyes were huge. "No, man," he said, and raised his hands. "I give up."

"Fuck that," Billy said, "you son of a bitch," and held the .45 out at arm's length and aimed carefully and fired. A black dot, not quite half an inch in diameter, appeared in the middle of Sonny's forehead, and he fell back and filled his pants and lay still.

A gun went off at the rear of the big room and Billy hit the floor, rolling to one side, as bullets snapped and popped past his head. He brought up the .45 and fired at the man called Track, who stood in the back doorway holding yet another submachine gun, but the shot missed and then the .45 locked open, empty.

From somewhere in the middle of the room came a burst of full-automatic fire. Track staggered, dropped his gun, buckled at waist and knees, and fell. Billy sat up and saw Janna standing next to DO IT's body, holding a machine pistol in a very competent manner.

"There is one more," she said calmly. "Outside."

Billy got to his feet, tossing the empty .45 aside. Mickey Wolf was just straightening up from Viva Villa's body, holding the dead man's weapon. "Here," he said, handing it to Billy. "You know more about these things than I do."

Billy started to run out the back door, changed his mind, and headed for the front instead, leaping over the dead Sonny and going out the front door fast just in case somebody was out there waiting for him. Nobody was. He went around the corner of the building and saw Spider getting into the van.

Billy figured they might as well let Spider go, but then the van lurched into motion and began rolling straight toward him. The driver's door swung open and Spider leaned out, his face wild. He had a machine pistol in his left hand and he was trying to drive and shoot at the same time. Most of his shooting was going all over the place but a few rounds smacked into the wall of the building, a little too damn close to where Billy stood.

Billy raised the MAC-10 in both hands and fired at Spider, holding the trigger down, emptying the clip, conscious of Janna coming around the corner of the building and firing too. The van swung suddenly to one side as Spider dropped his gun and grabbed convulsively at the air with his left hand. Billy and Janna jumped out of the way and the van roared past them and slammed straight into the side of the building.

Billy started to run back around the building to get Mickey Wolf and Sarah Aronson out, but then he saw that they were already outside, standing in the parking area. "Look out," he called, and everybody started running as the first lick of flame appeared beneath the wrecked van.

The explosion was not loud, just a muted *woomp*. An orange fireball, like a miniature nuclear explosion, blossomed upward for a moment. Van and building began to burn.

Billy looked at Janna. "Where'd you learn to shoot like that?"

"I did not tell you? I was three years in Red Army reserves." She looked at the MAC-10 in her hand. "Pfui. Cheap trash. You should see what I can do with Kalashnikov AK-47."

Sarah said, "Excuse me, but if the macho shit is over now—"

The others all turned to look at her. She had her right hand clamped tightly over her upper left arm. A red stain was spreading from beneath her fingers, soaking the sleeve of her bush jacket. Her face was gray and lined with pain.

"One bullet, I think," she said in a firm clear voice. "Through the muscle tissue, I don't think the bone was touched. Still, I'd like to be taken to some sort of medical facility."

Janna tossed the MAC-10 to the ground—Billy noticed she remembered to take out the clip and clear the chamber first—and moved toward Sarah. "I will look," she said. "We must take her to the city. Which way?"

"That way," Billy said. "I think."

"I'll get the Jeep," Mickey Wolf said. "I hope they left the keys in it."

A few minutes later they were rolling eastward along the old blacktop, picking up speed as Mickey Wolf worked up through the gears. Behind them the abandoned building continued to burn, sending up a column of black smoke into the clear desert sky.

17.

IT HAD GROWN larger, much larger, but it did not realize this. It had changed in many other respects as well, but it did not know this either. The truth was that even within its own weird frame of reference, it was very confused.

It had awakened from the brief period of dormancy with no clear understanding of where it was or what it had been doing. One of the side effects of metamorphosis was a temporary deterioration of memory; as far as it knew, it had always been as it was now.

But the memory loss was only partial. Certain recollections remained more or less intact; certain directions and locations had vaguely pleasant associations. So, disoriented by the changes still taking place within itself, it sought the comfort of old appetites and their gratification.

It found the valley again, and the dump site, without much difficulty. The first taste of radiation brought a satisfying rush, and it spent some time feeding, though in truth it no longer had any real needs of that sort.

Yet when it was done there was still an unfocussed restlessness. Inchoate new sensations and drives roiled within its rapidly-evolving consciousness; it felt compulsions it could not yet even identify, let alone try to fulfill.

For want of anything better to do, it began moving again, toward another place that held (as best it could recall) the memory of good times.

BILLY GLANCED NERVOUSLY around the hospital waiting room and said in a low voice, "I hope she remembers to tell them the right story. These places always ask a lot of questions when somebody comes in with a bullet wound."

Mickey Wolf shifted positions in the uncomfortable plastic chair without looking up. "What's to remember? We were driving across the desert when this stray slug came out of nowhere and hit her in the arm."

"Yeah, but do you think they'll buy that?"

"Why not? The desert around here is lousy with gun nuts and militia loonies and careless hunters and now and then the odd psychopath who just likes to shoot at passing cars. Unless somebody's come across the scene of our recent battle and there's a police alert out—which I seriously doubt—nobody's going to make anything of Sarah's injury."

Billy nodded and looked down at his feet. His G.I. boots had gone up in the fire, damn it, and now here he was in a hospital waiting room in his sock feet. It was embarrassing, even though nobody seemed to have noticed. He had a pair of moccasins in the Honda's topbox, but that was all. He wished he'd brought his Tony Lamas instead of leaving them back in Oklahoma.

He wondered if the Honda was still lying out there in the desert. His hat was in the topbox too, with his eagle feather. So was Janna's purse with her passport, and that damn stamp they'd gone through so much hell to get.

But he didn't want to talk about his own problems with Sarah in there with a hole in her arm, so instead he said, "I hope she's not hurt bad."

"It did not look serious," Janna said. "I think there will be no permanent damage."

Mickey Wolf grunted tonelessly. He was looking down at the floor.

Billy said, "Hey, Mickey, you okay?"

Mickey Wolf said, "We killed six men."

His voice was barely audible, not at all like his usual boom. All the same, Billy looked quickly around the waiting room again. But there was nobody near and nobody coming, so he said in an equally low voice, "We? I mean, no offense, but—"

"Oh, sure." Mickey Wolf put his face in his hands. "I didn't really distinguish myself, did I? Left up to me, we'd all be lying in a shallow grave out in the desert right now. Who am I to say anything about what you two did?"

He looked up, then, and his eyes were terrible. "I was a chaplain in Vietnam," he said. "I worked at a hospital and I saw the wounded coming in, and sometimes they died, sometimes while I was praying with them. But I never saw men just dying on their feet like that—" He shook his head. "I couldn't handle it, Billy. I stood there and watched and I couldn't move. Not even to push Sarah out of the line of fire."

Billy considered the possible things he could say. The truth was that the preacher had done exactly the right thing. People who tried to get in on the action, when they didn't know what they were doing, were a worse menace than the enemy. But it wasn't going to help Mickey Wolf's feelings to tell him that he would just have been in the way.

There was, in fact, nothing at all that anybody could say. This was something the man was going to have to work out with himself. Maybe he'd succeed and maybe he wouldn't; he seemed to have a pretty good supply of internal conflicts as it was.

Billy said, "Look, there's some things I'm good at, mostly because some people taught me. They're not things I'm proud of being good at, and they're not things anybody needs to be ashamed of *not* being good at. I mean, hell, there's some things nobody *ought* to be good at."

Mickey Wolf nodded heavily and went back to looking at the floor. Billy sat down on the waiting-room couch next to Janna. He hadn't really expected the words to do any good, but you had to say something. You couldn't just stand there.

THE AGENT WHO looked like Joe Piscopo said, "This is the worst fucking road I ever saw in my life."

His partner fought the wheel for a second as the car hit a pothole. "You been saying that," he said, "every one of these dirt roads we get on, ever since this assignment started."

The agent who looked like Joe Piscopo grinned. He didn't think he looked like Joe Piscopo, and it pissed him off when people said he did. He thought he looked more like Robert Redford. Or maybe that guy who used to be on *Hawaii Five-O*, the one Jack Lord used to tell to book 'em.

He said, "Yeah, well, it'll be over pretty soon."

The other agent gave him a narrow-eyed look. "You think so?" The dry cynical voice, the frozen face, everything but the .44 Magnum, and he would have carried that too if it hadn't been against regulations.

The agent who looked like Joe Piscopo looked at his

watch. "They've done it by now," he said. "Hell, those guys are back in town collecting their pay."

His partner said, "Shit!" and swerved too late to miss a huge hole. When he could speak again the man at the wheel said, "Tell you the truth, I didn't like that part of it. Not a damn bit."

"Sometimes these things have to be done. You know that."

"Then we ought to have the balls to do them ourselves. I don't like working with those punks."

The agent who looked like Joe Piscopo said, "You think you could have done it? If they'd told us to take care of it?"

"Why not? Anybody who can't do whatever's necessary, he ought to get out of the game."

They rode along in silence for a few minutes. The dust billowed up from the wheels in great blinding clouds; they could only see straight ahead, up the road toward Blacktail Springs.

"Whole business sucks," the man at the wheel said finally. "I'm telling you, I've got a bad feeling about this. I don't think it came down from the top or anywhere near the top. I think certain assholes—and you know who I mean—got a wild hair and decided to go cowboy on this one. You watch, there'll be some major shit come down over this business. And if they need a couple of fall guys to blame it on—"

The other man looked thoughtful. "You could be right. We need to start thinking about how to cover our asses if this goes rancid. Well, hey." He waved a hand in the direction of the road ahead. "We're almost done with our part. Get to that clinic, wave this bogus warrant around if any of those stupid blanket-asses try to stop us, and search through that woman doctor's office and living quarters. Once we're done and out of there, what can happen?"

He grinned again. "Those fucking redskins aren't going to give anybody any descriptions. Hell, us palefaces probably all look alike to them."

"Sure." The driver didn't look any happier. "Well, I'll be glad when it's all over, that's for sure. . . . "

He paused, staring at the rear-view mirror. "God-damned dust," he said irritably. "I can't see shit. You hear anything, like there's a big truck or something coming up behind us?"

The agent who looked like Joe Piscopo said, "What would a big truck be doing—"

There was an enormous roar and the world outside the windows went dark. The car lifted clear off the road and flew through the air. For an instant the agent who looked like Joe Piscopo believed they had been hit by a tornado, and he grabbed helplessly for handholds and wished he'd worn his seat belt.

Then—in the time it took the car to travel a hundred yards or so, bounce, and explode in flames—things were done to him and the other man, things they had never imagined possible, things that had never before been possible in this world.

"IT'S NOT ALL that serious," the doctor told Mickey Wolf. "Certainly not in any way life-threatening or permanently disabling. It's just that she's lost a good deal of blood, and there's shock as well—always is with gunshot wounds—and so I'd like to keep her here overnight. Just to be on the safe side, you know."

From the hospital bed Sarah Aronson said, "Hey, you don't hear me arguing. The way this thing hurts, I'm not eager to face the Blacktail Springs road. Especially in that damn Jeep."

Her voice was a little foggy and her eyes were half closed; she had already received a pain-killing injection. There was a big white bandage around her upper left arm.

The doctor looked at Mickey Wolf and then at Billy and Janna. "And you're certain none of you has anything to add to the report? Concerning how she came to be shot?"

They all shook their heads. "Just a stray round out of nowhere," Billy said, looking innocent as a chicken-killing dog. "Lucky it didn't kill somebody."

"All right. You understand, I'm required by law to ask. Has to be reported, and all that." The doctor tilted his head toward the door. "I think she needs to be left alone now. Besides her injury, she seems very fatigued."

Out in the corridor Mickey Wolf said, "Look, I'm going to stay around. Be here when she wakes up—you know."

"Sure." Billy looked down at his sock feet. "Only, well, I kind of need to get back out there and see if my bike's still where we left it. Even if it's wrecked, there's some real important stuff in it."

"No sweat." Mickey Wolf dug in his jeans pocket and handed Billy the keys to the Jeep. "If you aren't back by the time I decide to go home, I'll take a cab. Hell," he said, grinning, looking a little embarrassed, "I'm liable to spend the night here. If I can just find a softer chair."

LEONARD HOZIA STOPPED the pickup truck next to the reservation boundary sign and shut off the engine and got out. After a quick look up and down the road he reached in the open cab door and fumbled under the seat and pulled out a flat pint bottle of Kentucky Deluxe. He unscrewed the cap with slightly trembling fingers and raised the bottle to his lips and took a very long swallow, wincing and fighting for air as the cheap raw whisky settled into place and began to warm his insides. After a moment he took a second pull, coughed briefly, replaced the cap—his fingers had stopped shaking now—and put the bottle back under the pickup's seat.

It was around the middle of the day, early to be hitting the bottle. But his nerves had been very bad lately; there was just too much crazy shit happening on the rez, too many strangers coming around. Strangers always meant trouble, he knew that for sure. Even the ones who didn't seem to have anything to do with local affairs, like this Oklahoma Cherokee who was friends with Doctor Susan and Father Mickey. The tribal chairman had already called Leonard in last week and asked him what he knew about this strange Indian with the motorcycle, and had been pretty pissed off when Leonard had had to admit that he didn't know anything at all.

I'm going to move to L.A., Leonard Hozia thought. Get a real job. Fuck this place.

Thinking about this and that, he decided to have one more before heading back. He got the bottle out and uncapped it and swigged, holding it in his mouth a moment and enjoying the bite of the liquor before swallowing. As he screwed the cap back on, he glanced up and saw a big black crow flying northward above the road, its wings flapping lazily as it rode the cushion of hot air from the desert floor.

He stood for a couple of minutes watching the crow, for no reason except that it was the only moving thing in sight. Birds had it made, he decided. Just fly around and eat whatever they ate—bugs, mostly, wasn't it, and lizards and things like that, sure as hell no problem finding a square meal in southern Nevada if you were a bird—and never have to take shit off the FBI or the BIA or the tribal council or anybody else. Any time things got too tense, you could just up and fly away.

He watched until the crow was invisible against the bright sky, and then he turned, and then he saw the thing coming.

Heard it too, all at the same time, a great deep roar like every locomotive in Santa Fe's Barstow yards, and from the roar and the vague huge shape of the thing against the sky he thought at first it was some kind of storm blowing up from the south. But it was coming too fast for any kind of storm he'd ever seen or heard of, even a tornado, and there were no clouds anywhere in sight, though the sky directly above the thing was unnaturally dark.

It was, he estimated wildly, as big as the biggest hotel building in Vegas. Bigger, maybe, it was hard to tell because it seemed to have no definite shape. It was not raising any sort of dust cloud as it passed over the desert; in fact he had the impression it was not quite touching the ground. It was the blackest black he had ever seen.

For some reason he felt no particular fear. It occurred to him that he might start the pickup truck and see how far he could get before the thing caught him, but he gave the idea no serious consideration; at most he might buy himself five, ten minutes, no more. This thing was moving faster than any car ever made—and he wanted to be facing it when it happened.

At least, he thought, they can't blame me for this one.

In the last minute, as the thing bore down on him, Leonard Hozia unsnapped his belt holster and drew the old Smith & Wesson .38 that he had never fired in any official capacity except for shooting a couple of mad dogs. Without trying to aim—hell, the thing was right on top of him now and it was as big as a God-damned mountain—he emptied the rusty revolver into the swirling black mass.

Then it had him.

"I THINK IT was right along here," Billy said. "Help me look, will you? It'll be on your side."

He had the Jeep slowed way down, just about crawling along, not much faster than a healthy man could run. They had been looking for the Honda for the last several miles, and he was sure he must have passed the spot where the gunmen had run him off the road. Yet there had been nothing but sand and rocks and brush and, once, a wrecked and burned-out car a hundred yards or so off the road.

"Someone may have taken it," Janna remarked. "Not necessarily to steal it. Perhaps someone from the reservation saw it and brought it to a safer place."

"Yeah," Billy said, though privately he didn't believe that for a minute. He liked the Blacktail Springs Paiutes well enough, the few he'd met, but like most Indians he privately distrusted people from tribes other than his own. These western skins would steal a hot stove, everybody back home knew that—

"There," Janna said suddenly. "Isn't it?"

Even with her pointing, he barely spotted it: just a quick flash of sun on chromed handlebars, obscured by a thick patch of brush. He stopped the Jeep and jumped down.

The old 750 was farther from the road than he'd remembered, lying on its side in the sand like some dead metal beast, the single eye of its headlight staring blankly at the sky. As far as he could see there was no serious damage. A couple of turn signals had been snapped off in the crash, as had the right rearview mirror—he ground his teeth, thinking how much it was going to cost to fix everything; stuff like that cost more than you'd believe—and, when he hauled it upright, he discovered that the footbrake lever was badly bent, though not beyond repair. There was a crack in the right saddlebag shell but nothing a little fiberglass resin wouldn't fix.

"Looks okay," he told Janna.

"Will it run?" she asked.

"Let's see." He reached for the key and found it was still in the *on* position. Of course; he hadn't had a chance to turn it off after the fall. "Oh, shit—"

He didn't even bother trying the kickstart lever; that battery had to be dead as George Custer. Lying there with the ignition turned on and the headlight burning, it would have drained itself before dark.

"What I need to do," he said after a minute, "I'll drive up to Blacktail Springs and find somebody with a pickup truck—maybe I can get that big asshole cop to help me—and we'll come back here and get the bike and haul it into town. Any bike shop can charge the battery for me, won't cost much."

He opened the topbox and took out his black hat with the eagle feather and put it on. Just having his hat back made him feel better. He dug out his moccasins, the old center-seam style that Grandfather Ninekiller had taught him to make, and sat down on the ground and pulled them on. Wonder he hadn't stepped on a scorpion or something by now.

Janna was getting her purse from the cracked saddlebag. "Ah," she said, "my passport, thank God. I would rather face those men with guns again than go back to that immigration office."

Billy got up off the ground and she walked beside him back to the road, taking his arm. "That was incredible," she said, "what you did this morning. I have not said this yet." She squeezed his arm. "I said you were fantastic man. I did not know how fantastic you are."

Billy grunted, smiling at her, not really paying attention. He was thinking about how to get his bike fixed.

BUT A DOZEN miles up the road they saw another wrecked vehicle, a pickup truck, this one right in the middle of the road. It had not burned but it lay upside-down, wheels in the air, cab crumpled. When they came closer Billy saw the unevenly painted lettering on the cab door and realized which pickup it was.

"Hey," he said, "it's that cop's wheels. Leonard Whatsisname."

He stopped the Jeep and looked around, for no reason beyond curiosity. He assumed that the reservation cop had simply gotten drunk and wrecked the pickup, though it was hard to figure out how anybody could have rolled a truck on this straight flat stretch of road. Gone off the road, sure, but how—

Then he saw the body. Or rather he saw a foot and part of a leg sticking out from behind the truck, and when he climbed down and walked around behind the overturned vehicle, with Janna following right behind him despite his efforts to get her to stay in the Jeep, he saw that it was Leonard Hozia.

Not that the big cop was all that recognizable by now. It was the gunbelt, and the badge pinned to the khaki shirt, that identified him to Billy. Leonard Hozia wasn't decapitated or dismembered or even extensively mutilated, but much had been done to him. More than one reservation drunk, over the years, had threatened to take that gun away from him and stuff it down his throat; now someone or something had done exactly and literally that. There were other things as well.

The eyes were wide open in the blackened, distorted face, staring at the sky with a look more of resignation than surprise, as if Leonard Hozia had known all along that life was one day going to do something like this to him.

Janna said very shakily, "Billy, I don't know how much more I can stand. What is happening?"

He shrugged helplessly. Looking up and down the road, he wondered what to do next. Drive on to Blacktail Springs, or turn around and get the hell out of here? Immediate instinct said run, but would that do any good? What if the whatever-it-was had circled around and was now behind them? There was no outguessing a thing like that, that seemed to follow no understandable rules.

"We must go on," Janna said decisively, ending the mental debate for him. "The people at the clinic, and in the village, they must be warned."

As they walked back toward the Jeep, Janna said, "You will leave him there, like that?"

"Against the law to move anything," Billy said, climbing into the Jeep. But of course it wasn't that at all; he just couldn't bring himself to touch the body. "What the hell," he said defensively, starting the Jeep, "there's nothing anybody can do for him now."

Maybe, he thought as he put the Jeep in gear, there's nothing anybody can do for any of us.

* * *

THE PROSPECT DID not improve as they came to Blacktail Springs.

The first scattered houses and trailers looked much as usual; there were no signs of damage, at least, though it was hard to tell with the condition most of them were already in. But there were no people sitting on the dilapidated porches, no children playing; the dust blew and swirled across empty yards, and nothing moved except for odds and ends of litter tossed by the wind. The hairs were standing up on Billy's neck and arms. This was starting to feel very, very bad.

Nobody was in sight as they drove into the village, either, not so much as a dog moving about. The only sound was the humming of the cheap air conditioner on the tribal-offices trailer, and the constant sad whine of the wind. Billy shut off the Jeep's engine and sat for a few seconds looking and listening. "Like a ghost town," he muttered finally.

Janna said, "The clinic," and jumped down and started across the road. Billy got out of the Jeep and went up the steps of the double-wide trailer that held the tribal administrative offices. The door opened readily to his hand, and the lights were on when he stepped inside, but there was nobody at the desks and nobody came out of the inner offices to answer his hesitant call. He started to bang on the door of the tribal chairman's office, though he didn't really think anybody was in there either.

That was when he heard Janna screaming.

IT RETURNED TO the place where it had been.

The changes were coming faster now. It was bigger than ever and much more powerful; more focussed, too, and more conscious of itself. The time for trivial amusements was now over. The things it had just done had been no more than a regressive outburst, a last flare-up of immature capriciousness.

The changes were not yet complete; the final and greatest development was still to come, though close at hand. Its awareness was still imperfect. But within its consciousness there was now a growing sense of what it truly was and what it could do.

18.

WHEN THE GAGGING and heaving at last subsided, Billy straightened up and leaned back against the wall of the clinic's waiting room. A final dry retching spasm racked his insides as he wiped his lips with the back of his hand. Should have run outside, he thought, and realized immediately what an idiotic thought that was. In this place, now, a little vomit on the floor was not even a detail.

He reached out instinctively to take Janna's hand, but she had both hands to her face, so he put his arm around her shoulders instead. She was crying. He wished he could do that. For one thing it would make it harder to see the scene inside the clinic.

They had found the population of Blacktail Springs.

At least that was how it appeared; there was, under the circumstances, no way to take a count. There might have been thirty or forty human bodies in the dreadful crushed heap that filled the clinic's waiting room. There seemed to be more, where the tangled pile had overflowed into the corridor and the nearer examination room. It was impossible to make a guess.

Billy had seen carnage before, more than once. In the villages of northern Iraq the bodies of massacred Kurds had lain like raked-up leaves, and there had been mass graves nobody had bothered to cover up. He had seen the results of aerial bombardment and artillery fire, and the blackened remains of the crews of burned-out armored vehicles; he had seen these things over and over, during the war and for many nights that followed. But nothing in his experience had come close to this.

The dead were mixed and jumbled together as if deliberately stirred by some enormous finger. Not all the bodies were complete; many, perhaps most, had been dismembered, so that various unattached parts lay on top of the pile or stuck out here and there, or were scattered about the rest of the room. A head lay on top of the reception desk, on its side; Billy recognized one of the young white doctors from Cedar City. And there was so much blood that it was impossible to tell what color the walls and floor had been. . . .

He closed his eyes for a second, trying to pull what was left of himself together. "Out," he said through his teeth, and started to push Janna toward the door, but that was when the cry came from down the corridor.

It was a high, wailing cry, like nothing human, and for an instant a new wave of horror froze Billy's skin; but then Janna said, "Sammy!" and he remembered the child Sarah had shown him.

The cry came again. Janna started to move, her shoes slipping on the bloody floor, but Billy reached out and stopped her. "No way to get through," he said.

She stared for a moment at the mass of bodies that blocked the corridor. "The back door," she said. "Come."

They turned and ran, back out the front doorway and around the side of the concrete building. The clinic's rear door resisted Billy's first tug and he thought for a moment that it was locked, but then the sand-jammed latch gave way and the door banged open and Billy and Janna rushed inside.

Sammy lay on his bed in the little room, waving his stunted arms and making high-pitched mewing sounds. He appeared unharmed and untouched; there was no blood or other sign of violence in the room.

Billy and Janna looked at each other. "What the hell," Billy said helplessly.

"We must get him out of here," Janna said. "Can you lift him?"

"Sure." Billy bent over the bed and picked the child up. The small legless body weighed hardly anything. He had expected some struggle, but Sammy stopped thrashing and lay quietly in Billy's arms. Janna said, "Here, I will bring a blanket."

Going out the back door, Billy said, "Where do we take him? Plenty of empty houses around, or we could use Sarah's trailer." He looked back at the clinic. "Personally I think we ought to put him in the Jeep and get out of here."

From somewhere out in the street a familiar voice called, *"Ehena!"*

Billy went around the corner of the building, Sammy in his arms and Janna behind him, and saw the crow sitting on the Jeep's fender. *"Ehena,"* Grandfather called again. "Come here, children."

They walked quickly across the road, the dust sticking to their bloody soles. Billy said, "What's happening, *eduda*? I don't understand anything any more." He looked up and down the empty road and back at the crow. "Tell us what to do."

"First thing," Grandfather said, "you got to get out of this place. All three of you. All four of us," he amended. "I'm coming with you."

Billy nodded. "Okay." He started to walk around the Jeep and paused, looking down at Sammy. "How are we going to do this?" he asked Janna. "He can't sit in the seat, can he? I don't think he can even sit up at all." He jerked his head toward the rear of the Jeep. "Lay him down on the floor, maybe use that blanket for padding?"

"Hell," Grandfather said, "you can't just load this boy in back like a sack of potatoes. Specially on this road, where he'll bounce around and get hurt."

"It would be dangerous," Janna agreed. "We must sit him up beside you. Then I will sit in the back and watch him and help hold him in the rough places."

Billy considered. "Have to sort of tie him in, then. I don't think the seat belt's going to be much use, since he's got no legs. Can't even use his hands to brace himself . . . look in back, Janna, see if there's any rope or webbing, anything like that."

Janna went around and poked through the clutter of odds and ends in the back of the Jeep. "There is some rope," she reported. "It looks strong."

Together they managed to get Sammy into a sitting position in the passenger seat. Janna held the child in place while Billy devised an arrangement that would hold him securely without risk of injury. At least the child was able to hold his head up; Billy hadn't been sure he could even do that. Sammy was entirely quiet and passive throughout the operation. With his eyes closed as always, he might have been asleep.

Billy tied the last knot and studied the improvised harness. He had made a point of leaving the underdeveloped arms free, even though as far as he knew Sammy could not use them. Somehow he didn't like the idea of tying the boy up like a prisoner.

"I think that'll do," he said. "Till we reach the highway, anyway."

"Let's go, then," Grandfather said. "We don't have much time. Maybe we don't have any time at all. *Nula*," he added urgently, as Billy started to speak. "Hurry up. I'll tell you more on the way."

Billy climbed into the driver's seat and started the engine, while Janna got into the back of the Jeep. Grandfather half-hopped, half-fluttered over and perched on the back of the passenger seat next to Sammy's head. A few minutes later they were bumping back down the dirt road.

When the last empty house had disappeared behind them, Billy glanced over at Sammy. "How's the kid doing?" he asked Janna.

"I think he is all right." She grabbed at the seat back for support as the Jeep rocked over a stretch of sun-baked ruts. "Of course it is hard to be sure."

The boy did seem to be doing well enough so far, the crude rope harness holding him solidly upright in the seat. The crow was sitting on Sammy's shoulder now, the black feathers brushing the misshapen face. The child's eyes were still closed, but his mouth was turned up in what almost looked like a smile.

"Good boy here," Grandfather said. "Look how he's riding right along, not hollering or anything."

"I don't guess he knows anything at all about what happened," Billy mused. "Lucky for him."

"Don't be so sure, *chooch*. This boy knows a hell of a lot

more than you think. He just knows it in a different way from you, that's all."

"When we get to Las Vegas," Janna said, "we must take him to the medical center at the university. I know people there."

Grandfather said, "We're not going to Vegas. Not yet, anyway. You remember where the turn is, *chooch*? Just a little way up ahead, there."

Billy slammed on the brake and turned to stare at the crow. "Wait a minute. Not going to Vegas? Where the hell are we going, then?"

The crow returned his look with shiny black eyes. "This is the part you ain't gonna like, *chooch*. We're going down there where we went the other day. That valley where the poison stuff is. You know."

Billy opened his mouth to tell Grandfather there was no way in hell, but the dry old voice cut him off. "Damn it, boy, do you think I'd tell you to go there if there was any other way? This is something that's *got* to happen, or everybody's finished. Things about to happen, make anything you've seen so far look like a quail dance. It may be too late already, but we got to try."

Billy moved his hands helplessly on the wheel. "But what can we do about it? Two Indians—one of us dead—a woman, and a messed-up kid?"

"I don't know the answer, son. Like I told you before, there's things I know and things I don't. What I know right now is that you're supposed to go to that place, like I said." Grandfather pointed southward with his beak. "Like the A-rabs say, that's how it's wrote down. Now drive."

There was no arguing with a dead elder, of course. Billy would have driven off a cliff or crashed the main gate of hell if Grandfather Ninekiller had told him to do it. Still he hesitated. "Let me drop Janna and the kid off somewhere," he suggested. "No need for them—"

"You will not go without me," Janna said flatly. "We are together. Besides, what would Sammy and I do alone in the desert if you did not come back?"

"Everybody goes," Grandfather said with finality. "The boy too. It's all part of what has to happen. I can't tell you more than that."

Billy nodded, took a deep breath, and put the Jeep in gear. A strange peace had come over him now; his hands were no longer shaking and his pulse had slowed almost to normal. It was a feeling he had experienced before, in the moment of leaving the aircraft on a night jump over enemy territory. You told yourself, I am never going to get out of this alive, I am already dead, so there is no point in wondering about the details of when and how it will happen.

"Drive as fast as you can, *chooch*," Grandfather urged. "Best I can calculate, that thing's just about to go into some kind of big final change. Once it does, there'll be no stopping it."

"And then?" Billy said, shifting up. "What happens then?"

"Then," Grandfather said, "it's going to eat the world."

THE SHORT-CUT road was even worse than Billy remembered. He drove as fast as he dared but still the journey across the desert seemed to go on and on. His arms ached from fighting the wheel and his neck was sore from the constant whiplash bouncing. Behind him he could hear Janna cursing in English and Russian and Kazakh as she was tossed about; even Grandfather had to do a good deal of wing-flapping to keep his balance. Only Sammy seemed unbothered by the rough ride. If anything, the child seemed to be enjoying himself. Now and then, when the crow's wings touched his face or the back of his head, he made tiny chirping sounds, apparently of pleasure.

It was not long past the middle of the afternoon—Billy's cheap watch had not survived the motorcycle crash, but the sun was still high in the western sky—when they came at last to the riddled reservation-boundary sign and then to the old blacktop highway. The sky was clear, too, not a cloud from horizon to horizon; and yet the light was somehow growing dim, and the breeze off the desert felt unaccountably chilly. Above the line of hills, the sky was almost dark as night.

Billy gunned the Jeep down the highway, driving one-handed, holding his hat in place against the blast of the wind—whatever was happening, this was no time for a man to lose his eagle feather—and staring into the gathering twilight. If it got much darker up ahead he was going to have to turn on the headlights. Something touched his shoulder and he glanced around to see Janna reaching forward between the seats to cover Sammy's body with the hospital blanket. Her face was calm but very pale. Her black hair whipped and swirled in the slipstream.

By the time they rounded the end of the chain of hills and came to the ranch-road turnoff, the sunlight was almost gone. In its place had come, not the gray dimness of normal dusk, but something more like the weird greenish half-light that precedes a summer tornado. The hills looked distorted and blurred, and nothing had its proper shape. Even the sun, still visible in the darkening sky, appeared warped and out of round, and very far away. The wind was cold as death.

"Already starting," Grandfather said as Billy swung the Jeep off the blacktop and up the gravel road. "It's drinking up energy, getting ready for that last big change. That pile of radioactive trash wouldn't make a bite of what it needs now. Some way, it's pulling power from the sun's rays—that's why it's so cold and dark—but look!"

Billy had already seen it, reared against the darkening sky, up near the north end of the valley. And Grandfather was right: it had changed.

It was still that same infinite black; still the same shape-without-a-shape, too, though he thought its outlines seemed more solidly defined. But it was now so immense as to dwarf everything in sight, even the hills behind it; it covered, by Billy's guess, at least a couple of square miles of desert floor, and it rose higher than any building he had ever seen. That couldn't be right; it should have been visible for miles, towering above the line of hills, yet they had not even seen it from the highway. But everything was both impossible and possible in this place and time; both light and reality had been bent. . . .

Billy had stopped the Jeep, reflexively and almost unconsciously. But Grandfather shouted in his ear, "Drive, drive!" and he threw the Jeep in gear again and gunned it. Gravel and dust sprayed from beneath the fat tires and Janna grabbed at the seat backs for support. "Straight at the son of a bitch," Grandfather cried. "Keep going!"

Obediently Billy gassed the Jeep, charging up the gravel road and then out across the desert floor, heedless of rocks and brush and soft patches, no longer steering the bucking Jeep so much as aiming it. A crazy eagerness had taken hold of him; he no longer felt fear, only the desire to get there and get this over with, one way or another—

Halfway across the valley, the Jeep stopped. There was no warning of any kind; the engine simply ceased running and the Jeep rolled quietly to a stop.

"Should have known," Grandfather said as Billy tried vainly to restart the Jeep. "We got into that thing's field or whatever. It's sucking up so much energy, don't nothing work here any more . . . quit trying, *chooch*, it's no use."

They sat in the dead Jeep, staring up at the vast black shape that was now less than a mile away. Everything was strangely quiet; Billy had expected to hear the roaring again, but there was only a faint hum, down close to the bottom end of the audible frequencies. The only other sounds were the soft plinks and ponks from the Jeep's cooling engine. Even the wind had ceased to blow.

"What now?" Billy asked. "Get out and walk?"

"No time," Grandfather said. "It's about to happen, any second now. Can't you feel it?"

There was indeed a strange powerful something in the air now, an almost tangible tension and pressure: a sense of great and terrible imminence, like the aura of an impending earthquake. Billy's skin felt very tight. Yet there was no feeling of direct menace. The monster did not even seem to know they were there.

"What will happen?" Janna's voice was clear and calm; she might have been asking the time. "The world will end?"

"Pretty much," Grandfather said.

The great dark thing was absolutely still, now; it might have been no more than an immense artifact, erected in the desert by some race possessed by a maniac desire to build the biggest monument ever made. Yet its immobility had nothing passive about it. Rather it seemed to be gathering itself for some inconceivable climactic moment. A kind of nimbus of darkness had begun to develop about it, and seemed to be spreading outward. The humming sound was no louder, but there were harmonics now at the upper end of the scale, and the metal body of the Jeep had begun to vibrate.

Grandfather began to sing, a high soft repetitious four-tone song that Billy had never heard before. The language was not Cherokee; it sounded like that of the song he had used to doctor the tobacco. Billy wondered if he was supposed to join in. Instead he reached back to take Janna's hand.

But Janna was leaning forward, her head next to his. "*Bak!*" she cried. "Look at Sammy!"

Billy pulled his eyes away from the creature and turned his head. And felt a shock so great that for an instant he even forgot the horror at the head of the valley.

Sammy's eyes were open, gazing with keen and focussed clarity in the direction of the looming black thing. His features looked somehow different, more alive; the usually slack, loose-lipped mouth was closed and firm. As Billy watched, the undersized arms came up and reached forward, in a purposeful movement totally unlike their usual spasmodic flailing. The babylike hands were turned palm upward, as if waiting to receive something.

"*Awohali ugidatli hinuhsi!*" Grandfather's voice crackled with urgency. "Give him the eagle feather! Hurry!"

Black wings beat the air as Grandfather took off, hovering for a moment over the Jeep and then disappearing into the darkening sky. With jerky mechanical motions, without asking or even wondering why, Billy reached up and detached the big dark-tipped feather from his hatband and laid it in Sammy's soft hands.

Sammy's right hand closed immediately about the buckskin-wrapped quill; he raised the feather and began moving it through the air in a complex series of passes, keeping the tip pointed in the direction of the creature. His face was fairly glowing now. It almost seemed to Billy that an aura of light shone about the oversized head, like the picture of the Christ child in the Indian Baptist Sunday-school-room wall when he was a boy. The dark-lashed eyes were very bright as they stared at the towering blackness.

Janna's hand touched Billy's shoulder. "Look, Billy," she said in a soft wondering voice. "Look around."

All around them, all over the floor of the valley, small shadowy figures were beginning to materialize in the dim light. Children, tens and then hundreds of them, perhaps thousands; they stretched off in all directions, farther than Billy could see. All were facing in the same direction, toward the great black thing at the valley's north wall.

And such children . . . Billy saw the flat, high-boned faces of the Asian heartland, and others like those of his own people; there were tiny, birdlike Japanese children and dark, heavy-browed Australian natives and fine-featured, bronze-skinned Pacific islanders, all mixed up together, standing almost shoulder to shoulder across the desert floor.

Not one was whole in body. Some were bent and twisted like very old people; some lacked arms, or like Sammy had deformed limbs, and some stood on bent, too-short legs, while others, lacking feet or legs, sat in the dust and were held up by those beside them. He saw faces that were barely identifiable as human; he saw great twisted masses of scar tissue on faces and bodies—nothing was hidden; the children were all of them naked—and grotesque, unidentifiable growths sprouting from necks and shoulders and torsos. Many of the small heads were hairless, their bald scalps covered with angry patterns of scars.

"Where did they come from?" he said, almost in a whisper. "How did they get here?"

Janna shook her head. "I think these words no longer have meaning. I think there is no more 'where' or 'here'. Something has happened to reality in this place, and there are no more explanations, only what is."

She said it in Russian and Billy did not understand it all, but he was not really listening anyway. "Who are they?" he said.

"You know who they are," Janna told him. And this time he did understand, and after a moment he nodded, and reached up to put his hand over hers where it rested on his shoulder.

Now Sammy raised his tiny arms high as they would go, the eagle feather held above his head. There came a soft murmuring from the multitude of children, a wordless rustling like a wind in green leaves, that ran the length and width of the valley; and the small faces all began to shine with the same strange light that illuminated Sammy's face. Their eyes still looked toward the head of the valley—or rather their faces were turned that way; many of them had no eyes—and Billy found himself caught in the power of their massed gaze, turning his own head to look in the same direction.

The enormous black impossibility still stood there, unmoving and, as far as Billy could see, unchanged; and it was still surrounded by the same dark aura, which by now had spread to cover a great area of the sky. But now the darkness was surrounded by a band of light so intense that Billy had to half-close his eyes to look at it. It seemed to be a barrier of some kind; the zone of darkness had stopped spreading, and there were vague ripplings and roilings within the murk, waves of deeper darkness that flowed outward against the band of light and then fell back upon themselves like surf against a reef. The humming sound changed slightly in frequency; the high harmonic grew louder.

"My God," Janna said. "See what is happening."

Slowly, almost imperceptibly at first, the halo of light had begun to constrict, forcing the darkness inward upon itself. As Billy and Janna watched, the bright band grew even brighter, tightening irresistibly, while the darkness contracted and grew ever more agitated within itself, the waves of blackness battering faster and faster, uselessly, against the ring of light. The outlines of the creature had grown blurry again; the humming and its harmonic had begun to falter and break up.

They're killing it, Billy thought with something far beyond wonder. The children are killing it.

The dark aura was half its present diameter now, and the light was closing in with increasing speed. From over the valley floor came a soft, high, fluting sound, like the upper register of a pipe organ.

The end came very fast. Suddenly the light rushed inward, like a noose snapping tight, driving the dark aura before it, and then there was only the immense blacker-than-black body of the thing itself, barely visible through the dazzling light that now surrounded and enveloped it. A single impossibly high whistle drilled through Billy's head, while the ground shook briefly as if from a subterranean explosion.

And then, just like that, the thing was gone; and, a fraction of an instant later, the light too was gone, and the sun was shining in a bright blue sky, and a warm breeze came down the valley and brushed a lock of Janna's hair across Billy's face.

After a moment he lowered his eyes to the valley floor, hearing Janna's voice beside him: "The children! Where are the children?"

The children had disappeared. The desert was now covered with butterflies. Big butterflies, small butterflies, all the sizes in between, all the bright colors and all sorts of harlequin markings; scores and hundreds and perhaps thousands of butterflies, turning the dusty valley floor into a patchwork carpet. Their wings moved gently as the sun warmed the earth; then, all at once, they began to take off, rising in a single great fluttering swirl of fragile vivid wings, up and up, to vanish at last into the blaze of the bright afternoon sun.

19.

THERE WAS A small sound beside Billy. He turned in his seat and saw Sammy looking at him. "Hello," Sammy said in a high clear voice. "This is yours."

He was holding the eagle feather in his outstretched hands. As Billy took the feather, Sammy turned his head and said to Janna, "May I please have something to eat?"

Janna looked into Sammy's eyes, which were now no more and no less than the eyes of a bright young boy. After a moment she reached out and stroked his thick black hair.

"We have nothing with us," she told him. "But we will all go, now, and get something. Is that all right?"

"All right," Sammy said cheerfully, turning back to face forward. "I'm hungry."

Billy turned the key, wondering whether the engine would start. It did. Carefully, worrying about soft sand, he backed the Jeep up and got it turned around, pointing back toward the distant highway. During the long slow ride back across the valley—he couldn't believe he'd driven full-tilt over this ground without turning over—he looked around for Grandfather, but the crow was nowhere to be seen.

As they came to the highway, Janna reached over the back of the seat and gave him a quick hug. "It is over," she said in English. "Now we can go on with our life."

"Over?" Billy ran the Jeep up onto the blacktop and turned right, in the general direction of Las Vegas. At least he hoped it was the direction of Las Vegas; he realized that he didn't really know where this road went, in either direction. "How the hell do you figure that?"

He waved a hand in a gesture that took in most of the state of Nevada. "I guess we just helped save the world, but I don't think anybody else knows it. I don't even think the world ever knew it needed saving. We sure haven't bought ourselves any help with the shit that's sure to come down."

Accelerating more or less smoothly, working up through the gears, he said, "We left a bunch of dead people at that burning truckstop—all right, that probably won't ever be traced to us, but somebody sent them after us, somebody might decide to make another try, who knows? Then there's that awful business up at Blacktail Springs, a whole tribe of dead Indians and any number of ways we could be tied to it. God knows what kind of a loony theory the cops are going to come up with, but I bet they're going to want to ask us some heavy questions."

He looked back over his shoulder at Janna. "In fact there's all kind of people going to be asking questions, and you know something? We're going to have to come up with some damn artistic lying, because the truth just isn't going to do at *all*."

"I know all this," Janna said calmly. "So what is your point?"

"Well, hell." He reached up and shoved his hat down more firmly on his head as the wind tried to take it away. "I just don't know where we go from here, is all. Those old stories never tell you what the Monster Slayers did with themselves afterward, do they? That's what I mean," he said. "What are we going to do?"

"Do? I told you, we will go on with our life. After all we have been through today, you are worried about a few tiresome policemen? Pfui," Janna said. "We will deal with whatever and whoever we have to deal with."

Billy popped the Jeep into top gear and leaned back as the speedometer needle slid up past the legal limit. "I hope you're right," he said.

"Of course I am right. That is all anyone can do," Janna told him. "To go on with life. The rest is detail."

Soaring high overhead, in the body of an enormous eagle, Grandfather Ninekiller looked down on the tiny speck that was the racing Jeep. *"Howa,"* he said.

THE END